AERIE

The Chinjoka Saga, Book One

Jon Keys

Askari, Dhala, and Gyam grew up as childhood friends during happier days for the Chinjoka, an Iron Age people with the ability to shapeshift, but now they must learn their place among the tribe while dealing with both a devastating plague and war with the Misiq.

Ena is a young warrior for the more savage Misiq, a tribe whose cruelty exemplifies their deity—the Angry God. The Misiq, also shifters, have declared a genocidal war against the Chinjoka, blaming them for the disease devastating both tribes. As a result, they are locked in a battle for survival. But when Ena is shown compassion by those he means to harm, he begins to question all he's ever known.

A chance meeting changes their lives, and maybe their tribes, forever.

A NineStar Press Publication

Published by NineStar Press
P.O. Box 91792,
Albuquerque, New Mexico, 87199 USA.
www.ninestarpress.com

Aerie

Printed in the USA
First Edition
February, 2018

Print ISBN: 978-1-948608-12-1

Also available in eBook, ISBN: 978-1-948608-04-6

Warning: This book contains sexually explicit content, which may only be suitable for mature readers.

Chapter One

DHALA'S WORLD OVERFLOWED with desperation as he filled a bowl with crystalline water trickling along the edge of the sky portal for Gyam's aerie. His attempt to spot Gyam in his flyer form was thwarted by the dense early spring fog that limited the visibility of the surroundings. Even the river running along the cliff was hidden from Dhala's sharp eyes.

Assigned to be the Saat responsible for the last two Athru, Dhala took his worker caste's responsibility of caring for Gyam and Choro with much weight, especially since Choro was in the final throes of the deadly plague that had devastated the Chinjoka over the last few cycles. As Choro's health diminished ever more rapidly, Dhala and Gyam had become ever more desperate until, before first light, Gyam had left on the final attempt to gain their friend and mentor more time.

A gust sent a spray onto Dhala's face and moistened the nest of short curls framing it. With the bowl having long ago been filled, he wiped the water from his skin and sighed.

"You can't will him to travel faster, Dhala."

Startled from his dower mood, he grabbed the bowl of fresh water from the trickle and moved to Choro's side. "I'm so sorry. I was lost in thought." He dropped a soft piece of trade cloth into the liquid, squeezed it almost dry, and ran it over the man's face. Choro's labored breathing echoed through the room, a symptom of how far the disease had progressed. Dhala found some solace knowing they'd had no new cases for a cycle. But sadness overwhelmed him each time he allowed himself to consider Choro losing his battle against the sickness.

With a hand withered to little more than talon and sinew, Choro caught his wrist. "Dhala, I'm neither fevered nor in need of cleaning. We both know my time is limited. Gyam set himself on this task hoping to change my fate, but this sun cycle is likely my last."

Dhala scrubbed the tears from his face and scowled at the feeble figure lying before him. With a fierce determination, he grabbed the older man's hand between his. "Choro, you will live. Gyam will find an osa herd, and the fresh meat will give you the strength to last until we discover a healing." Dhala glanced out the cave opening to the fog-swathed valley that stretched to the forests surrounding Mother Falls high in the mountains to the north. Nothing of Gyam was visible, but he turned to Choro filled with a stubborn glint. "Soon. He must return soon."

Choro lay back with a rattling breath. "Fledgling, we have not cured what is killing the Chinjoka in all the cycles since it began. Each caste suffered losses. Once I am gone, Gyam is the last Athru. None of the fledglings show signs of the Athru change, and the responsibilities weigh heavily on Gyam."

Dhala dropped his gaze as Choro reminded him of his greatest shame. But there was a gentle touch on his chin, and he lifted his head. He took the elder's hand in his, and Choro smiled sadly.

"It's no fault of yours that you never left the Saat caste. The Father of the Twins decides who takes to the sky, who are the protectors, and who cares for others. We are all born with the abilities of the Saat, and many become able to shift to the protective plates of the Onija. But the few who are gifted with the faculty to shift into one of the Chinjoka flyers guard us from the sky. We all stop where the Father decrees."

Dhala sighed again but released Choro and moved the bowl aside. The elder was right. Dhala needed to accept his place and the disappointment of never becoming one of the Athru caste as his father always believed he would. He would never develop the stone-hard plate of the Onija, much less the ability to become the taloned and winged protector of the Chinjoka.

Dhala's father held several unique beliefs, including that the earthbound Saat were as important as the soaring Athru. When he was a child, Dhala spent many hours with his friends, climbing the precipice above the village as the Athru flyers glided across the azure sky. He'd loved the time among the heights, regardless of the season, but warm summer mornings were his favorite. By afternoon, the sun would heat the rocks, making them uncomfortable, but during the early mornings, the breeze coming from the warming grasslands northward to the cutleaf forest made it easy to imagine what flight over the last Chinjoka settlement would be like.

He glanced again to the outside, thrilled at the rays of sun cutting through the dawn haze and bringing the river far below them into sharper relief. The dry-fit stone wall that formed the flight path for this aerie glowed with the golden light of morning.

"He's fine. Gyam is the strongest Athru I've met during my time in the aeries. When the Father takes me, he will need your help."

Choro's reference to the afterlife made Dhala cringe. He and Gyam had been determined to heal Choro of the plague since his first symptoms. Anyone who'd shown signs of the disease had left on the Long Flight with no exceptions. Dhala lost far too many of his friends, as had most of the Chinjoka. But when Choro showed the difficulty breathing that was the typical first symptom, Dhala fought with ferocious determination to save his friend and advisor. Choro's downward spiral caused Dhala and Gyam to drift apart. They'd been among the best of friends since they were fledglings, but Choro's terminal condition left Gyam bitter and unpredictable.

The result might be different if their only Athru healer hadn't been one of the first to die. Others tried to find a cure, including his mother who was a well-versed Saat healer. The failure to determine a cure made people doubt their skills and, in some cases, blame the spread of the disease on the Saat healers. Regardless of the truth, no healer had been successful, and most had stopped their efforts, for fear they might be blamed.

"He comes."

Dhala glanced at Choro, who nodded toward the aerie's sky portal. An instant later, the slow beat of wings came closer. Dhala swept the room with his gaze and found everything to his satisfaction. He moved close as Gyam landed on the rock opening. Dhala couldn't keep from gasping in awe any time he saw Gyam.

Each smooth wing was as long as Dhala's height. The muscles across his shoulders and down his torso flexed with each swipe of his webbed appendages. Dhala stepped away when Gyam thrust his elongated muzzle toward him and screamed a high piercing call, demanding attention. Dhala wanted to clasp his hands over his ears but knew instead he would do as Gyam demanded. Gyam tensed and released another scream.

Dhala dashed forward and grabbed the blood-dripping osa heart from Gyam's taloned hand. The fresh organ from the small grazer still quivered with the final throes of life. He rushed to Choro's side, ignoring Gyam's cry.

He knelt beside the older man and offered him the fist-sized heart. Choro preferred the meat of the smaller grazers, and a freshly harvested heart was a special treat. Both Dhala and Gyam hoped it would give him more strength, but Dhala feared it was Choro's last meal. More of Choro's presence in this world disappeared with each breath.

But he wouldn't give up hope. Dhala arranged Choro's bedding to make him as comfortable as possible while he enjoyed the treat. Choro sank his teeth into the morsel with clear relish as blood coated his fingers. Dhala couldn't help but smile at the elder attacking the tidbit with the same enjoyment as a fledgling with a sweet treat. A short time later, Choro finished and glanced around him.

Dhala squeezed out the cloth he'd been using earlier and handed it to Choro, who took it with a grin and wiped himself clean. Once he'd finished, he lay back on the bed, closed his eyes, and sighed.

His voice rolled across the room. "Delicious, Gyam. That was the best osa I've eaten in many seasons."

Dhala glanced over his shoulder to find Gyam in the midst of his change from his Athru form. The webbing was absorbing into wings, which were disappearing into Gyam's muscular body, and interlocking scales were becoming supple skin as Gyam left the form marking him as Athru. Dhala relished the beautiful body being revealed to him. When front paws and talons became work-roughened hands, Gyam made his final shift to leave his Athru form and stood nude behind him. Dhala tried not to stare but lost his struggle. Usually, Gyam covered himself, but today, he held his loincloth in one hand while watching Choro. His stout, muscular body demanded Dhala's attention until he realized how inappropriate he was being, especially given Gyam's current state. Dhala was painfully aware of the attraction he'd had for Gyam since they'd both grown beyond fledglings, but he would keep his role as Saat for Gyam and Choro during his time of sorrow for them all.

He wrenched his gaze to the ailing man and got a smile and quick wink. Caught staring at Gyam, Dhala dropped his attention to the floor. A slight rustling served as warning when Gyam walked past him, making the last tie on his loincloth before kneeling at the side of Choro's pallet.

"Elder, how are you feeling? Did the osa help?" Gyam asked.

Choro smiled and tapped Gyam's cheek. Gyam grinned, and Dhala caught a glimpse of his friend from cycles past. He leaned in to give Choro a kiss on each cheek, but Choro's gaze included both of them.

"It was warm and delicious, exactly what I needed. We must be honest. In spite of all your work, there is no cure. I am not long for this flight. My wings are tattered and bones are brittle. I will soon be with my mate. Both of you must accept this."

Hot tears rolled down Dhala's cheeks as he listened. He knew the truth of Choro's assessment. His body was failing. Dhala's gut twisted with grief, and a sob leaked from his lips.

Gyam turned on Dhala and snarled. His face elongated and his canine teeth grew as his emotions overtook his body. But before anything happened, Choro spoke.

"That's enough, Gyam. You two stretched my life further than any of the others who have fallen victim to this illness. For that, I thank you. But the time is here."

Gyam motioned at Dhala as he spoke. "He's given up. He's letting you die."

Choro glared and sat up. Dhala scrambled to change his bedding to make it easier, but Choro waved him away. The movement threw Choro into a coughing spell that left him gasping for air.

"Please, Elder. Don't strain yourself. I will do as you wish," Gyam said.

Choro again motioned them off, but not before Dhala saw the flecks of blood on his lips. He lacked none of the weight of his role as elder Athru when he turned to Gyam.

"You will be the last Athru. You need your friends. You have been together with Dhala since you both ran free of clothing during the warm moons. You've protected and guarded each other through your time together. Now you have let this come between you, and it must stop. Dhala is your friend even though he is Saat. You have grown up together and must regain your ability to work together. Athru, Saat, or Onija, you are all Chinjoka. This disease has almost destroyed our people. So many have died, and only one village remains. You must rebuild the people. You cannot succeed without all three castes who make up the Chinjoka."

Choro lapsed into another coughing fit. This one left him flat on his bed, sweating and gasping for air. He covered his eyes with an arm and tried to breathe. A morning breeze curled around them, bringing a mix of scents of the Chinjoka Basin, from the verdant growth of the shortgrass plains in the south to the crisp scent of the great cutleaf trees nourished by the Pilea River. The single wisp of air reminded Dhala of everything at stake for the Chinjoka nation. Dhala moved closer, pushing an immobile Gyam aside. He checked Choro's pulse and found a weak thread. He ran his hands down the older man's neck, but halfway along his path, Choro grabbed his wrists with the strength of a failing butterfly. The silent command left no doubt. He met Dhala's gaze and nodded.

"Soon. But not now." His gaze moved to encompass both of them. "You look like the gods are testing you. Both of you should rest, but I know neither of you will listen. I plan to sleep and won't argue with either of you any further."

With that, Choro sank into his bed and closed his eyes. Dhala waited but worried. He moved when Choro parted his lips.

"If you check my heartbeat, Dhala, I will hurt you in ways to prevent any enjoyment with a mate for the rest of your life."

Dhala drew away and turned at a snort from Gyam. His dark eyes twinkled as he looked at both Choro and Dhala. "He's not making idle threats. Even as he is now. Come. We can build up the fire and plan the evening meal. I asked a group of Onija caste hunters to bring the osa carcass. We must be ready for its arrival."

They had created a bed of glowing coals when a voice came from the passageway carved into the interior of the cliff as a way to reach the upper caves.

"I could use a little help here! Gyam picked the biggest Twins-blessed osa in the entire basin."

Dhala recognized the voice as another of their friends. Askari was of the Onija caste and one of the most successful hunters among the Chinjoka, but as a warrior, he was unequaled in the village. The plates he formed as Onija were as strong as iron but as mobile as Dhala's soft skin. Dhala should have known it would be him who retrieved Gyam's kill. That the three of them had been inseparable since they began to walk made it even more certain that Askari would be the one who would retrieve Gyam's take. Even though the Father had spread his gifts through the castes as they went through puberty, bodies changing in line with their castes, their friendships had remained. They rushed to the path and found Askari balanced precariously while gripping the carcass he'd thrown across one shoulder. Dhala moved down the first few steps, grabbed the carcass by the stag's straight-spiraling horns, heaved it upward, and settled it onto his shoulder. Once the body was securely in place, he carried it into the aerie.

Askari followed a few steps behind him, and as they reentered, he spared a glance toward Choro's sleeping form before turning to the other men. Dhala stripped to his breechcloth and used his long knife to cut openings in the hind legs' tendons so he could hang the osa from the tripod kept for that purpose. With practiced knife work, he peeled the hide from one side while Gyam worked on the other. With a soft crackle, he pulled the skin loose around the neck and glanced toward Askari. The plates from his Onija shift were still prominently displayed over his torso and brow. While scales proved invaluable in protecting one from the Onija caste during battle or hunting, they limited Askari's finger mobility. The limitation made tasks requiring fine dexterity more difficult. Askari maintained his distance from the work being done, but Dhala knew his friend too well to allow him to avoid the dirty work of butchering the carcass.

"Askari, wake up and shift back from your Onija form. You can help." He gestured his knife toward Gyam. "We want osa for dinner. The rest needs to be spread on a drying rack."

Askari closed his eyes and skewed his face in an expression Dhala recognized as he shifted from his warrior form. Once Askari began, it took little time before his skin was as smooth, flexible—and vulnerable— as Dhala's. He flexed his fingers a few times before pulling his side knife. Askari's skill with a blade was evident by the speed the meat was prepared. With the three of them working together, butchering proceeded with well-practiced efficiency. As often as the three of them had hunted together, they should be skilled at sharing the work.

Dhala checked on Choro and saw his chest rising and falling. Signs of life, even if his breathing was shallow, gave Dhala hope. He had the urge to evaluate further but considered Choro's earlier threat. He found the others cleaning the osa blood from their hands. Askari held out the bowl of water he'd filled earlier.

"Here, use what's left, and I'll get more."

Dhala nodded and let Askari pour the cool liquid over his hands. He rubbed them together to loosen the drying bits from his skin. Once that was done, Askari splashed more water onto Dhala's hands. After a few repetitions, Dhala was clean, and the pottery bowl was empty. He dried himself on his tunic and nodded to Askari.

"Thank you. We appreciate your help."

Gyam glanced up and one brow lifted. But a moment later, he returned to the task he was trying to complete. His knife flashed in the light as he sliced the loin free from the backbone, cut the meat into thick slices, and threaded them onto fire-hardened skewers before hanging them over crimson coals. The meat was soon sizzling and filled the aerie with delicious aromas.

They tended the meat, constantly turning it to get a perfect sear on all sides. But while they did, Dhala kept a continual watch on Choro. All three friends worked to carve what remained into thin strips and hang them from the drying rack Dhala put in the small fire's draft. The sun approached its peak when they finished. The skewered loin had cooked to perfection. Askari had always claimed a talent for cooking. He'd often said if Gyam had no choice but to eat his own cooking, he would learn how to do a decent job with its preparation. The smells of food had Dhala's stomach growling, but he checked on Choro first to see if he might be interested in eating.

He walked over and squatted beside Choro's bed. When he leaned forward to shake him awake, Choro's eyes fluttered open.

"I'm still here, Dhala. The aroma of cooking osa was enough to keep me. It smells delicious. I haven't eaten a meal from Askari in too many moons."

"You will enjoy his cooking many more—" Dhala's throat tightened, and he could not complete what he and Choro both knew was a lie. The older man patted his hand and smiled sadly.

"I relish sharing this meal with you. Bring me a piece of that delicious meat, fledgling. Invite the others to join us. I think we'll have the best meal we've had in seasons." He studied Dhala and continued. "Be certain to put out an offering of the osa to the gods, especially the Father. Their favor is needed by all of us."

Dhala rushed away, glad to be focused on anything other than Choro's rapid decline. The others turned to him as he approached. He glanced at them as he brought his emotions under control.

"Choro says the meat smells delicious and would like for us to share the meal with him," Dhala said.

Askari leaned closer and whispered, "How is he?"

Dhala motioned toward the sleeping area. "He asked me to assure the offerings from the successful hunt. I will take care of their placement on the fire. Go. Sit with Choro and enjoy sharing our meal with him."

Dhala drew his blade and carefully sliced thick pieces from the osa's mineral-rich liver. After adding more wood to the fire, he dropped the raw meat into the searing hot coals. As the scent of the roasting delicacy filled the aerie, Dhala began a simple chant of thanks every Chinjoka was taught before their first blooding. As the last of the flesh turned dark, a breeze blew across the fire, hiding it in the smoke. Once Dhala's sight returned, no trace of the meat remained. He hesitated but then joined the others with a shake of his head.

The three young men gathered the food they had prepared and sat on the floor surrounding their elder. Dhala brought small drinking bowls, one for each of them, filled with clear water Askari had brought from the river while they cooked. The mood was somber; everyone had seen the disease progress too many times. Choro only nibbled at his meat before setting it to one side. He lowered himself into the bedding and stared toward the open sky as they finished the rest of the meal.

"There are so few of us left. I don't know how the Chinjoka can survive. Our gods have deserted us and the sickness destroyed the tribe until we are tempting targets to our enemies," Choro whispered. The others fell silent as they explored their own dark memories. Blood-laced saliva and the gradual failure of the victims' ability to breathe were the symptoms burned into the memory of any Chinjoka. The number of people Dhala had eased onto their Long Flight left him numb. Even at his young age, he remembered when the plague began. Hysteria made a bad situation worse. Early, when so many were dying, terror ruled people's actions. Saat healers suggested any possible cure or at least a way to stop its spread. Its progression was slow but always fatal. It didn't seem to spread through contact. In many cases, some members of a family would not develop symptoms, while their fathers, mothers, brothers, or sisters perished. The Athru healer who might have been able to develop a cure died in the first wave of fatalities. Saat healers could do nothing, but ignorance and malice caused them to be blamed for the disease. The first season was devastating for the Chinjoka, physically and emotionally.

One village had thrown a Saat healer from the burial heights in a confused effort to gain attention from the Father. Choro, and the other Athru caste who lived then, championed the Saat healers. But people still feared the illness that was wiping out entire villages, and the healers' fear of retribution led them to stop aiding, not only those afflicted with the plague but other diseases normally not considered serious. This caused more deaths, this time from lack of rudimentary healing. The last of the plague victims received the best possible care. But even with the finest healing, like Choro was given, the ending was too predictable. And too tragic.

The small group finished their meal, and Dhala cleared the remains, dropping them into the cooking fire. The other two sat near Choro to fulfill any request. Dhala studied them, trying to think of anything to make Choro more comfortable. But he'd done all he could. To give Dhala something to occupy his thoughts, he began the work of tanning the osa hide. First, he brought a frame from the storage room. He cut a thin strip from the outer edge of the skin and made small slits along the edge. With care, he laced the pelt to the frame, stretching it into place.

"You have a skill to appreciate, Dhala. Don't forget others take note of your labor," Choro said.

Dhala faltered at his task. Tears flowed again as he met the gaze of the elder. He broke contact to refocus on his task even though emotions overwhelmed him. One thing he had learned early in life, emotional and fragile Chinjoka suffered short and miserable lives. He nurtured the strength to continue even when overwhelmed with impending loss. This was no different as he focused on scraping the hide clean, fingerwidth by fingerwidth.

But his walls broke and loneliness poured into Dhala. Too overwhelmed to continue, he let his hands drop to his side as he wept. No one chastised him for his lack of control, even though it was certain everyone heard. His strength waned as his sorrow leaked out as salty tears.

A light touch shocked Dhala, and he turned to find Gyam standing beside him. He stiffened, expecting a reprimand. But no rebuke came. Gyam instead knelt beside him and hugged him. Dhala returned his embrace. During that moment, his friend since birth returned, and the formal Athru of recent seasons vanished.

"He will be fine. I think the fresh meat brought him new energy. He will recover. Don't grieve for him."

Dhala schooled his expression before meeting Gyam's gaze. Unable to lie, he spoke a different truth. "I believe Choro is one of the strongest Chinjoka I've ever met. If anyone can conquer the disease killing us, it will be him."

Gyam patted his shoulder and flashed a smile at Dhala.

"Exactly. Now, one of us will sit with him so we are close if he needs anything. Otherwise, we will continue our day."

"Of course, Gyam."

Dhala tried to add more, but his knowledge of the Saat healing was too limited to enable him to sense the state of Choro's rapidly deteriorating health. He nodded and turned to his work.

WRENCHED AWAKE IN the darkest of night by a sense of dread, Dhala glanced into the inky darkness, trying to find the source of his unease. A thick layer of clouds masked the moon and stars so that little light entered through the portal. It resulted in a black so complete he couldn't see a handspan from his face.

Then, he heard it again. A rattling breath followed by a tight grip. Choro held tight as a thready whisper twisted around him. He leaned closer to try to understand. With his ear almost against Choro's lips, he understood the words.

"My time has ended."

A shuddering sigh came from deep inside Dhala. He held Choro as he sent his silent pleas to the Father of the Twins. Deep inside his being, he sensed these were Choro's final moments. He didn't know what else to do than give what comfort he could. Choro's gasps for air became more desperate with each passing second. Light flared from the fire, and a shadowed figure joined him. He glanced to see Gyam's square jaw and expression of determination. He looked first at Choro and shifted his gaze to Dhala.

"Do something! He can't breathe."

"Gyam, he's leaving for the Long Flight, and we can do nothing about it."

"No! You must heal him!"

Dhala started to explain again when a dark noise came from Choro. With strength he hadn't exhibited in moons, Choro brought Dhala's hand onto his chest and pulled Gyam's on top. He glared at both of them as he fought to pull in another breath. But with a final throaty rattle that would be with Dhala forever—Choro died.

Dhala left his hand in place as sorrow flooded his being. The tears flowed again, landing drop by drop on the body of the kindly man. Gyam snatched his hand back, breaking contact with Dhala. The action added to the ache, but it was time to block his emotions again. After waiting a little longer, he lifted his hand from Choro's chest, sat on his heels, and wrapped his arms tight, trying to console himself.

He wiped his face and looked around to see Askari building their fire into a bright and warm spot in a night with no pleasure. Once the flame illuminated the dwelling, Askari lit a small lamp and slipped into the storage area. The rustle of things being moved stopped a few moments later, and he returned to the room with a white bundle under his arm. He sat the lamp on a niche carved into the rock wall, walked to Dhala, held the bundle out, and inclined his head. A moment later, Askari looked up and gazed at Dhala.

"It's Choro's life shroud. He told me where it was so I could give it to you when this day happened. It's finished. He showed me how to do the last of the embellishments after he was unable."

Dhala's throat clenched tight as the supple and heavily decorated shroud slid across his palms. The soft weight identified it as the work of a skilled artisan. It was beyond beautiful, but its purpose kept Dhala on the verge of breaking. His duty was clear, however, and he refused to dishonor Choro.

He opened the bundle of white leather and found what he expected. Gyam stepped away but appear to be ready to help Dhala should he need it. This was one time Dhala wouldn't suffer the help of anyone else, not even Askari and Gyam.

He laid the shroud to one side, brought a bowl of clean water close, and bathed the cooling form. He performed the duties according to tradition. While not his first burial, it would be one of the most painful.

Dhala walled away the overwhelming sense of loss that kept the knot in his gut and the next tear poised to fall. Dhala's entire focus remained on his duty to bind Choro in the rich, ceremonial garment Askari had given him. The light of predawn had strengthened when he was finished. Dhala hoped he'd prepared Choro as a highly respected elder should be presented. He stepped back to inspect his work, and someone's arm wound around his waist. A quick glance confirmed his intuition: Askari was at his side. His tear-stained face told Dhala that he was also grieving.

"Your skill would have made him proud."

Dhala fought for control before turning. "It will be time soon to do his death keen. Then the mourners give their tribute. The ascent to the burial crags begins at dusk. There is no time, and little reason, to feed my pride."

Askari drew his lips tight, but Dhala allowed it to pass without comment. Once he finished preparing the body, he cleaned the aerie while Gyam and Askari stared at the central fire pit. Dhala put what he needed to take to the lower levels in a net bag and carried it over one shoulder. The other two seemed determined to spend the rest of the day staring into the flames.

Dhala stepped onto the inner pathway and plunged into the wash of dark gray. The steps of the village were a nondescript color smoothed by the touch of countless sets of hands and feet. Gyam's aerie was high on the cliff. It would typically be the home of a number of Athru and would have a constant flow of traffic from the lower levels. Now only Gyam remained to utilize Dhala's skills as his Saat helper. He found the steps with the surety of long practice as he hurried down the steep treads. Soon he completed his descent along the well-worn path to the Saat warrens. The door cover opened with no effort, and he crept inside so as not to disturb the occupant.

"Dhala?"

He should have known his mother would be awake and working in the first light. She had not quit giving aid to those who needed it and maintained all her healing herbs at the height of their potency, unlike the other Saat healers. But she was not foolish. She was cautious in how she provided her skills. It was her famous relaxing tea that made treatments possible. One dose and the detail of what occurred became very fuzzy. The more perceptive of her patients didn't ask. His mother filled a small leather pouch with a handful of dried herbs as she smiled at him. She motioned toward the pot nested on one side of her glowing hearth.

"Osa stew is cooking, and I added herbs from the gardens to help fortify us through this day. Eat your fill."

Dhala's stomach roiled at the thought of food. "Choro is on the Long Flight. During the darkest hours last night. I need to prepare myself for the day of mourning."

"Yes, I know. I sensed him leave."

A deep sob rattled Dhala at the agonizing event put into words. He wrapped his arms tight to hold himself together. His mother sat her work aside, moved to her son, and held him. As the worst of the sadness diminished, she released her hold and gave him a peck on the cheek.

"Go. I'll send food for the three of you. I made flatbread yesterday from the groundnuts we harvested during the season of color." She stopped and cocked an eyebrow at him. "It's my hope the discord between you and Gyam is resolved."

Tension set his nerves on edge at the memory of their exchanges in recent days. "I don't know if he will ever forgive me. He blames me for Choro's passing."

His mother remained silent, but the disapproval directed at both of them did nothing to resolve their issues. As the silence tightened, he stood frozen, uncertain of what to do.

When the tension in the room became too thick, his mother let the discussion drop and motioned him toward the inner chamber. "Hurry. The keening begins soon. Few burials have a singer from each caste. Choro deserves the honor."

Dhala snapped his lips shut and moved to the back room. He found a bowl filled with clear cold water, his clothing lying beside it. He stripped and washed himself of grime, tears, and sweat from recent days. Once he finished, he felt better. He pulled out the rawhide container holding his ceremonial clothing and began making his selection. The breechcloth he chose fell almost to the ground. The material was dense with dyed quills forming a complex geometric pattern that spanned from his waist. Sewn to the fabric were also the translucent teeth of osa fawns in rows as well as sikari fangs. His footwear was not the open sandals he typically wore; these were heavy, laced to just below his knee, and decorated similar to his breechcloth.

Satisfied with his appearance, Dhala pulled on his richly decorated ceremonial leggings that had seen too much use in recent seasons. After tugging the more subtly embellished overshirt onto his slender body, he rejoined his mother.

She glanced toward him and smiled. "My son looks handsome today. Maybe Gyam will realize what he's missing."

"Mother! I'm Saat caste and he flies over the cutleaf forest. Our union will never happen. Even if it were possible, he holds me responsible for too many of his problems."

She snorted, sounding disgusted. "Foolish fledglings. We need a healing Athru to save us from the sickness. Unless something happened since I saw you last, you have not grown scales and wings to join their ranks."

Dhala shook his head. "No. I would have told you first. My body isn't even the right shape to be Athru."

She motioned again. "No one knows the paths the Twins provide for us. Our people are dying, and we must find a cure or the Chinjoka will be gone from the basin. You must follow the path set before you even if it is not the one you envisioned for yourself."

He nodded, kissed her cheek, and raced up the stairs. He had no desire to hear his mother's platitudes today.

When he reached the aerie, Gyam and Askari were both in their formal dress. He found himself at a loss for words, so he maintained his silence. Gyam remained aloof, treating Dhala as if he were invisible. Askari gave him a pat of encouragement as he walked past. The last ray of sunshine pierced the doorway, and Gyam stepped onto the outcropping that fronted his aerie, many spans from the brush and rocks below.

He began the keening with a high piercing whistle that tore through Dhala's carefully constructed walls. As Gyam shifted into a wordless call to the gods, Askari joined him. Their voices were distinct but intertwined in harmonies signifying a great man had passed. Dhala could almost see the flight of Gyam's song. It spoke of aching heights and powerful stoops. It was the song of a raptor.

Askari brought a different element to the call with the power of the earth and a sense of responsibility. It spoke of the role of Onija as warriors and hunters. It wasn't difficult to sense the earth's tremble as the Onija massed their strength to protect the Chinjoka.

Dhala's time to join the call came, and he instinctively sensed his role. His light trill began a call for peace and harmony, for healing and growth. He sang of the Saat as the support to the other castes. He knew his place, but his chorus told of the worker caste. There were bits that surprised Dhala as they left his lips. This new harmony talked of calm strength and the value of the Saat.

Their timing was perfect as light flooded the space, touching the shroud surrounding Choro. The tune created by the three told the story of the freedom of gliding on the summer thermals, skill with spear and bow, and satisfaction of a successful harvest.

Other notes joined them as Chinjoka added their own trills to the base provided by the trio. Soon the entire valley filled with the sounds of Choro's mourning song. Rising notes bound themselves together before drifting apart. The refrain faded as Dhala whistled his final notes.

The other two trailed their songs until only silence wrapped around them. They stood unmoving until Gyam nodded with a note of finality.

"The other Chinjoka will join us soon, and we will carry him to the highest crags for a proper Athru burial."

Dhala and Askari locked gazes, and Askari looked at Gyam. "Are you certain? The high recesses need at least two Athru. Do you think you can carry Choro alone?"

Gyam shot a venomous glare at Askari before replying. "I will do this. I will carry Choro to his final resting place." He leveled an emotion-filled stare at Dhala. "Some of us fulfill *all* of our duties."

Distress pooled inside Dhala, and his heart ached at the accusation, but he refused to respond. He retrieved an awl and osa sinew and knelt to close the burial shroud. The bundle of dried tendon fibers lay beside him. He pulled a strand free and ran all but the tip through his mouth to moisten it. After pulling them from between his lips, he studied the damp fibers, requiring nothing less than perfection of his craftsmanship. This work normally fell to the deceased's helper Saat. As the closest Choro had to such, the task fell on him.

He gathered the edges of the hide and pressed the awl through the soft layers, and then for the next step, pressed through the moistened end and pulled it tight. He'd finished only a handful of stitches when Askari squatted beside him.

"I can help. You aren't alone in this."

Dhala paused from his work to study his friend. Askari's expression told him the offer was serious.

"No. This is my duty." He refused to let it overwhelm him. "Not only was he an Athru elder, he was my friend and mentor. He deserves the best of my efforts."

"I would stay with you, if you would bear it."

A warm sensation flowed over him. "Yes. I would welcome that."

As the sun fell lower on the horizon, something rustled in the dimming light opposite the fire. He started to call out, but Askari's light touch stopped him.

He leaned in and whispered, "It's Gyam. He struggles with the loss."

Dhala focused on his task and, after a few more stitches, spoke softly. "He is not the only one who has suffered."

"Your mother told me when I first led war parties against the Misiq, I should never judge the depth of someone's grief by their outward display."

"That sounds like something she would say. Misiq fighters leave an overwhelming swath of death and sorrow whenever we encounter them. I do not see the similarity."

Askari smirked as Dhala returned to his work. Gyam blamed Dhala for the elder's death, but there was little Askari could do about that. Dhala had done everything imaginable, but they'd still lost Choro.

The sun eased its way down the western skies, disappearing beyond the rim of the White Cliffs of the Chinjokas' lands while Dhala focused on the task before him. Time slipped away as he gave his best effort to the work he was doing, only dimly aware of the times Askari tried to feed him. In some part of his being, he knew Gyam and Askari were preparing in their own ways, but his only focus was completing his task. His hands cramped and the sun slipped beyond the horizon when he threaded in the final stitch.

He rocked onto his heels and checked the work he had done. Disappointed to see a few flaws, but knowing he'd done his best. Askari stood, brushed himself off, and looked at Dhala's work.

"It's amazing," he said a moment later.

Gyam stirred from the position he'd held since Dhala began his task. He looked over the effort. Without meeting Dhala's gaze, he said, "It will suffice. Prepare the Chinjoka for a high burial."

Dhala nodded and walked from the cave.

THE COOL OF early spring filled the evening, but Gyam wasn't chilled. The ends of his breechcloth drifted away from him with each breath of air. Cradled in his arms was the body of his mentor he had carried from the aerie Choro and Gyam had shared. His grief washed over him again and again. But he would not appear weak. Dhala displayed his emotions at every turn, but Gyam would not allow the grief to overwhelm him.

The last of the people climbed to the base of the burial crags. He would take Choro's remains to the heights. He had sworn so to his mentor. Gyam blocked any other thoughts as he surveyed the crowd again before turning on the narrow trail. The light of the fading sun made the treacherous climb even more hazardous. He tested each step before trusting it with the weight of his burden. The almost breathless whispers from the village followed him as they did. The soft oaths from missteps were proof to the treacherous nature of the climb, even to a people who resided in the cliffs.

His breath became labored, and the steep climb had his legs burning as if buried in fiery coals. The weight of his burden was no less taxing on his arms and chest. Deep inside, he understood he was being stubborn about many things. But reasonable wasn't something he could manage. His focus was only on the ritual that remained.

Only the final sliver of the sun persisted when they came to the first of the niches holding Chinjoka. No one asked him to go higher, but Gyam refused to do anything less for Choro.

The trail narrowed until it was wide enough for only a single person. Gyam climbed higher while others dropped by the wayside, deciding the heights were great enough. But Gyam had his goal. Choro would rest with the greatest of the Athru.

Gasping for air, heart pounding, he reached the point where the path ended in a sheer drop. He glanced back to find Askari and, to his surprise, Dhala. But his focus remained on his task, and he would not accept any physical weakness.

He eased the body on the flat stone beneath their feet and stared at the other two. With an impassioned glance, he turned into the strong breeze. The valley floor was far down the mountainside, yet the winds brought him scents of spring. He called on the Goddess of Life and Fire, and began his change.

Gyam's skin thickened and became scales the deep-red of a coal buried in the flames. His hands and feet elongated and grew claws capable of killing an osa with a single swipe. His thick muscular body stretched and lengthened until he towered over even Askari. His chest grew larger to provide the air Gyam needed in flight.

The breechcloth fell in a pool around his feet as his hips became narrow, similar to those of the sikari packs, needed to hunt down the fleet osa. His genitals sheathed themselves between his legs as the final scales formed a brow ridge above each eye. The creature Gyam became stretched an arm over its shoulder and sliced through one of the twin mounds forming over his shoulder blades. He twisted and lanced the opposite one open with his other hand.

The wet flaps of skin grew larger with each beat of Gyam's heart. A moment passed before he tested them with a few strong strokes that lifted him from the ground. He gave the others a single command.

"Prepare him."

Speech vanished in an animalistic scream that filled him with power. He became as much raptor as Chinjoka.

He tucked his legs against his torso as he flew a few lengths higher while Dhala and Askari prepared the shroud for its purpose—a place for Gyam to sink his talons into as he carried Choro's remains to their final resting place.

Once everything was prepared, Gyam swooped down and straddled the body. He found this shape's emotions much more primal. But this form had no problem expressing his displeasure at what he had gone through over the past sun cycle. He roared at Askari and Dhala. Neither of them flinched or moved away. Gyam approved.

With infinite care, he grasped the shroud in his talons, their needle-sharp tips piercing the layers of hide with no difficulty, but it did not tear. He noted the distance to his destination. His wings unfurled, and he flexed them several times. Once certain the transition had been successful, he cut great swaths through the thin air. Each downstroke built in power until he rose several lengths above the stone precipice with his burden held tight.

Wind pummeled him from all directions. Sheer rock walls in a variety of configurations contributed to the always-shifting conditions. Through time, wind and rain had sculpted the crags into magnificent forms from the gods. Their solid gray masses contrasted against the azure spring sky. Buffeted by the turbulence, he struggled toward his goal, straining. His wing muscles burned with fatigue long before he reached the cluster of niches hidden among the columns of stone.

But the lower Athru burial caches didn't fit Gyam's needs. His determination to place Choro in the uppermost of the resting places was overwhelming. He passed by several other pillars of rock presenting themselves as possibilities, but his pledge sent him to higher and more dangerous funeral caches. The winds buffeted him as each downward stroke of his wings drove muscles already screaming from exertion.

He reached his goal as the fire in his wing muscles threatened to destroy him. He strained to reach the rock shelf when the wind shifted directions and swept him away from his destination. His outstretched wings caught the brunt of the blast and twisted him to one side.

The flight would have been challenging enough, but the extra weight left him struggling. Constant buffeting by the winds exhausted him to the point of failure. Gale-force gusts rolled him again. With wings tucked, Gyam allowed himself to drop for a moment. A glance downward brought the sight of length after rocky length of cliffs only too glad to crush him should he fail.

He fell enough to stabilize his flight, but as he did, he caught the concern on Askari's and Dhala's faces. He lashed his head about, focused more than ever on his destination. With wings pumping, he crept toward his goal, a fingerwidth at a time. The burning muscles screamed as he clawed his way through the turbulent skies.

His fatigue built with each snap of his wings. The world shrank to insignificance but for the pinpoint of rock that was his goal. He groaned at a slight loss in altitude and knew his time for success was dwindling. He curled inward and, with a final effort, drove higher. The effort cost him as he scrambled for purchase on a treacherous landing. He pulled himself forward until he and his burden rested on the unstable layered stone.

Gyam lay gasping on the cold rock, refusing to think how close to disaster he had just been. His overexerted muscles needed time to recover. But his task demanded more from him, and he would fulfill his quest.

Studying the surrounding landform, he found what he'd been searching for: an Athru burial cache. With great care, he lifted the remains he had carried and took the first unsteady step toward his destination.

The last part of the ritual was the most difficult. He must commit Choro to the high reaches, and the finality of his loss tore at his heart. The burden in his arms didn't compare to the weight of losing his mentor. Alone on Choro's windswept final resting place, Gyam released the emotions he had kept in careful containment. Tears ran across the fine scales covering his face, blinding him as he moved closer. Wave after wave of loss washed over him. He reared his head and bellowed his anger with all the force of the animal side of his Athru form. Resenting a life with no other Athru, he found the responsibilities a heavy burden. The fears and uncertainty became more than he could deal with. A sob choked him as he found a resting place for Choro.

Folding his wings against his back, he crouched lower until he could ease his burden into the opening. Gyam finished his task and paused in silent prayer to Pilea. He needed the fire from the Twin to survive his trial. Having placed the shroud-covered body into its cairn, he used his blade-sharp foreclaws to stack fist-sized rocks until the grave was covered.

The light faded before he finished, but his heat vision was enough to allow flight once the final stone settled into place. He waited, his wings furled tightly as he gathered his thoughts. Done with his reflection in pity, he stood and walked to the edge. After looking down at the seemingly endless drop before him, he bugled his cry of rage and threw himself from the cliffs.

Wind rushed past as Gyam relished the freefall. He enjoyed the rush of adrenaline for another heartbeat before snapping his wings open. His powerful backstrokes broke his fall, and he shot over the river that ran along the base of the cliffs. Once he'd regained control, he back-winged and flew over the people making their way down the cliff by dim yellowed torchlight.

He raced up the sheer stone cliffs, screaming his agony at the loss of another Athru, of this Athru. Most of the villagers drew back from his cry. But at the top, he found both Dhala and Askari waiting where he'd seen them last. Neither withdrew as he voiced his rage again and again. With a growling scream, he recognized the two who meant most in his life had refused to desert him in spite of his attempts to drive them away. Gyam refused to acknowledge their support, having just completed last rites for his mentor. Instead, he released the tethers on the animal side of his being and allowed it to voice his emotions. He would begin his healing process only after he gave himself to the blackening sky, which perfectly echoed his mood. Without another moment of reflection, he flipped over one shoulder and winged away toward the open grasslands.

Chapter Two

ASKARI SHARPENED HIS hunting knife while he sat in Gyam's living quarters. The soft scrape of metal against stone created a comforting sound within the confines of the stone aerie. It also helped mask Gyam's frantic pacing, which carried him across the space in a few quick strides. He'd hoped Gyam would calm himself during the handful of days since the burial, but nothing had changed. His searing glances toward Dhala only intensified. Askari tried to talk to Gyam, but it had as much impact as discussing the issue with the cliff face. Mention of Dhala made Gyam's temper flare to new levels.

Askari felt sympathy for Dhala, who struggled to give Gyam the care expected as part of the duty Dhala agreed upon. But Gyam became more difficult with each passing moment, and Askari wondered where this was going. A soft sound from the direction of the steps brought him back to the present. He cringed, expecting yet another damaging reaction from Gyam. After a pause, Dhala stepped through the doorway, and the moment Askari had dreaded unraveled.

Gyam turned away with a barely audible hiss that left Askari chilled. He prepared himself to rescue Dhala, but Gyam's only reaction was to cross his arms and watch the other man as if he were a carrion eater. Dhala avoided the gaze and carried the food he'd brought to the fire. Askari noted he'd brought enough to feed them for several days, a variety of foods, some fresh and needing to be eaten soon. But he also brought a large jar of anpar. The fermented mix of vegetables was well liked by Askari, and the version made by Dhala's mother was his favorite.

Dhala's hands shook as he went through his tasks. Gyam's attitude was obviously affecting him. But then, Gyam's mood was a challenge to all of them. Dhala was the most affected, but his attraction to Gyam had been obvious for cycles, at least to Askari. He'd recognized it long ago and understood Dhala would do whatever he could to satisfy Gyam, but so far, nothing had succeeded. One thing Askari was certain about: Gyam distancing himself from Dhala was having a devastating effect.

There was a curse, and an instant later, the crash of breaking pottery yanked his attention to the scene before him. Dhala looked stricken. Spread across the aerie's floor was the contents of the anpar container. Dhala must have dropped it, and the pottery shattered against the stone floor. Askari readied himself, fearing the accident would send Gyam into a rage.

Tiny, almost imperceptible tremors shook Dhala. They reminded Askari of the shaking of a newborn animal. Dhala seemed to lack the strength to struggle any further. He was close to breaking, and Askari tried to aid his friend.

"Don't worry, Dhala. It was an accident. I'll clean the mess." He'd taken only a single step when Gyam's voice filled the room.

"Enough. I don't need help. I can care for myself."

Dhala looked like he would have been less shocked if Gyam had screamed and hit him with his hunting bow. Dhala appeared distraught, but instead of breaking, he drew himself into a dignified stance.

"As you wish, Gyam. I can find a replacement if you would prefer."

Gyam pinched the bridge of his nose and stood for several heartbeats before speaking. "No. I want to be alone. Choro is gone, and I don't need help. Why would I need assistance from you or anyone else?"

Dhala never flinched. He left without another word. The footsteps faded until he could hear them no more. He frowned at Gyam.

"Are you going to drive me off next? Since you've sent Dhala away, I'm the last of your friends. And for what purpose did you spew the worst of your venom at Dhala? To prove you need no one? He cares for you. He would battle an entire band of Misiq if you asked him. In return, all he asks for is—"

"He knows his place as I know mine. There is a reason the Father created three types of Chinjoka. They are not to mingle."

Anger and frustration festered in Askari, his patience exhausted by his thick-skulled friend. He fought the need to slap the back of Gyam's head; perhaps it would knock free the webbing that must fill his skull. He narrowed his eyes at Gyam.

"The three make a whole. How far we shift dictates how we best serve the Chinjoka. You could not make scales capable of deflecting a spear strike any more than I could change into your flyer form. No caste is more important than another. Each serves its role. You know this but continue to battle change. Once, you knew the importance of the three castes and embraced it. The three of us have been closest of friends for as long as any of us can remember. Now you're allowing your bitterness to destroy the efforts of many seasons in order to hurt someone who cares for you."

Gyam ground his teeth as he glared at Askari. The torrent of expected excuses never came. Instead, Gyam walked to the sky portal and studied the portion of the basin surrounding the Chinjoka cliff dwellings. Askari stood silently as he scanned the land spread before him from the gray-green of the plant life that grew on the banks of the river along the base of the Chinjoka's cliffs. The blue haze muted the details of the far reaches of the basin. Much of what was hidden to his eyes, his other senses showed him.

The fitful breath of wind brought him the trace of cooking fires preparing the day's food. He could catch the murmur of the last of the Chinjoka mixed with the rattle of head-high brush that shook softly with each breeze. Askari relished the simple signs of life and honored Gyam's moments of silence. Once Gyam had taken ample time, Askari turned to face him while he leaned against the wall.

"He would come back. Even now. You need only to ask."

They stood looking over the lands as the wind twisted again around their bodies, making the ends of their breechcloths dance as if they had a life of their own. Time passed until the silence stretched to an uncomfortable level.

"I do not need help. Besides, what good would it do me? Choro had the undivided attention of the Saat, especially Dhala. It served no purpose. His death is no less permanent. Any of us could be next." Gyam studied the Chinjoka territory as it unfolded before him. "Would it change anything?"

Askari stared at him for a long moment before moving to the steps and leaving Gyam to his mood.

DHALA SAT IN the afternoon shade creating a new pottery vessel for his mother. The sun streamed into his workspace and flooded the cliff face behind him. He'd promised to replace the one he'd broken in spite of her protests that the work wasn't necessary. He'd used the past several days preparing the clay and searching along the river to find the materials he needed. The effort gave him a sense of accomplishment. At least he could do something.

He'd spent the afternoon digging clay from the river's banks and laying the pieces to dry on an ancient hata skin. Once it was dry, he'd pounded the hard clay into a powder and mixed it with the finest of the sand to be found.

Once everything was combined, he added water in tiny amounts until it was the perfect consistency, and worked the clay to remove any air bubbles he might have introduced during its creation. As he did, he thought back to the days his parent had taught the three of them how to create the pottery used by the Chinjoka. He'd enjoyed even more that it was one skill Gyam never mastered. He'd finished the initial work by evening, knowing his skills would be tested the next morning.

His clay was the consistency of leather when he checked it the next day. Once he had his working area arranged, he spent a good part of the morning making short coils and forming the pot round by round. As he went higher, he used his smoothing stone until the individual coils became a thin wall perfect for his needs. The vessel was for anpar and had its own set of requirements. The most critical of which was a curved shape to allow the ingredients to be packed inside and a well-fitting lid to seal the container. He knew from earlier experience his challenge would be fitting the lid. With past attempts, his mother sometimes rescued the day, but this time, he refused to rely on others.

I will do this if it takes until the hata migration comes through the grasslands.

"The shape is developing well. I could fill that with anpar."

Dhala rolled his eyes and then peered at his mother. "I'll make it work. I don't need help at every point. Your son is no longer a fledgling."

"No one would doubt you. You've always been strong-willed. You can become anything you want."

Dhala paused from his efforts and muttered. "Not anything. My body refuses to take on the shape of the Athru form."

He kept his eyes down, not wanting to see the pity that must be on his mother's face. When her silence stretched beyond what Dhala could bear, he glanced over. To his surprise, she had left. He looked around to find her. He would have welcomed her opinion, but she had disappeared into the dark tunnels trailing back into the cliff face.

After a few moments, he stiffened his determination and refocused on the work before him. The afternoon sun beamed against his back as he cut the lip into the vessel. The clay was past ideal with the sun drying it faster than he would have liked. He dipped his fingers into the small bowl of water beside him and flicked droplets onto the pot to slow its drying.

"You can't hide making pots for the rest of your life."

Dhala lurched forward, almost smashing the fragile piece he'd been working on all day. He allowed himself a moment to regain his equilibrium before turning to Askari.

"You almost ruined a day's work. You're stalking me like when we were fledglings."

Askari chuckled, a sound that surprised Dhala with its lightheartedness. "You were always easy prey. Your focus was on one thing. You'd never last as an Onija. You would be captured by the Misiq while you were hunting mkali."

Dhala blushed but flicked his clay-coated finger at Askari. "It wasn't a Misiq. It was you with cutleaf fronds hanging from everywhere. And you know I love roasted mkali."

"And you have the scars to show for your obsession. Every time they boil out of their burrows because you've disturbed them, their fist-sized bodies swarmed over us until they looked like a thatch of brown hair, sharp claws, and gnashing teeth. The one time we hunted them, we bled from scores of their tiny bites."

"Roasted mkali. You should go hunt a brace of them for dinner. I will even do the work of cleaning and cooking them. You are exaggerating their ferocity."

Askari chuckled again. "No, I remember that day very clearly and have scars as evidence. Not even if Tayi was cooking them would I be willing to risk being gnawed by the tiny tribe of bloodletters."

Dhala let a soft chuckle escape. "I still say they're delicious. If it were up to you, we'd be eating only from the gardens."

"I don't get bitten in the garden, and the harvest is tasty."

Dhala rolled his eyes again, but kept any other comments to himself. He finished the lip of the jar as Askari squatted beside him. Without glancing to his friend, Dhala eased the vessel to one side and worked on the lid.

"He regrets what he said. He'd welcome you back if you asked," Askari said.

Dhala slowed his hands to a stop. A deep sigh filled the air as Dhala tried to mask the flood of anger his friend's statement caused. "He told me to leave because he didn't need help caring for his aerie. Should he decide he needs a Saat, I'm sure the elders could find him a suitable one."

Their gazes locked as Askari's expression shifted to disapproval. He stood and shook his head. "You're as stubborn as he is."

"He's not the only one to lose an important person in his life when Choro joined the Long Flight. I'm sure the last of the Athru caste will have no trouble finding a Saat to serve him."

Askari walked away, his anger evident in his stride.

Without a glance to his friend, Dhala clenched his teeth and focused on his work. The inner turmoil made the task even more difficult than usual. His struggle for control showed in the first lid. It was far from what he needed. Frustration washed over him as he tossed the failed piece aside and began anew.

The last of his control evaporated when another attempt was the farthest from fitting of all he'd done that sun cycle. He held it in his hand, contemplating his failure for a moment before smashing the lid against the stone wall he faced.

"It's never easy making two different things fit each other."

Dhala sighed, his chin dropping to his chest. As much as he didn't want his failures known, his mother would have been the one he dreaded most. "I can't seem to master the technique. I know what I said earlier, but could you show me again?"

His mother studied his work, turning the half-dry pot with careful dispassion. But she handed it back to him with a shake of her head. "No. You said you didn't need my help, so I'll let you continue."

Dhala's jaw dropped at his mother's refusal. His gaze followed her as she disappeared into the warren, and he waited, hoping she would return. But she would hold him to his statement to finish the work without her help. He must finish the task he'd set. Focused on the remaining clay, he scowled and began again.

The day slipped into evening, and he realized how exhausted he was as he sat with his shoulders cramping, watching the fire burn low. The empty bowl that had contained the stew his mother made for their evening meal was long ago emptied. He'd struggled with piece after piece, taking out his frustration on the failed works by smashing each one against the wall.

The time would come to regret his childish expressions of frustration. But smashing the failures into blobs gave an outlet to his anger. Given no other choice, he picked up one of the final bits of clay and started again. He paced to the dwindling flames and moved more wood to the hot embers. His thoughts drifted to Gyam as he studied the material in his hands. Maybe that's why the situation with Gyam bothered him so much. Like the clay, Gyam refused to work with Dhala. The request to leave had left him with a gnawing sensation of failure.

He clenched his jaw and sat down with his clay, placing the thin coils one over another until he completed a rough lid shape. He worked with great care, focusing all his energy into the effort. Outside the bright circle of light given off by the fire, the world no longer existed for Dhala. A short time later, he held the most elegant lid he'd done that day, perhaps one of the most beautiful he'd ever done. He cradled the piece in his hands, awash in awe he had created something showing this level of mastery.

With a smile of satisfaction, he retrieved the almost-dried storage vessel and sat it between his knees. His smile grew as he held the new lid over the opening before easing it in place. He leaned back to admire his work, pleased with the results.

The lid shifted with an audible click, and before Dhala could discern the reason, the top slipped again and fell through the opening. The hollow thud filling the surrounding darkness seemed louder than the scream of an injured hata. He knew the results without looking. His perfect lid was a misshapen blob at the bottom. Waves of failure crashed over him. *Can I not even create a competent anpar container?*

"Do it again."

His frustration boiled over at his mother. "I've done them all day and into the night. I did the best lid I've ever done, and it failed."

"Do it again."

"There's little clay left. It might not be enough."

His mother stared at him and lifted one eyebrow.

"Fine."

He grabbed the last ball of clay and worked it without looking, his gaze locked on his mother. But swirls of emotions twisted through his system, leaving his stomach knotted and his body shaking. In spite of the sense of failure and worthlessness building in him, his fingers dug into the soft material and formed the rough coils.

He glared at his mother. "This is a waste of time. I've failed with each attempt."

The fire flared for an instant, and she took the appearance of one of the Dark Lord's followers. Dhala was not in the frame of mind for this brand of learning. The sight only inflamed his anger. His hands moved with strength and certainty, ignoring the delicacy of his earlier approaches.

When he spoke, he was close to shouting. "I tried, Mother. What else can I do? My best is not good enough. Something so simple as a lid to an anpar storage jar. I did more lids today than most people complete in a full season."

"And what happened?"

"I created a beautiful lid. A beautiful useless lid. It became another blob of clay I dug from the bottom of the jar." His hands blurred as he put his focus anywhere else. His emotions boiled to the surface, but he refused to be overwhelmed by them. The struggle lasted a moment before he walled over the flood of failure he was experiencing.

The piece he held in his hands was complete. Dhala wanted to turn and destroy it as he had so many. A rattling sigh leaked from him at the thought of the people he had failed, including his mother. He would at least prove to her that he hadn't quit.

"Show me."

His breath caught as he opened his hands. What he held wasn't the work of a fledgling. Instead, it was the work of a competent craftsman. It didn't have the delicate beauty of the other piece, but it was solid and useful. He found himself drawn to the work.

"Try it."

He looked at her and arched his eyebrows. She nodded and motioned toward the jar. With a shrug, he sat the lid in place. It nestled in with easy familiarity. It fit. Not only did it fit, it paired with the jar in a way that the beauty of the earlier one couldn't match. Yes, it was simple and utilitarian, but it served its purpose with dignity.

"But the other was so beautiful," Dhala couldn't help saying.

"It didn't fit. It didn't complete the pairing. This one, made without harsh judgment, is the one for your jar."

Dhala looked around the space and to his mother. "What now?"

She smiled at him. "You will sleep. When you wake, you're helping me in the gardens."

"And what are you doing?"

She chuckled. "Beginning my day. The new day is close."

He peered around them, and the gray of predawn brought the surrounding features into being. When he turned to his mother, he rocked for a moment before giving her a childish smile.

"Yes, Mother. I think sleep sounds like an excellent idea."

SEVERAL DAYS HAD passed since Dhala's success with the pottery. The result left him lacking the willingness to do more than what was required. He found himself in many solitary endeavors, isolated even from other Saat. He relished the quiet. In spite of what he'd told Askari, his infatuation with Gyam had not lessened. He drew Dhala like a flasher bug to the evening fire, with similar painful results.

In the early-morning quiet, he worked on the section of the communal garden assigned to his family. In spite of there only being the two of them, the elders gave his family a large section. His mother fed many of the families among the Chinjoka and believed wholesome food to be one way to keep the people healthy. The full stomachs that resulted did nothing to discourage the decision. The larger space also left room for the medicinal herbs she scattered through the garden. These rounded out many of the plant pharmaceuticals she used in her subtle healings. The others were plants that refused to tolerate the confines of cultivation.

As he worked his way down each row of green plants, he couldn't help but think about their small family. Tradition would have relegated them to the edges of the village and the worst spots in communal hunts. When Dhala was a toddler, his father had died during one of the annual hunts. His mother didn't talk about it, but others told a quiet tale of how his father's bravery that day saved several other people.

With their family reduced to just two, it would not have been unusual to move them to the smaller warrens to allow space for larger families. But his mother's status as a healer warranted her location in the center of the village so she could be reached quickly by someone in need, whether they nested in the highest aerie or the deepest warren.

"I have herbs I need you to gather for me. It will soon be the season for the heat fevers. This is the perfect time to harvest certain plants."

Dhala managed not to sigh as he stood and turned to her. He dusted his hands against the leggings he'd donned that morning and gave her a forced smile. "Of course. Just tell me what you must have."

She handed him a mesh bag and listed her needs. He realized he must focus or he would neglect something from her exhaustive list. She seemed determined to refill her entire store of herbs in a single day.

"The blue fledgling tears are only found near the spires. And only take one of three. We don't want the Father to think we do not appreciate his gifts."

Dhala sighed again, loud enough for anyone who was close to hear. "Mother, I know the harvest rituals and which plants are where. This task will take days."

She darted into the cave and returned with a small bundle. "Here is your bedding. You don't have to rush. Some plants can only be harvested at certain times of the day."

Dhala reached out for the pack she offered, fighting to keep the many comments running through his mind from emerging. He recognized a diversion, but if he didn't get the plants she asked for, she would be unhappy. No one liked to displease her, least of all her son. Not that she did anything. Nothing that resembled confrontation. No one enjoyed disappointing his mother. She added a net bag to his supplies, and he managed not to let any more sounds of discontentment leak from his lips. He leaned forward and kissed her on the cheek before turning and leaving the warren. Time to begin his journey. His needs had been addressed.

His path took him north of the village. He would travel first to the most distant gathering places and work his way back toward his home, harvesting from the crags last. He'd seen too many burials to enjoy the high grounds. He wasn't pleased with the way his mother had manipulated him into leaving, but as he moved farther from the village, he found his tension lessening. When he traveled alone, he must always be vigilant, but he enjoyed being away.

Regardless of how he denied the effect of Gyam's rejection, he felt judged by everyone he passed, especially the Saat. They either showered him with expressions of disdain or pity. He couldn't have said which was worse, but the combination put him in a dark mood. He resolved to focus on the task assigned to him. The glances, judgments, and pity meant nothing.

Dhala froze in midstep and crouched low at the sound of scurrying across the dried leaves. He eased the throwing stick from his breechcloth and scanned for his quarry. Motionless, he watched the grass before him. The moments ticked past as he waited. Something was close. He needed it to make the slightest of moves for him to locate and identify his quarry.

There. In the thick brush.

He leapt forward as an entire flock of runner birds erupted from the high grass. He drew back and let fly with the knob-ended stick. It spun in an arc toward the animals. He burst into a run when the throwing stick hit one of the small plump birds. He grabbed the injured animal and dispatched it in an instant. He put the take into his net bag, glad to have his evening meal.

Dhala navigated the steepening paths until he was inching his way across the loose broken layers of stone forming part of the eastern boundary of the Chinjoka territory. He used the rest of the day to gather the herbs found in the rough landscape. Harvests from these rare plants varied from a leaf or two of low-growing succulents that had spread through a treacherous old rockslide to the gray, fuzzy flower buds of the snow petal. Emphatic about the bud's unmatched ability to stop bleeding, his mother stressed the snow petal's importance as a treatment for deep wounds. Already well aware of the value of the treatment, he took as much as possible without damage to the plant. He layered his harvest in stiff hide carrying cases to protect the precious material. But this landslide held the largest patch of the plant he'd ever seen, and he had been gathering medicines with and for his mother since he could scramble over the rocks.

He timed the conclusion of his work to arrive at a campsite Dhala had used on many prior occasions. It was not only one of the few flat sites nearby but also had a source of water trickling into a grove of trees dwarfed by the severe weather of the high altitude. Of more importance to Dhala, their diminutive branches provided a windbreak from the snow-tinted winds that swept from the high mountains once the sun sank below the western rim. The winds that wouldn't warm until the last of the snow melted during the tallgrass moon.

He cleaned the small fire pit he had used when he spent the night on previous trips and gathered the material he needed to start his fire. He carefully arranged the tinder and pulled his firestones from the small pouch at his waist. His first few attempts, he had difficulty getting the hot sparks to land in the right spot, but then the strike was perfect. A bright, hot glow hit the tinder and a wisp of smoke drifted upward. He lay almost on top of the smoldering pile. With a few gentle puffs of breath, a yellow flame burst into existence, and he fed the flames gradually larger bits of fuel until he had a respectable fire going.

He cleaned a spot for his bedding, and by the time he'd finished that task, the fire was becoming what he needed as a cooking flame. He rolled a few dense rocks into the hot coals. By the light of his fire, he prepared the bird. With two thin sticks for tongs, he fished out several small stones from the fire and dropped them into the bird's cavity. The rocks sizzled, and in a short time, the aroma had Dhala's mouth watering. Next, he pulled the rest of the stones into a pile and eased the meat onto them.

Dhala focused on the cooking as dusk gathered. The darkness settled around him until all that was visible were silhouettes of the distant mountains. The fire brought on a sense of contentment and safety in spite of the solitude of the farthest crags. After the day's work, the simple pleasures of a delicious meal and a night's rest held great appeal.

Tempting aromas wafted around him, and Dhala decided the bird had cooked long enough. If it wasn't completely cooked through, partially raw worked too. Using his sticks again, he moved the meal to a large flat rock to cool. Despite his best intentions, the aromas overwhelmed him, and the meat had cooled only slightly when he began stripping pieces of meat from the small carcass.

A short time later, he sucked on the last thighbone, enjoying the tastes of succulent flesh. He nursed the marrow from each bone before tossing them into the red coals. After giving himself a few moments of contentment, he arranged his bedding to its best advantage and cataloged the day's harvest. Some were tiny amounts he put in envelopes made from finely woven grasses. Others were large plants he bound at their bases and rolled in pieces of softly tanned osa hide.

He had most of the items he needed from his mother's litany. He lacked one or two more herbs he would gather as he moved from the crags to the cliffs that served as home for the Chinjoka. Satisfied everything was in order for the next day, he lay with his head against his arm and recalled the multitude of changes in his life since Choro's death. He considered each possible place he could have chosen differently and how it might have changed the results. He knew the answer to his obsessive question, but that didn't keep him from asking himself more until the fire faded to a few winking crimson spots and exhaustion overwhelmed him.

Dhala woke to the soft scurry of nocturnal animals seeking shelter in the early predawn and gave himself time he rarely allowed at the village.

But the gray light had brightened only slightly when he slipped from his bedding and checked for any signs that might signal intruders. The Chinjoka's valley might be a sheltered area, but one didn't live to Dhala's age without exercising caution. Sikari packs were infrequent in the valley, but a chance meeting with the bone-crushing jaws of the four-legged eating machines would be fatal. Like the quarry he hunted, Dhala learned early always to be aware of his surroundings and everything in them.

He readied himself. Even though he was well inside Chinjoka territory, he arranged the campsite until no one could tell it had served as his overnight shelter. He threw the bedding roll over his shoulder, along with the net bag and its precious cargo. He kept his steps to the rock outcroppings to hide his footprints. After a few lengths, rough terrain hid his back trail, and he moved faster.

One realization Dhala arrived at through his obsessive examination—he'd wanted the impossible. His obsession with Gyam was pointless. Athru did not life bond with Saat. Gyam had told him often enough. He would never become Athru. The time for him to change form to Athru, or even Onija, passed long ago. His mother had always left him believing his destiny was to gain the ability to shift to the Athru form. Disappointed when it didn't happen and his friend had completed their change, he had pressed onward. Season after season, the change never came for him. He'd celebrated with Askari when his plates first appeared, even helping him spread the lotion his mother gave him when the tiny scales enlarged and caused Askari to claw at his skin as the itching became almost unbearable.

The change wasn't easy for Askari. Dhala talked him through the process over and over again, repeating the instructions his mother gave the others. He'd kept his own anguish hidden behind thick walls so his friend had never known his sorrow. Then, the plague struck, and caste became less important than the masses of people who were sickening and dying. The only Athru healer died in the first wave of the plague. Later, people blamed the Saat healers for being unable to cure the disease. The dark looks became threats and even more dire.

His mother refused to stop treating patients despite the danger. She continued to heal any injured and made people comfortable as the sickness took them.

The other Saat healers no longer treated the sick, saying they had lost the ability. But she faced down distraught people several times and continued to help any who asked. But she never gave false hope. She only said she would give what comfort she had.

Those seasons filled with turmoil. The other two Chinjoka villages became too small to defend themselves against Misiq attacks. When the survivors from the devastated villages appeared seeking help, she was a passionate advocate for providing them shelter. She calmed fears that the newcomers would bring new cases of the plague. Voices such as his mother's won the day. Sadly, his village had contained more than enough empty spaces for all the refugees.

Dhala rammed his toe into the edge of a flat stone, the pain jarring him from his melancholy. He bit down against the waves of discomfort and waited for them to subside.

That's what I get for letting myself become lost in the past. I'm lucky it wasn't worse.

As he studied the surrounding landscape, he realized he had moved toward his final destination. The air became chilled as he climbed higher, feeding the morning ground fog that curled around his feet. The ash gray fog revealed only the occasional glimpse of the rugged ground he traversed. He checked his bearings and studied the lands surrounding him. Mists oozed from the peaks to his north. The gray mass devoured the lowlands many spans below him as it spread across the upper valley. Winds from the high peaks swept through them. He stood while the morning mists curled through the valley below him as if it were alive rather than a provider of life. Dhala allowed himself another moment before turning toward the heights.

He moved higher, searching for the final herbs that had been requested. After traveling a few spans farther down the game trail, he spotted a small cluster of the blue flowers his mother had demanded.

Relieved to have found the last of the items, he readied the leather bag designed for this herb. In fact, he only needed the tiny blue flowers and blue-green leaves, so the small scattered clusters would more than serve. He pulled his short harvesting knife from the pouch and gathered as the Father had dictated by taking only a fraction of the plant material. The sun moved higher in the sky by the time he'd harvested what he needed. He gently shook the bag to settle its contents, then tied the container shut.

As he moved back to his feet, a piercing whistle filled the air and caused Dhala to jump. When the call assaulted his ears again, he recognized its source. It was a mkali guard sounding an alert. It didn't take long for Dhala to spot the rocks that were home to a colony of the aggressive animals.

These were the mountain variety and much larger than the ones he'd hunted in the valley. He'd denied his concern about the bites from these animals to Askari but agreed with his friend's assessment. They were vicious. He had only hunted them once, the time Askari liked to recall. Several of them decided the mkali would be good prey. It turned out they had chosen poorly. The other mkali pull dead or injured ones into the colony, so it was difficult to get a morsel to eat. When an entire colony of the fierce animals were biting whatever they could reach, it was difficult to think of hunting them again.

A third note pierced the sky, and he spotted small faces peering at him from every crevice of the colony's rocky home. Dhala chuckled. He'd never hunt the mkali again. He was certain he'd have nothing to show for it but another set of scars, only from larger teeth. And besides, he had to respect any animals that protected their own with more savagery than some people he knew.

"Little brothers, let me pass. I have no intention of battling your warriors. I might be Saat, but that doesn't make me foolish."

The creature who'd triggered the alarm cocked its head to one side but issued no other sounds. It studied Dhala before leaping with a chirp and diving into its den. The others followed in rapid succession. Even with none of the animals visible, he was under no illusion he wasn't being watched.

He changed his focus from the animals to his own journey. Dhala was close to the burial grounds, and he hadn't needed the mkali to guide him. The Chinjoka didn't carry Saat or Onija to the air crags. Only the Athru, like Choro, received that honor. But the crags were sacred.

Do I have the strength for this?

As he turned, having decided his course of action, the now-familiar whistle sounded behind him. He glanced over his shoulder at the fist-sized animal. Their gazes met, and , against its nature, the mkali turned and bounded up the path. Dhala scowled. *I will not take directions from a favorite roasted morsel.*

It paused, turned to him, and Dhala swore the sound the animal made was more reminiscent of skyfire during a storm-moon wind gale. He stood in shock. This wasn't the playful antics of an animal with a brain the size of his thumb. This was likely the Father ordering him to the heights. Otherwise, it was one or both of the Twins, and Dhala wasn't certain that path held any fewer hazards. He had hoped to avoid intervention from any of those that dwelled beyond.

With a sigh, he started on the path that would take him through the Chinjoka burial grounds. He tried to prepare himself, but that goal seemed impossible.

THE SUN HAD scarcely moved by the time he stood on the flat, circular stone. One whose purpose he knew well. He stood at the sacred altar created by the Twins for Chinjoka last rites.

He turned slowly, at the edge of the barren, windswept plateau and stared at the delineation marking the change in the Chinjoka lands between the cutleaf forest and the beginning of the grasslands. As he stood on the precipice, winds howling against the cliff face raced upward to lash against Dhala. He'd been there too many times in the past seasons. Even though the village was close, the heights seemed to be in a different land.

Dhala spoke to the rugged cliffs. "You knew my tasks would bring me here. I've been here too often. I don't want to revisit the spirits resting in this place."

The winds dropped, and a tendril of mist uncoiled toward him, sweeping the dais of leaves and debris. As it dissipated into the thin mountain air, Dhala sighed. It was time he made offering to the worlds beyond this one as he had many times before.

First, he laid his carrying bag next to the small opening in the center of the stone and brought out his firestones. Then he stripped until only his calf-high shoes and breechcloth remained. Dhala gathered a fistful of twigs and finer materials and soon had the center filled. Once everything met his satisfaction, he lowered himself beside the small fire hole. In an attempt to delay his effort, and failure, he made minute adjustments in the materials.

He clenched his eyes shut to block out the thoughts flooding him. He relegated himself to the task, grasped his firestones, and struck them together. The impact sent white-hot sparks showering over the fire-starting material. He leaned forward, breathing into the bundle. A wisp of smoke struggled upward, and he blew again. The red glow shone for a moment before extinguishing. He shook his head and prepared again. The second time was a similar failure.

He rocked back on his heels and examined the stone, trying to work out a solution. But he couldn't find a reason for its refusal to catch fire. He searched the immediate area for more tinder but found nothing other than rock and the odd green sprout poking its way through the gravel. But as he worked farther away, he spotted an oddity among the more familiar. A ball of thin fibers.

Dhala picked the bundle up and studied it. It was a seedpod but unlike any he'd seen. Dried and devoid of the individual seeds of a typical cluster, this was a perfect bit of tinder.

He rearranged the hearth with his new discovery. With the firestones held close, he struck them together. A hot spark again lodged inside the tinder. He leaned in to breathe on the ember when a breeze raked across the rocks and ignited the flames.

He fed it small twigs and bits of grass until a fire crackled. The breeze continued for several more moments before coming to a dead calm. Thin threads of smoke emerged from fine cracks in the stone he had never noticed. With the middle as an apex, tendrils of white formed four transparent screens, one to each of the cardinal directions. As it reached the outer edge, it contained the entire stone. The blaze he'd tended should never have been able to create such a space, but it did.

As he tried to discover the source of his mystical smoke, a familiar voice came to him. A voice lost years ago. He stared into the haze now encompassing him to find Aroha standing before him.

Shock and fear filled Dhala, leaving little space for any other emotions. As the dark-haired figure drew closer, he called out. "Aroha? Is that you?"

The figure shook its head. "I'm sorry, but no. Aroha's spirit went to the Long Flight seasons ago. We'd hoped his form would be comfortable for you. But I can be others."

The figure changed shape, becoming Choro. He kept that form for an instant before changing to other people from Dhala's past. All buried in the heights.

"Please. Stop. Who are you? Why are you torturing me with images of all the people lost to me?"

The form became Aroha again, but the face echoed lifetimes of sadness as he turned to Dhala. "I didn't intend to torment. The only shapes I may use are from those who have already taken the Long Flight. Without a strong soul rider, you could not bear the sight of my actual appearance."

Dhala's gut knotted. "Who are you?"

"I am Voda. The one you call the God of Waters."

Dhala's legs might not have held his weight if he had been standing. But his next reaction was a flush of anger that threatened to roar out of control. He pursed his lips and met the turbulent blue eyes staring at him, instead of Aroha's beautiful brown eyes. It sent his fury roaring even higher. He struggled not to release his anger.

"You are troubled, Saat. Ask what you will. There will be no punishment. Be warned. You'll not like certain answers."

The dams burst and a torrent of words and accusations threatened to rush out. He bit off a few words. "We need a cure. Why do you let your people die?"

"We are not here to remove your challenges. Life is growth. Without struggles, there is no growth."

Dhala was speechless for a moment. But only a moment. "You've allowed the Chinjoka to be decimated by the plague. From three villages, now we are one. The plague you sent upon us isn't a challenge. It's a death sentence for all the Chinjoka." He looked at Voda as something else came to him. "Even now? You aren't here to save us. Isn't that right?"

The only sign that Dhala's words had any effect was the unrest in the Twin's eyes. His reply came in a measured beat. "The sickness is not our work." He waved Dhala into silence when he tried to speak. "No. I will speak now. The gods mourn the deaths, but it's the Chinjoka who must find the cure."

Dhala exhaled in a gust, the anger leaving him for the moment. "Is there a cure? Nothing has slowed it. We tried everything from the combined knowledge of all the castes."

"Yes, Father has seen a treatment is possible. But we have no knowledge of how to discover it."

Dhala nodded, relegating himself to the path they already traveled. But Voda startled him when he continued. "I said earlier that I am not Aroha. Which is true. But when he passed into the next world, some of him stayed."

Dhala swallowed hard. He had spent many sleepless nights wondering about Aroha's feelings when he left on the Long Flight. Aroha had been a close friend through his entire life. They had shared a bond with each other that was almost as strong as the one that existed with Askari, and Gyam. At puberty, it was Aroha he'd explored his sexuality with...and he had been the first to die from the sickness. The loss of his intimate friend had been a horrible ordeal, but what Dhala worried about more was if Aroha understood the truth.

"He knew. It wasn't as he would have liked. But he knew."

Dhala stepped back with a choking sob. "What? How?"

He received a sympathetic shrug. "There are things we can foresee and others we cannot. Aroha knew your love for him and understood it was not the depth of love he would have preferred. He realized the one your soul ached for was Gyam. He understood your heart more than anyone else. His desire for you was great, but he recognized the two of you were not a soul flight."

Dhala scrubbed at the tears flowing down his face and studied Voda. But there was nothing else to say.

"He was happy. Aroha understood you couldn't give him more. But he was content."

"What would have happened—later?"

The God of the Waters shrugged. "Does it matter? He found happiness with you. He relished your times together as young lovers. Nothing else matters."

Dhala gazed at the being giving him this information. "I am thankful to hear this. But why?"

"It is important for you to understand you need not feel guilt. But you will make important choices over the next seasons. You need to do them without the weight of losing Aroha."

"What? What must I learn?"

The form in front of him faded, but he had no trouble hearing the final comment. "You have free will. You always have free will. The choices will be yours."

Chapter Three

ENA MOVED WITH the stealth of his people, the Misiq. He hunted in his battle form. The patterned fur hid him well as he had traveled through the forest, which covered most of the Misiq territory, and his senses in this shape were much stronger than that of his two-legged mode. As part of the early force sent to attack the Chinjoka, he could perform his assigned task more efficiently in this variation. He stood atop the cliffs marking the western boundaries of the flyer's lands. His battle form's long tail writhed around him like something alive as he studied the enormous basin stretching as far as he could see. The wind blew toward him, and he inhaled, testing it for critical information. The scents played through him, allowing him to identify the odors. From the various evergreens that blanketed this end of the valley to the family groups of osa scattered through the area, he could name the scents drifting to him, and there was no taint of Chinjoka.

With morning's arrival, it came to Ena that he was making the same mistake as someone on their first patrol mission. Granted, the Chinjokian ground troops were fierce, but the death from the sky had been responsible for the failure of the Misiq to wipe out the ones who had spread their wasting disease. Before Ena's birth, the Ruling Council had declared a genocidal war against the Chinjoka. But the flyers were fierce warriors and struck down many Misiq with their diving attacks. They'd learned to avoid openings in the forest canopy where they were vulnerable to aerial assaults. Ena reared onto his hind legs and shredded the space in front of him with the deadly claws on his forepaws. His twitching tail showing the level of his agitation and disquiet. He dropped to all four feet and stepped into the dappled shade of the forest's edge, his coat hiding him well. Once he was comfortable with the location, he sank to his belly and studied the surrounding sky. As he did, he let the fitful gusts of wind continue to bring him the secrets of this region for many spans.

While young, Ena knew well the fatal consequences of the disease, for both sides. It had transformed their once-peaceful trading partners into their most-hated enemy. But he was familiar with the slow death to which the sickness condemned the Misiq. He'd lost many friends through the years as they fell to the fatal disease. Ena's emotions were in turmoil. He knew stories of the times before and how the two peoples had worked together. But now to save the Misiq, the Chinjoka must be eliminated.

He served as scout for his group of warriors, renowned for his tracking skills—both visual as well as his sense of smell. He changed locations several times through the afternoon, but nothing out of the ordinary came to him. He was surprised. He'd expected the patrols of the Chinjoka who shifted to flyers to be more of a presence.

He turned toward the Misiq encampment as the sun disappeared behind the trees. He'd located nothing noteworthy but would rather have what contact he must have with Upseeri before his meal. It made for a more tolerable evening.

He raced deeper into the forest and soon found himself within scent distance of the Misiq camp. He stopped and prepared himself to shift. His fur rippled and swirled as if he were in the middle of a storm-moon tempest while his body reabsorbed the thick, double-layered pelt. Popping like a Chinjoka whip sword, his tail disappeared. His body changed to the consistency of soft clay as it shifted from the form of a large feline predator back to his two-legged form. The night stubble of a beard appeared an instant later, as did his belted kilt with the metal demarcations of his rank among the Misiq.

Having re-formed into his two-legged shape, Ena worked through a series of stretches to eliminate any stiffness. Once he was satisfied there were no more lingering problems, he adjusted his clothing so he didn't look as if he had just emerged from his den. Ena slipped from the cover and stepped with authority along the main path.

He neared the almost invisible fire and noted Upseeri stood nearby. He knew from the hulking form of Annao, Upseeri's second, and the way he was abusing his authority over the new scouts that he prepared to spread his poisonous nature through the warriors. Ena found the man disgusting and recognized his cruel nature. Annao lost his entire family to the disease and that he was one who blamed the Chinjoka. He also dispatched captives in the most horrific way he could devise.

Ena despised him, but had done nothing about it. Annao showered accusations against a warrior who was barely of age to change form. "Leave him, Annao. He finished the tasks given to him. Not everyone can make the same claim."

Annao tensed, and it appeared for a heartbeat he would shift to battle form and challenge Ena. But when their eyes met and Ena welcomed his challenge, he glared. "Upseeri is making plans with real warriors on how to wipe the Chinjoka vermin from the lands of the Great Ones. He doesn't have time for a scout with no ability to track a lame flyer."

Upseeri appeared between them and scowled at the large Misiq. "That's enough, Annao. Finish your tasks." With his displeasure clear, Annao stomped away. Once he had disappeared into the brush, Upseeri turned to Ena.

"He's a dangerous man to challenge. Use care," Upseeri said.

Ena cocked his head and stared at Upseeri for a time before speaking. "You chose him as your second. If he is untrustworthy, then why?"

Upseeri studied Ena and the forest surrounding them. "He is loyal because he sees it as his mission to eradicate the Chinjoka. So long as our enemies align, he is useful. Once that changes..." He shrugged with no further comment.

They stood without speaking until the tension grew and Upseeri shifted his gaze. "We will scout this area more closely, but I believe it is a good base. The flyers cannot see us through the thick forest canopy."

Ena cocked an eyebrow. "In the past, the Chinjoka have found a way to locate us. Why would this time be different?"

Upseeri smirked at Ena. "We will make our shelters deep and hide their entrances. No Chinjoka flyer can see into a span-deep Misiq den."

Ena kept his silence, but he didn't believe they had given the Chinjoka the credit to which they were due.

Upseeri took him from his thoughts. "It's far to the west of any attack we currently have landed, but I want you patrolling the White Cliffs."

Ena considered for a moment why Upseeri decided to send him far from the Misiq forces to patrol the nearly impassable western boundary of the Chinjoka territory. But with no firm basis for a complaint, he didn't question the mission he'd been given. "As you wish, Upseeri. I see no reason it should be a burden."

Chapter Four

SINCE THE OTHERWORLDLY event at the heights, Dhala had searched for what he was to become. He developed new skills and honed those he already had. He ached to press his gifts to their limits. For the past several days, he'd worked with the bowyer. He succeeded at scraping the cured stave into the rough shape of a finished bow but found the process mind-numbingly tedious: scrape a pass or two, the flint dulls, knap a new edge, scrape again.

Although focused on his work, he sensed when Askari squatted beside him. Neither said a word, each waiting for the other to begin the conversation both of them understood was coming. Dhala set his resolve. If Askari wanted to take their talk down the path of Dhala's infatuation with Gyam, then he would be the one to start the conversation.

"Stubborn stupidity is not a trait mastered only by my friend Gyam. It seems to be a trait shared throughout the entire Chinjoka nation," Askari said with an air of innocence.

Dhala stopped, considered his words with widening eyes. Then he snorted and his shoulders shook with laughter. His initial chuckles escalated until his entire body trembled. Once his amusement at his friend's blunt observation had quieted, he met Askari's gaze and smiled.

"Are you trying to be certain the entire village was offended?"

"It was time for you to laugh again. If offending everyone was the way to keep you from acting like a sour old man, then I will," Askari said.

"You won't make friends saying things like that, especially with one stiff-necked Athru."

He made a rude noise and grinned at Dhala. "They all deserve it. They gossip like old people sitting in the spring sun after a long cold season. No facts, just making up things and pretending they're right."

Dhala nodded, a slight smirk on his face. "Well, at least he made his wishes clear." He turned to Askari and cocked an eyebrow. "And don't defend Gyam. He is the most stiff-necked person in the entire tribe. Gods help us all if one of the rules he thinks he knows so well is not done to his idea of how it should be done. He should be bait for a mad Misiq in full battle form."

Askari's face turned solemn. "Don't mention them; we don't want to call unneeded attention on us. The Misiq haven't attacked in several cycles, and I would prefer to leave it that way."

Dhala tilted his head in agreement but never let his eyes shift from Askari's. The silence drew out too long, and Dhala sighed, bringing up the topic he hoped to avoid. "I know you came to talk to me about returning to serve as Gyam's personal Saat, but Gyam made his wishes clear. He doesn't need or want me to help him any longer. From what others have told me, he wants no Saat to serve the traditional role."

Askari stared at him for a moment before dropping his gaze. "I think..."

"You think if I beg him, he will let me return."

Askari exhaled deeply. "I had hoped you would be willing to help him." Their gazes locked when he turned back to Dhala. "Would it be that terrible? Working with Gyam again? You were so proud when he selected you to be his Saat."

"I was young. The three of us have been friends since we could crawl. When we started through puberty, all I wanted to do was be with him and fulfill his wishes. I was in love with Gyam. I would have done anything he asked of me. So long as I could breathe in his scent, I was happy to do what he needed."

"Dhala, were you..."

Dhala barked out a harsh laugh. "By the Father, no. He was far too aware of proper behavior. I've tried to seduce him since I was too young to understand what I was doing. But he never noticed. Even Choro tried to play matchmaker and told him of times in our history when Athru and Saat have bonded."

"And what would Gyam do?"

"Either ignored us or, on rare occasions with Choro, he would argue against it being proper."

Askari sighed. "I've heard stories of bonds between all the castes. I don't understand why Gyam is so determined to be formal with this."

Dhala shrugged, ready to bring the conversation to an end. Askari would work on new arguments for Dhala to return to his service of

Gyam. The litany of reasons and excuses was about to begin again when a flash of brown slammed into Dhala, off-balancing him and knocking him onto his back.

Askari chuckled as a small boy climbed onto Dhala's midsection. "You stopped working. Can we go now? I have a new fishing spear. You said we could use it. I'm ready to go. You said we would go when you finished with the bow."

Dhala clamped his hand over the small child's mouth for a moment of silence. "Jua, we will go. But my friend Askari stopped by because he wanted to speak with me about an...issue." He glanced at Askari before continuing. "He wanted to ask me for a favor. But I was telling him I'd already promised to take you spearfishing."

Jua turned and studied Askari before nodding. "You can go too. Dhala has a bunch of spears. That's what he said."

"Oh, I'm sure Askari is far too busy to go fishing with—"

"Not at all. Fish sounds delicious, and the river is full from the spring melt. I haven't been fishing since—" His eyes flicked to Dhala. "—since the last time Dhala took me and another of our friends."

With great solemnness, Jua looked at him. "Did you take a fish?"

"As I recall, we all fell into the water and splashed around until we were blue. But we got enough fish to feed everyone. Tayi wrapped us in a hata skin robe, and we all huddled together under it while we ate every fish we caught."

Dhala frowned at his friend. "We were lucky. The redtail were spawning and so thick it seemed possible to walk from one side of the river to the other without wetting our feet."

"I'm sure it will be fun. There are lots of fish in the river now," Jua said. He slid off Dhala and stood in front of Askari with his arms crossed. The boy was wearing only his breechcloth, his bare feet in constant motion from excitement. "Dhala told me fishing is serious. We need to feed our people and give thanks to the fish for allowing the hunter to spear them."

Before Askari could reply, Dhala tapped Jua's shoulder. He glanced back, and Dhala nodded him toward their home. "Why don't you go ask Tayi to give you the spears. We'll go now. I can work on the bow later, and this way, we will have fish for our evening meal."

Jua cocked his eyebrow at Askari and trotted to the warren without ever looking at Dhala.

Once the child disappeared, Dhala turned to Askari with a grim expression on his face. "His parents were among the last sickness fatalities at Many Stones village. He's been passed from one family to another ever since. Mother asked for him to shelter with us."

"Tayi is planning to adopt him, isn't she?"

Dhala's grin left little doubt about how he felt about adopting Jua.

"He seems fine, considering everything he's been through."

"He's afraid he won't have a home. Some people who fostered him were unhappy about the responsibility. But Mother wants him to decide."

A muffled crash came from inside the dwelling. Jua had found the spears. He turned to Dhala. "Where did he get the spear from?"

"The last family helped him make it, but he didn't use it. So I promised I'd take him. Unfortunately, I became busy."

The boy came running out, trying to keep his hold on the three spears he had as his breechcloth blew out behind him.

"Dhala! I have the spears. Tayi says these are your favorites."

DHALA EXPLAINED AGAIN how Jua should stand above the pool that formed in the river above the village, and it took all of Askari's control not to burst out laughing. They had been at their task long enough to be well past midday. Askari had made a few attempts at spearing the migrating redtail but discovered he had lost his ability to judge his throws.

Jua took it as a personal insult that the fish didn't impale themselves on the tip of his youth-sized spear. And Dhala seemed no less determined that the boy get at least one fish during this outing, which resulted in two people with a single mission.

"Remember, the fish isn't where it seems to be. Aim below it."

"I know. I know. Quiet."

The fierce look of determination would be humorous if Jua's expression wasn't of a person giving their ultimate effort. It didn't matter that he was less than half of Askari's height. He would succeed in taking a fish, regardless of the effort it took. One of the larger fish drifted upward. Jua drew back, and when the fish paused, he threw his spear.

With a flick of the tail, Jua's quarry disappeared into the pile of brush blanketing one side of the eddy. Frustration washed over Jua's face as he pulled the cordage to retrieve his spear. He coiled it behind him and crept forward until the icy water lapped against his bare toes. He crouched over the water, frozen in position as he waited again.

Askari glanced toward Dhala and lifted his eyebrows. The slight shrug from his friend told him all he needed. Neither of them saw a high chance of success. But they were both willing to let Jua decide when they would quit. After a half day of fishing, Jua showed no signs of giving up.

There was another soft splash, followed by a muffled curse that forced a chuckle from Askari. "Well, at least he's learned the language of spearfishing."

"He's had opportunities to hear such talk from the older boys, trying to impress each other or a potential mate."

Askari snorted with another outburst from a near miss. "It sounds like he's got them in the correct order."

Dhala nodded, but more than a little sadness tinged his smile. "He's a good fledgling. Jua refused to leave his parents' sides, feeding them and keeping fresh water nearby. He slept beside them to make certain they had what they needed. The others were afraid he might be a carrier for the sickness. That's why my mother took him in."

Askari was about to ask another question when a high-pitched squeal came from the waterside. They raced to the river and found Jua in the freezing cold water up to his waist, trying to wrestle a speared fish close to his own height. The determined fledgling was not only hanging on to the fish but also his spear and cordage.

Dhala and Askari splashed into the water to help. Askari slipped his hand into the animal's gills while Dhala pulled a shivering Jua to the bank. Once they all stood on the riverbank, Askari held the fish up for everyone to admire. It was huge, larger than any he'd seen during this redtail spawn. He turned to Jua with no small amount of wonder.

"Twins bless us! This fish is huge."

Jua shivered, struggling to get the words out of his mouth because his teeth were chattering so hard. "I saw a big shadow. And I waited, just like Dhala said. I was real patient. He was about to turn away. So I threw and it hit. I promise. I heard the spear hit."

Dhala patted him on the back and squeezed his shoulder. "You did a good job. Now let's get you to the warrens to change into dry clothes and warm up. We don't want you sick. Besides, you have a fish to eat tonight."

The fledgling wrapped his arms around himself and led the other two back to the sheltering cliffs. As they started on the pathway home, Jua halted and turned to them. "It's my fish, right? So I can do whatever I want?"

"Of course," Dhala said.

"I want to share it with Askari and Gyam. Tayi said they are your best friends."

"Jua, Gyam might not come."

Askari waved his hand. "He'll come. I'll tell him personally Jua wants him to come."

Dhala's jaw muscle flexed. "And if he doesn't want to join us?"

Askari lifted one brow. "I will be very persuasive."

ASKARI HAD BEEN looking for Gyam since he left Tayi and Jua preparing the fledgling's fish for that night. He'd expected to locate Gyam with no problem, but he'd been wrong. He was running out of places where Gyam might be when he spotted him in a deserted part of the village.

There he is. How could it be so difficult to find one Athru?

Askari raced after the stocky, dark-haired figure striding ahead of him. If this had been anyone other than Gyam, he would have thought they were trying to avoid him.

"Gyam. Wait. Gyam!"

The man kept his pace for a few steps farther, then his stride broke, and he stopped. Askari half expected him to look and act contrite. Instead, his black eyes flashed anger. Askari came to a stop a step away, and some of the plates in Askari's torso transformed into tough protective scales as Gyam triggered a partial change in him.

"Oh, by the gods, Askari. There was no reason to call your armor to protect yourself. I will not attack you."

"I didn't call for the change. It happened when I got close to you."

Gyam tensed, ready to argue. But after a long moment, he relaxed. "I could see how my mood might trigger a protective change. I apologize for that. But you were looking for me. To what purpose?"

Askari recalled his task, his battle scales disappearing as he grinned at Gyam. "Jua wants you at his first blooding. He speared one of the biggest redtail I've ever seen."

"Jua? The fledgling that lost both parents?"

Askari rolled his eyes at the Athru's feigned disinterest. "Yes, Jua. The fledgling I saw you playing hoops and spears with."

Gyam's mouth opened and closed several times before shutting to a thin line. He glared at Askari. "I know you are behind this."

"This time the mighty Athru is wrong. Jua asked for you and me to share his first kill. I didn't trick the fledgling."

"And you expect me to believe it will only be you, me, and the boy?"

"I suppose that is asking too much, isn't it?"

"I will not share a meal with a lazy Saat. If he were to try flying from the high cliffs, it would not sadden me."

"So the years of friendship between the three of us mean nothing? You have decided the two people who have been there for you through every crisis you've had in your life are no longer important to you?"

"You're aware of my feelings. You have tried to change them often enough."

"Choro couldn't be saved. He didn't blame Dhala; why do you insist on labeling the plague as Dhala's fault?"

"He could have done more. He could have tried harder."

"So you, an Athru of the red flyer form, are a healer?"

Gyam bristled. "You know the only Athru healer died in the first wave of the sickness. He was a green-scaled flyer, and a healer of great repute. I have no skills in the healing arts."

"And Dhala is also not an Athru healer; he can't even master the shape-changing ability of the Onija. He has no armor, no wings and talons, but you expected him to perform miracles. Tayi tried to save Choro, and she is a skilled Saat healer. But we can only do so much."

"They should have done more. They should have healed him."

Askari sighed again. "I'm not here to argue about something you refuse to see. But I am here to offer you the honor of sharing the first blooding of a fledgling. Are you going to honor his request?"

Gyam glared at him for several moments before nodding. "Yes. I won't let my disapproval of the person he shelters with dampen his day of honor."

Askari refused to gloat over his triumph. Without another word, he began retracing his footsteps to Jua's celebration. He'd only traveled a short distance before he sensed Gyam at his side. He resisted the urge to glance toward the Athru, knowing the smirk now on his face would mark his satisfaction. Even now, he sensed one side of his lip curling upward.

As they moved closer to Tayi's warren, the aroma of baking fish wafted through the air. The single sniff, mixed with the aroma of herbs that lightly accented it, had Askari ready to devour the entire catch by himself. Jua launched himself at the two of them as they came into sight. He wrapped his arms around Gyam's waist and hugged him. Then, as if he thought he was not solemn enough, he released Gyam and stepped away. After a moment, he nodded.

"Welcome, Gyam. Thank you for coming. I hope you will enjoy the food we have prepared."

Askari smiled at the fledgling's seriousness. He wondered how long he had been practicing with Tayi's assistance. She would help him make the night into an event he would remember for as long as he lived. Askari planned to assure it was a night of good memories only.

I swear to the Father, if anyone disappoints this child tonight, I will tie them in front of a charging hata herd.

Jua stood for a moment, looking at them before he sprinted through the doorway. Loud whispers that Askari couldn't quite decipher drifted from inside. Jua reappeared, walking to them with a drinking bowl in each hand. He held one out to Gyam, who accepted it with great dignity, and repeated his action with Askari. Once he'd delivered the drinks, he again ran into the warren.

Both men sipped their drinks. It was one of Tayi's special herbal mixes: cool and refreshing.

"I'd forgotten how good Tayi's teas were."

Askari glanced over in time to see Gyam take another healthy drink. His look of satisfaction was genuine. Askari had seen it before. Then a much louder conversation erupted inside the warren.

"Dhala, you said you would share my first kill."

"I know, Jua. But I'm not sure—"

"No. You said. You told me you would."

"Jua...."

Askari turned toward the entrance. "Dhala, come. Join us. The fledgling invited all of us, and we accepted."

He chuckled as Jua said, "See!"

Dhala appeared and moved opposite Gyam. The three sat in the tense atmosphere. But then Jua appeared with a drinking bowl, which he handed to Dhala, and even Dhala found the fledgling's joy infectious. The child dashed inside, leaving the three sitting around the cooking fire. Jua's fish was covered with a thick layer of clay and buried in the hot ash and coals. The scents curled into Askari's nose, and his stomach made a loud grumbling noise. Both of the others glanced at him.

"Sorry, but that fish smells so delicious. Tayi's cooking is always good."

As if on cue, Tayi appeared, carrying a bowl filled with wild greens she had gathered that afternoon mixed with vegetables roasted on the hot ashes. The scents filled the air as Askari lowered himself to the ground and eased his drinking bowl to the rock beside him. She brought the baked fish from the fire using a set of implements she'd no doubt created for the task. Jua stood at her elbow with a stack of wooden planks, which Tayi took from him as she motioned him to a seat by the fire.

"Sit. I will make certain everyone has their food."

He nodded and scampered to his spot. Askari couldn't keep from smiling. He well remembered his own first blooding dinner. He had been just as excited as Jua was tonight. He glanced at the other two men. The same people had shared his meal as surrounded the fire on this night. He grinned at both of them with the memory.

Tayi broke the clay crust and peeled it away, exposing the succulent fish. Steam rolled from the exposed pink flesh as she gave each of them a generous portion, then took the last one for herself.

A moment passed before Tayi motioned to Jua. "First bite is yours, Jua."

The young man studied his food for several moments before breaking off a piece of fish. He held it in front of his mouth and blew to cool the morsel. Then he lifted it to his nose, inhaled deeply, and smiled before popping it into his mouth. As he chewed, his eyes closed and a soft moan escaped his lips. By the time the fledgling finished the bit of food, everyone was smiling.

"How was it, Jua?" Tayi asked.

"Delicious. Very yummy delicious."

The boy pulled another bit free, cooling it for a heartbeat before it disappeared into his mouth. Tayi motioned for everyone to begin their meal.

Askari didn't need a second invitation. The smell of the food was an almost intolerable temptation. He didn't bother to cool his food as he scooped a chunk of flaky fish and filled his mouth.

He regretted his haste within a heartbeat. The steaming meat seared the inside of his mouth and left him panting and fanning to cool the food he'd stuffed inside it. His contortions and air sucking soon had everyone smiling.

Even Gyam grinned. "You never will learn, will you, Askari? Typical dense Onija, you think your thick scales protect you from everything."

Askari brightened as he thought about Gyam's comment. "Wonderful idea, my friend," Askari said as he focused on his hands. After a moment, they were armored. He pulled off a thick piece of fish and held it while it cooled. A short time later, he was licking the last bits from his fingers.

Dhala snorted and looked toward Gyam. "He doesn't seem to have improved with time."

Gyam ate another bite of fish as he seemed to consider. "No, you're right. He's no better than when we were at his feast of first blooding."

Askari tilted his head downward, careful to hide his smile. Their relationship was regaining the closeness it once had. At least that was his hope.

Chapter Five

DHALA ENJOYED THE warmth of the sun on his bare back. The previous night had left frost on the village's upper ridges, and the highest peaks appeared to be coated with light snow. But the day had built its warmth, and by the time he was working their garden plot, he no longer felt a chill.

While he worked, he kept an eye on Jua. His mother had adopted the fledgling a few days after his blooding feast, and in the days since then, he had become an integral part of their family. Dhala sensed relief from others in the village when they realized they would not be asked to house the orphan. It had been subtle, but some families avoided Jua. Worse, the child seemed to understand they were shunning him, and it was through no fault of his own.

As a result, Dhala took the boy with him whenever possible. When they were alone, Jua was eager to do anything Dhala asked of him. This morning, that meant he helped Dhala working the garden. Jua had stripped to his breechcloth and was moving with great care through the plants, pulling each weed he found. Few escaped his scrutiny.

Dhala enjoyed the quiet work. It wasn't difficult, but it freed his mother to spend more time caring for the medicinal garden near their warren. The village might have their suspicions about her special garden, but no one speculated about it to anyone else. Besides, her restorative broths were in demand from all three castes. Because of the need, Tayi grew, harvested, and preserved a wide variety of herbs on her patch of ground.

The sun was only halfway down the afternoon sky when they finished their work. The boy rose to his feet, wiping the sweat from his brow with a dramatic sweep of his hand. "It's hot. I think we did a good job. But it's hot."

He smiled down at the boy, knowing what he was hinting at. He stretched, unknotting muscles that were tight after spending half the day bent over, working.

Once the last contracted muscles lengthened, he sighed with relief and patted Jua on the shoulder. "It is hot, and we've worked hard. Tayi would appreciate it if we cleaned ourselves before entering the warren."

Jua nodded with great gravity and walked toward the river. He headed to the large pool the river carved along the base of the cliffs. The water was cold, but a short time in, it would leave them both feeling better. Dhala followed close behind at first, but soon, the boy was sprinting down the path. He chuckled when he stepped through the shrubs in time to see Jua leap through the air and hit the still water with an impressive splash.

Dhala stripped and walked into the pool. The icy water that had seemed so inviting earlier caught his breath as he slipped farther from the bank. He crept through until ice melt lapped above his knees and gave himself time to adjust. Jua dove and ducked through the water with as much agility and grace as the fish he'd caught a few days earlier. Dhala gritted his teeth as he moved deeper into the pool until the chilled water lapped around his genitals, and he sucked his breath between his teeth. He paused for an instant before taking another step and finding himself in water up to his navel. As his body tried to adjust, Jua surfaced beside him.

"Come on. It's great. You'll love it."

"It's cold."

Jua stared at him for a heartbeat, then splashed water on Dhala, soaking him.

"You little squeaker!" Dhala roared. He dove into the water, trying to catch his playful tormentor. He thought he'd trapped Jua several times, but he would always slip away. They played long enough to wind both of them, or at least Dhala thought they had.

Dhala floated with only his head sticking above the cold water. The chase removed the last of the chill from his body. He paddled around the pool, enjoying the quiet.

He froze in place, discord flowing through his system. A few heartbeats later, the village drum beat out the urgent message. Dhala listened for a moment before splashing toward the shore. Scouts had spotted the hata in spring migration.

He glanced back to find Jua swimming behind him. The two of them reached the shallow bank and climbed to the narrow beach. They raced to their belongings, put on sandals, and grasped their other clothing before sprinting toward home.

Dhala found his mother preparing large carrying baskets for the hunt. She looked up as they burst through the entrance and into their sleeping space.

"The hata have returned. The scouts are back with word the herds are here. If nothing happens, they will arrive tomorrow before the sun is at its highest."

"We were at the river when the drums sounded." Guilt washed over Dhala that he'd taken time away from his tasks.

His mother paused long enough to squeeze his shoulder and said, as if she read his mind, "You deserve a break. You work hard. It did no one harm." She smiled and pushed him toward his area. "But now, we must prepare. Our bows must be readied and you need to check your bull spear. I want the caches filled. This will be a good hunt."

Dhala nodded and moved to begin his preparation.

THE APPEARANCE OF the hata marked the beginning of the new grass moon. The great herd blanketed the grasslands east of the Chinjoka Basin. As they traveled through the region, what they didn't eat, their massive hooves ground into the earth. The Chinjoka needed the meat from this hunt to renew their stored food. The spring migration was also critical for the fiber left hanging from anything strong, or lucky, enough to be left standing. Once the herd had moved northward, the members of the Saat clan would search for their shedded underfiber. Traditionally, it was fashioned into some of the clothing for the flyers. It was said the hata fiber transitioned to flyer and back with great ease. The hata were critical to the Chinjoka food supply, and they watched with eager anticipation for their arrival twice each cycle through their migration.

Dhala glanced upward and scanned the sky for a glimpse of red against the ash-gray clouds. He spotted Gyam, looking like a falcon riding the summer thermals. His brilliant red coloration muted with the distance. There was no question he was where he was needed for this hunt.

Dhala found himself in a mix of Saat and Onija hunters. The castes wouldn't have mixed in years past, but at this time, their survival was at stake. And it would be foolish not to allow skilled Saat to participate in the hunt. The day might decide the fate of the Chinjoka.

He once again studied the passageway where they expected the hata to be thickest. The oftentimes shoulder-high grass gave the Chinjoka hunters hiding areas to ambush the hata. As the hunters surrounding him slipped through the grass to disappear, Dhala moved to his spot.

Satisfied everything was ready, at least those things he had control over, Dhala searched out his mother. He found her helping the people who could no longer take an active role in the hunt, preparing for the hard work that always followed. But he knew once she was satisfied with the level of preparation, she would take up her bow and join him.

Dhala also caught sight of Jua. Even without seeing his face, he knew the decision not to allow him to participate in the hunt had upset the boy. He wanted to hunt with Dhala. Being sent with those who weren't capable of facing the herd had been a blow to Jua. Disappointed didn't begin to encompass his feelings. Unhappy as he was, he'd understood he was not ready to hunt the great herd. Many of these animals would be mothers with calves, fiercely protective mothers. Hunters knew the females were the most dangerous animals in the spring hunt.

He turned to find Askari coming toward him.

Once they were close, he nodded to Dhala. "Everyone's ready."

Dhala knelt and put his hand against the ground. The earth vibrated with a multitude of heavy hooves crossing the valley toward them. "They're coming."

They sprinted to their positions. Dhala nocked a hunting arrow the length of his arm into his recurve bow and squatted into the grasses. He glanced over to see the tip of one of Askari's spears hovering just below the top of the grasses. They disappeared from sight in a mix of sere brown fall foliage and the deep green spring grasses. It was the lush green growth that fed the herd as it moved into the cooler summers of the northern range as well as escaping the hordes of biting insects that infested their winter grazing lands during this season.

The first massive gray beasts topped the rise and made toward the easiest crossing through the rough hills for several sun's walk in any direction. As the leading edge of the herd moved toward the north, the winds shifted until it came from behind the hunters. One of the cows threw up her head in alarm.

Voda's cock! She scented us!

An instant later, the cow let out a bellow that carried for spans. The animals went on alert at the lead cow's warning, and the stampede began. The hunters leapt from their hiding places, yelling and waving their weapons as they tried to drive the other hata against the animals in front. The frothing herd was in full panic as they bore down on the last of the concealed hunters. The herd grew closer, and Dhala's heart pounded with the beginning of the annual hunt.

Hunters along the front edge selected targets. Sometimes, several hunters would concentrate their arrow fire on a single animal. But the hata were difficult prey. Which was the reason the Chinjoka had developed their bull spears. The spears were longer than twice the height of a tall man, with a leaf-shaped iron head. One came into play when its carrier ran toward the charging hata. The Onija stopped, bracing the shaft of the spear against the ground and aiming the tip. An instant later, the enraged animal hit the spear and sent the spear-carrier flying as a vicious pain-saturated bellow erupted. But before Dhala saw the outcome, Askari screamed at him.

"Dhala! Bull! On you!"

He spun to find his quarry only a handful of lengths away, hooves pounding against the hard earth. He drew the bow to his cheek and released. The feathered shaft sprouted from the hata's thick neck. It seemed oblivious to the wound and continued to bear down on Dhala. He released a second arrow toward his target. This one sank to the feathers but there was no change in the bull's wild eyes. Dhala reached for another shaft, racing from its path as he did.

He slapped the third arrow into his bow. The gray shape was charging him far too fast for him to take aim. He stumbled, catching himself but losing the arrow he nocked. With his quiver half full and no time to aim and fire, he grabbed the end of his bow—prepared to use it as a club. Dhala's focus shifted as events unfolded in a blur.

A mass of red slammed into the enormous bull from above, knocking it to its knees and giving Dhala the moment he needed. He knew it had to be Gyam. He scrambled away as another figure ran toward the struggling bull. Dhala identified a fully shifted Askari in the next heartbeat. He drew back, and the palm-sized scales typical for Askari rippled in the sun.

Askari braced the butt of the enormous spear against the ground and tilted the hand-long blade at the charging animal. The animal dropped to its knees when it impaled itself. But its bellow of battle sounded an instant later as it regained its feet.

Dhala scrambled away from the battle taking place only a few spans away, and in his haste, he found the arrow he had lost earlier. He quickly nocked the arrow and fired it as the embattled animal struggled to regain its feet. Other Chinjoka released a shower of shafts. The massive quarry seemed impervious to the arrows bristling from his hide. He swept his head left then right, his enormous horns clearing a wide swath around him. Askari backpedaled from the arm-long horns, but the tip still hissed along his plates.

Dhala stepped forward, trying for an impossibly difficult eyeshot to bring it down. But there was not a clear shot regardless of where he positioned himself. He sensed Gyam circling high above, certain he was searching for an opening to bury his talons deep into the animal, which would give Askari time to escape uninjured.

Suddenly it appeared, an open instant. A moment of stillness in the trampled grass and Dhala shot at the beast's engorged neck artery. He released the arrow, and it buried itself deep, severing the artery as Dhala had hoped. The new injury drove the bull to increasing levels of frenzy. It bellowed, looking to attack his tormentor, enormous horns slicing through the air as his lifeblood pumped onto the crushed grass.

Then the unexpected. Askari faltered. The man, who never made a misstep, moved wrong and a bicep thick horn slammed into Askari's torso.

Askari's plates crack with audible snaps, and a muffled cry came from him. Dhala's sole focus was on the events unfolding. The bull caught Askari under his arm and sent his limp body cartwheeling through the air to crash against the hard earth with a sickening crunch. The prey-turned-predator spun again, sweeping a horn down Askari's back, snapping his plates one by one.

Dhala raced to help. He released an arrow, and the tip pierced the beast's eye. It shuddered. Dhala prepared another arrow, drawing the bow when his prey was struck from above. Gyam in flight form was impressive enough. In full battle fervor, he was magnificent. His long foreclaws drove deeper as he screamed his anger. With that, he clamped his teeth onto the base of the brute's skull and sliced through until he struck bone.

The hata bull bucked, trying to dislodge Gyam, but Gyam only sank his teeth deeper. Dhala tossed his bow to one side, and waited as close as he could for a chance to rescue Askari. Just one pause, an opening, that's all he needed. This wouldn't worsen.

Then it happened. The bull dropped to his knees again. Dhala shot in during that instant of time, grabbed Askari, and dragged him away as fast as his legs would move. Other hunters surged past to help Gyam. But he didn't care. Several of Askari's chest plates were moving in ways that should have been impossible, and blood dribbled from both nostrils. Askari's injuries were severe. Once he pulled his friend to a safe location, he turned to find Jua and his mother racing toward them.

She knelt close to Askari and opened the bag she carried at her waist. She cut away his tunic and assessed the damage with a light touch. After a moment or two, a rumbling moan escaped Askari's lips as he turned. Dhala breathed a little easier, but the injured man never opened his eyes. He glanced at his mother, who hadn't stopped checking his injuries. Without looking up, she answered his question.

"It's bad, horribly bad. Several major plates are broken to the point he can't shift from his armor. With his body armored, all I can do is treat the obvious wounds. But the bull hit him at top speed, and I have no idea what other damage those blasted scales he is so proud of might hide. I need him at the warren so I have everything at my fingertips."

Time meshed into a swirl of confusion and concern as they prepared to move Askari. He refused to let the bliss of unconsciousness overtake him as Dhala would have preferred. The carrying litter materialized, but it seemed the task took a lifetime. They eased Askari to the platform and soon were moving with as much speed as possible toward the village and home.

The sight of his mother sprinting ahead to prepare for Askari was a relief. Once he was resting comfortably on the bedding, the room emptied. Dhala was uncertain what to do next.

He paused, trying to bring logic to the chaos when a small voice overwhelmed everything else. "Is Askari going to die like Mom and Dad?"

Panic filled Dhala at the child's words. He had the same fear, but he couldn't say the words out loud. He glanced over to his mother, but all he got in answer was a slight lifting of her eyebrows. Uncertain of how to offer comfort, he turned to Jua.

"The bull hit him hard. He has many injuries." Dhala stopped. The child's lip quivered, and Dhala's resolution melted like snow in the fire month. "But Askari is stronger than the bull. We'll heal him."

Jua chewed his lip for a heartbeat, and asked for the response Dhala dreaded. "Do you swear by the Twins he'll get better?"

He couldn't do it. He refused to let any doubt shift into the boy's thoughts. "Yes, Jua. I promise."

His mother shook her head but said nothing. She pulled out a small water basket from her pouch and handed it to Jua. "Fill this basket with river water. Clean, nothing but clear water. Now go. Hurry."

The fledgling sprinted toward the stream. Once he left, Dhala turned to Askari's still form. The task before him was overwhelming.

"Finish cutting his tunic free. Be careful not to bring him any more pain. We need a small fire too. This medicine must be heated to be the most effective," his mother said.

She turned without another word, dug through her pack basket and the pouches of medicine filling it. Dhala glanced at his mother frequently as he cut the breechcloth loose and let it fall to the floor.

Focused on his tasks, Dhala pulled out his fire-making kit and began his work. The sparks were hot, and he soon had a small fire going in their fire pit, feeding from the bits of twigs and dried grasses. A moment later, a respectable flame burned. He was glad he'd accomplished that task as Jua hurried to them. The boy moved with care to keep from spilling the precious water.

She accepted the water basket with a nod of acknowledgment and poured from it into a cooking pot the size of Dhala's fist, which she sat on the edge of the fire. She stirred it with great care before turning to Askari.

"What more do you need, young one? Perhaps something to relax so these scales you are so proud of can become skin again," she said.

She wasn't speaking to Dhala, but he hoped if he was silent she would allow him to stay. Then he'd be close if she needed his help. Askari's labored breath echoed through the warren. He wanted the healing to progress quicker but knew she was working to get the best healing.

She brought out another small bowl, a drinking bowl, and began her ritual of mixing water and herbs again before putting the new combination beside the first. Her hand moved in an intricate dance over each one, passing her palm over them to pull the scents to her and test her mixtures. With a nod, she pulled the larger pot from the flames and sat it at Dhala's side. She caught her son's gaze and lifted her brows before motioning to the bowl she'd sat beside him.

"Clean his wounds with this wash. The herbs will help keep any wound fever to a minimum." She dug through her pack again, and handed Dhala an absorbent piece of leather. He moved so he could see Askari's injuries. He had cleaned the most obvious wounds when he felt a presence beside him. Without looking, he knew it was Gyam.

"How is he?"

"One of the largest bulls in the herd tried to gore and trample him. How do you think he's doing?"

Gyam's face grew dark, and he twisted his features. "Askari is very—"

Dhala cut him off with a hand motion. "I am helping Mother. Your hovering is not useful. We are doing our best."

The darkness gathered on Gyam's face. Before he exploded in frustration, Dhala's mother laid her hand over his upper arm. He spun to her, the storm of his fear and anger still filling his expression. He stopped himself, took a deep breath, and exhaled in a gust of breath. When he again met her gaze, it was obvious his emotions were at manageable levels.

"Gyam, we appreciate your concern, but Dhala and I are doing what we can. Without a Father-marked Athru healer, our options are limited. But the gods blessed the hunt. Many of the hata gave themselves to the Chinjoka harvest. We do not want to dishonor their gift by leaving anything for the scavengers. Help those who need assistance with the harvest."

She tilted her chin away from them, and Gyam's gaze followed to see a family working hard to process a calf they had brought back to their portion of the warrens, four comprised three fledglings, similar in age to Jua, and their grandmother.

Dhala's mother spoke low. "They lost their parents and grandfather to the plague. The village provides what it can, but the end of the cold season is lean times for many. The meat, bone, and hide from the calf the grandmother has taken will serve them for several moons. But they are having difficulty harvesting each usable part from the animal."

Without a glance back, he started toward them, and once he was close, he stopped. "Jua, come with me. Tayi, and her son, are taking care of Askari. We are needed elsewhere."

Jua looked to Dhala for permission. He patted the boy on his back. "Help Gyam. If anything changes, I promise to send someone for you. It will take several days to ready all the hata who sacrificed themselves to feed the Chinjoka. I need a sharp-eyed warrior to help keep the sikari away."

Jua and Gyam left. Both seemed lost in their thoughts, and Gyam wore the permanent scowl he had adapted since Choro's death.

"They will be fine if we do our job as healers. We have achieved our first goal of getting Askari to the village. He won't like it when he awakens, but he will have to stay in our warren until he is healed."

Dhala bobbed his head in acknowledgment and focused on cleaning all of Askari's injuries.

Chapter Six

GYAM STOOD WITH his toes curled around the rock shelf at the lip of his sky portal. The cool breeze didn't have the usual comforting sensation. Several days had passed since Askari's injury during the hunt. He was not healing as fast as Gyam would have liked, and his fears washed into all parts of his life. Through the time since they'd brought Askari to Tayi's warren, he had not awakened. Gyam checked on the state of his friend as often as possible. But he knew his presence didn't help, and worse, he feared it irritated Tayi.

"Do you want me to get something for our midday meal?"

He glanced at the boy and couldn't keep from smiling. "Yes, Jua. I think the food we prepared this morning should be ready."

Without another word from Gyam, the fledgling grabbed the carrying bag he kept with him constantly since Askari's injury and plunged down the steps to Tayi's cooking area. So far as Gyam knew, Jua's bag held nothing more than a set of eating bowls, which he kept spotless. After each meal, he scrubbed them with river sand so they were as pristine as when they emerged from the kiln. Before Gyam began the descent, Jua was already in the cooking area Tayi used as a communal kitchen.

Gyam entered the warren a few moments later and paused. He and Tayi glanced at each other, but no words were exchanged. He slipped beside Askari, who still had the signs of someone just this side of the Long Flight. He moved away from Askari to scan from the warren's wide opening. Even from the bottom of the cliffs where Tayi made her home, the Chinjoka Basin could be seen from the cliff base where he stood to the hazy opposite chalk bluffs, which marked the western boundaries of the Chinjoka lands since the people first came into this world. Beyond that boundary held the dense forests of the Misiq people, once valued trading partners, but during Gyam's life, they had become merciless enemies. If a Chinjoka happened on a Misiq warrior, only one walked away. In recent moons, he'd added the duty of checking the far borders to his already exhaustive surveillance flights, using the Athru's level of sight, which ranged from the detailed distant sight of the great birds to the ability to see the heat of a living body. These allowed him to find any invaders long before they threatened the village. On foot, it took many days, but he could fly the distance and return before the sun traveled halfway across the sky. For the past several cycles, his searches had yielded nothing, but his overwhelming sense of responsibility drove him to continue. The duty became a habit Gyam didn't want to change.

As he stood in Tayi's warren, he focused his sight and began to develop the muzzle and eyes of his Athru form. He sensed the stretch as his head and face elongated a fingerwidth or two while his orbits widened and his dark eyes shifted into multifaceted red spheres, which pressed against the underside of his closed lids. He gave his body a moment before easing his eyes open.

The colors were always different through the sight available to him when he was in his flyer form. Now he saw a crimson overlay on all the warm-blooded forms he viewed. The first time it occurred, the change left him huddled in the back corner of his parents' storage area, with his clothing sweat-soaked from fear. His parents were of the Onija caste and couldn't understand the cause of his terror. To his great fortune, they took him to Tayi, who brought him to Choro. Discovering that Gyam was normal, and part of the Athru caste, relieved his parents. When Choro offered him a place to live, the fears of both his parents were eliminated.

As he matured and his powers grew, he became comfortable in being a permanent member of Choro's aerie. The older man's kindness and insight eventually moved Choro to be the most important person in his life, including his own family. His parents tried to comprehend, but their son, who could change into a giant winged predator, frightened them. By the time he passed his rite of manhood, he saw them and his sibling only during festival days. Each member of his family was lost during the waves of sickness until none remained. In a final insult from the gods, the last wave of illness had taken Choro.

The solitude left Gyam with an incurable ache. And now one of his best friends was dying from the injuries the hata inflected. Deep down, hidden in a place where he didn't need to study it, resided his understanding that he had rejected his only other friend.

Jua returned, and Gyam changed back to his two-legged form. He waited, giving himself time to adjust. But he refused to wait long. The air filled with delicious aromas from the steaming bowls of Tayi's stews.

Jua handed him a hot bowl filled with appetizing food. The warmth of the ceramic vessel was comforting against the chill brought on by his change. He'd often asked if the chill was the reason Athru can only change completely once in a sun cycle and left a flyer in a much weakened and vulnerable state for days afterward. That was the limit Choro had drilled into him since the first day of his training. If he stayed shifted too long, he lost his ability to change for many days. He had done that one time and one time only. Circumstances forced him to shift more than a day's walk away from the village with no more ability to change than Dhala for days afterward.

"How is it?"

The sound of Jua's voice jerked Gyam to the present and the small boy seeking his approval. "It smells delicious. I recognize the aroma of Tayi's stew."

The fledgling ducked his head, and Gyam saw his ears turn as red as live coals. Gyam clasped his arm and squeezed. "That was smart of you. Why venture further when the best food in the village is just below us. Remember how delicious your first blooding was?"

Jua smiled at the mention of the best event so far in his young life. "It was delicious. I'm ready to go spearfishing again. I will share whatever I catch."

Gyam sipped his stew, enjoying the flavors washing over his senses. "Something this delicious could only be from Tayi's pots, and we will go spearfishing again soon. But right now, we have fresh hata. I've been smelling ribs roasting since shortly after sunrise, and they will be delicious."

Jua nodded in agreement as he sipped from his bowl. He paused and stared into space. Gyam was close to asking if he was all right when the boy began. "Ribs are the best part of the hata. My mother made the most delicious I've ever eaten. She cooked them until they were tender and tasty." Jua stopped eating, a small sob catching in his throat. "I miss her."

Gyam leaned close and patted him on the back. "I know how you feel, Jua. Trust me, I understand."

Dhala rushed to Askari's side at the sound of a light cough. He ran through the points he needed to check. He didn't like the signs he found as he inspected his friend. But in spite of everything, Askari still lived. Dhala hadn't been certain that would be the case as they carried him from the site of the accident.

He relived the interminable journey they undertook to transport Askari to the bed where he'd been since. They'd used a fresh hide as a carrying sling, moving with great care to keep from causing more injuries. By the time they had him settled into the warren, he had slipped into the deep sleep of the mortally wounded, with his breathing almost imperceptible.

Over the past few days, depression filled Dhala. He didn't know how to help. He wasn't a healer. Their only Father-blessed healer had died seasons ago. He didn't know what he would do if he lost Askari, his best friend and defender.

"Close the doorway and tie it shut."

Dhala turned to his mother, his nerves in turmoil. "What?"

"Do as I tell you. Close the door flap. No one will question our actions. They know we are trying to comfort Askari."

"But—"

"Do it! We have little time."

Rebellious anger filled Dhala, but he pushed it away. His mother never acted like this. Something had changed, and she needed his help—and privacy. Without another word, he pulled the osa-skin door closed and laced it shut like they would in the snow months.

He found his mother had stoked the fire, warming the room and filling it with light. She'd also set several hata-tallow lamps around the area to add another layer of illumination. The white pallor of Askari's skin caused Dhala's stomach to twist and roil.

"He still lives. But he won't survive to see the next sunrise if we don't help him."

Dhala nodded, wondering what was happening. But it was clear she had a plan.

"Bring me my healer's bag."

He trotted to the shelf holding her bag, grabbed it, and knelt beside his mother. She took the bag from him and sifted through it, taking each item out and aligning them in a particular order. Time crawled for Dhala. He wanted to scream for her to hurry. But he knew she moved with as much speed as was prudent. She removed the last item, and Dhala hovered, ready and eager to help.

Even though her bag should've been empty, his mother searched through its recesses. He was close to pointing out she had already removed the bag's content when she pulled a stiff rawhide envelope from a hidden pocket. The packet was about as thick as his finger and the length and width of his hand. Covered with bright geometric decorations, it was unlike anything he'd seen. He wanted to study the patterns, but this wasn't the best time to break from the routine she had set into motion.

She adjusted several lamps for clear light and unfolded the unusual container. Each side opened until it exposed a handful of blades, each one tied to the bottom layer with meticulous care. He leaned closer and realized it held both iron and flint blades. None longer than his finger, and most far shorter. He looked at his mother for explanation.

"They are the healing knives used by our ancestors since the Chinjoka flew to this world from the fourth."

"Healers? But..."

She sighed. "You knew I could treat some ailments and most injuries. I didn't give you more details to protect you. The sickness that has killed so many—our gift doesn't work against it. I have tried since the pestilence struck and the Chinjoka began dying in droves. Injuries such as Askari's we can help. The others wouldn't understand our limitations. Because of their fears, we must keep the tools of our magic hidden. The herbs and skills are important, but they help hide our magic when we need to create it. What we share is not the Father-blessed magic the green Athru has. But the gift flows from Voda as surely as he sends summer rains. We saved people and worked with the green flyers when they lived. But fear overwhelmed the Chinjoka."

He reached toward the knives but looked to his mother for confirmation before making contact. "Yes, touch them. Those are yours. I made them for you. But it will be your duty to care for them."

Askari gasped, his body seizing and his low moan filled the warren. Panic flooded Dhala. "We have to help Askari now. We shouldn't have waited. Tell me what to do."

"Calm yourself. The healing is not without danger, and I had to be certain it warranted the risk. Askari is a strong man. I'd hoped he would recover on his own. Your action is simple enough. You will carve a glyph into your body that will open a gateway to send you through to heal him."

"What glyph? How?" Fear raced through him like skyfire from a summer storm.

Her hands darted in like a striking nyoka, pulling a small blade free. She pressed it into Dhala's palm. "Carve the glyph you are given into your inner thigh. It must be shallow, or you will open the great blood pathways there."

Ready to do whatever it took to help his friend, he hovered the blade over his leg, and looked up, fighting down the expanding panic. "What do I cut? Which glyph do I need to use so I can help Askari?"

"Each healing is different, each given to us by the Water Twin. Voda will give you the symbol you need."

Askari's body seized, and his back arched as he gasped for air.

"How do I do this? You are experienced. Wouldn't it be better if you performed the ritual?"

"You are closer to Askari. The healing will be stronger coming from you."

"But how can I save him?"

"Cut! Trust Voda."

He pressed the blade against his skin. The sharp pain shot through him as the iron bit into his leg. Blood ran from the wound as he waited the aid of the gods. It dripped from his leg as he trembled with the fear he would be found inadequate. He shook, but a sense of calm washed over him. Before Dhala understood what was happening, his hand moved of its own volition. The signet showed more of itself with each stroke of the blade. Blood from the incisions pooled for a heartbeat and ran in trails down his thigh as he carved the needed symbol until he completed it with a final decisive cut. He saw the pulsing of an almost severed artery and began to tremble. His heart pounded at the bloody series of cuts on his leg and questioned the wisdom of what he'd done.

Dhala's breath caught and escaped in a rush. He studied his leg to find each cut transformed into a thin blue line. His next inhalation filled him with energy, and his vision became a complex series of overlaid colors and texture. He glanced toward his mother, unsure of what to do next.

"Work on his chest. See where the blood pathways are broken and reconnect them. Focus there first."

Dhala nodded once and turned to Askari. With intuition as his guide, he laid his hands on his friend's chest. The layers of color and texture he'd seen positioned themselves over the man's torso and sank inside. When the last layer settled into place, the scene shifted for Dhala.

Once his sense of self stabilized, he found himself perched on the head wall of an enormous valley. As his vision unfurled, he found a land filled with lush grasses, tall trees, and a multitude of intertwining streams.

Dhala launched himself from the cliffs, hoping his instincts were right. His wings tucked against his back as he dove toward the valley floor.

Wings? When did I grow wings?

The landscape rushed past in a blur. His iron-tough leather wings snapped open a few spans above the treetops, and he sailed across this new land. He relished the sensations he had never expected as the sun kissed each wing webbing and warm air washed over his face.

The moment fled and the land under him became more ominous. Grasslands carried the scars left by the ravages of fire. Much of the forest lay twisted and broken, worse than any storm he'd seen during the high-winds moon. Plant life died as he watched. It came to him. This dying world was Askari.

What can I do? How do I start his healing?

Then he remembered His mother's words. Askari's lifeblood was the most critical. It flooded his lungs.

Floods! They would represent Askari's blood flow—if I can discover the reason for the floods.

He found his objective. The lands surrounding the river were inundated. Not the gentle rise of the spring floods that deposited new soil in the gardens. No. These lands seemed damaged beyond repair.

He landed on a boulder in the midst of the high swirling water. How could he stop this? Could he contain the flood? Something surfaced a few spans from him, and the top of a huge flat head shot through the water toward him. He tensed, ready to launch skyward should the creature move closer. He didn't know his vulnerability there, and refused to speculate and be wrong. But he recognized the creature crawling onto the stone with him. It resembled a piwa with its thick fur, long tail, and enormous gnawing teeth. But it towered over Dhala, several times the size of the piwa he knew. While the animal studied him, there was no sense of threat.

Are you the guardian?

Dhala started at the voice inside his head. But he realized the creature standing before him awaited a reply. After a moment, he remembered this form wasn't able to create speech. He focused on how to share his thoughts.

I'm not sure. What is a guardian?

We hope it is you. Otherwise this one has little time left.

I must be the guardian because I want to save Askari. What do you need me to do?

Our dams are broken, some destroyed. We must repair them.

Do the repairs! Time is short.

The dark ones keep us away. Several have died from their attacks. If we lose any more, we will be unable to finish the work needed before this one is on the Long Flight.

Dhala realized a benefit of speaking mind to mind: he could "see" the animal it called the dark one. Teeth and muscle with a long tail that propelled it. He was certain it was quick and deadly.

Show me where the dark ones are the most formidable.

The thick-furred animal turned and reentered the pool with a single fluid movement. Dhala tensed and launched himself into the sky. He followed the broad head slicing through the water. Between the webbing on its wide feet and the long tail, it was able to move with great speed. It seemed only an instant passed before they reached one of the larger breaches.

With several strong strokes of his wings, Dhala lifted himself above the treetops. *There they are. I see why the pseudo-piwa called them the dark ones.* Their forms made long dark shapes that darted through the water on all sides of the breach. He circled several times, considering how he could best attack these creatures, because attacking them was the only choice available.

He recalled the great fishing birds snatching redtail from the river. Before he lost his nerve, he unsheathed his hand-length talons, twisted in flight, and plunged toward the largest of the shapes. At the last moment, he balled his feet, slammed into the animal's head with the full force of his diving body, and rammed his foreclaws into the animal, just behind its head. As he winged away, he glimpsed his victim rolling downstream.

With powerful wing strokes, he climbed even higher and plummeted toward a second target at a blinding speed. He snapped his wings open and bound with the creature. His talons sank deeper until one lethal tip pierced its skull and, with a shudder, the creature expired.

He climbed again, searching for more prey. To his surprise, the dark ones were scattering. The piwa attacked the stragglers. Dhala spread his wings and spiraled upward on the thermals that existed in this strange land inside Askari. He glanced over, exhaustion filling him, wondering if these piwa still needed his help. But as he circled, piwa flooded the area and began repairing the worst of the breaches.

Go, guardian. We can carry out repairs. We will help him resist the call of the Long Flight. You need rest. Go.

As the familiar voice faded from inside his head, he looked up to discover a spiraling tunnel through the dense clouds that had formed during their short battle. As he pumped his wings toward it, he realized the piwa was correct. He was at the limit of his strength. As Dhala flew higher, he was careful to marshal his resources. He glanced downward again, and his world went white.

ASKARI KEPT HIS head still as he scanned the room. When he'd first awakened during the night, he'd tried to get up. His vision had filled with points of light, and his stomach blanketed him with enough pain to remind him an angry hata had trampled his midsection.

The room in Tayi's warren was dim, but faint sounds of activity were clear. He turned slightly, all his bruised body could take. Shafts of light shot around the edge of the stiff door cover. *They must think I can't handle the light of outdoors.* In the next instant, the cover opened, and he discovered they were right.

The door cover dropped, and he realized he was no longer alone. At first, the soft voices were not intelligible, but a short time later, they moved closer. He strung together words as he gathered his thoughts to speak, but heard his name mentioned and remained silent. He mimed unconsciousness as they stopped beside him. They stood silent before Tayi spoke.

"Check his points of life. His heart should have a strong beat."

Two fingers ran along the left side of his neck. When a second touch echoed it on the right, there was a feeling he struggled to describe. It took all of his will to keep from reacting. The touch vanished to reappear on the inside of his thigh. Dhala was checking his life force flowing down each leg. Askari braced himself for another touch, but it never came.

"His heart seems stronger. The blood runs eagerly. Do you think I can..."

Askari cracked his eye open, enough to make out the dusky outlines of the other two. Dhala had done something that made him the focus of Tayi's anger. But neither seemed willing to budge.

"I almost lost you last time. It will take many days before you recover your strength. Leave yourself more energy to return to us. To me. You almost died trying to heal Askari."

There was a long pause in which Tayi never relented her rigid stance. *What happened? How had Dhala endangered himself?*

Tayi continued. "It sounded normal. Your description, or the basis of it, fits with my experience. But I am always myself. Not—" She paused and looked thoughtful. "—not as you described yourself. I don't know what it signifies."

"More needs to be done. I know better what to expect. I need to heal the plates before they become fixed in place."

She sighed but nodded. "Very well. Use care in selecting the location of the new glyph. But the symbol should be simple. Remember some glyphs will fade while others are permanent. The blue tattoos of healing were a mark of honor in days past, but no longer."

"Yes, Mother. I remember your cautions. There will be no battle."

"All right. I will keep Jua occupied."

She left the space, and Dhala watched her retreating form until she moved out of sight. He sat lamps around Askari and lit each one with a brand from their fire before seating himself beside Askari.

Dhala removed a small flat case from a spot above him and opened it. Inside, it was filled with a variety of small blades. Dhala selected one and bared his thigh. He pressed the sharp edge against his skin, and it parted as if by magic. As he worked, the trickle of blood became a steady stream.

The sight of Dhala cutting into himself repeatedly almost made Askari break his silence. By the time he finished, blood seeped from a wide area of lacerated flesh. He feared for Dhala's safety, but when Askari spoke, his world went black.

His wakening thought was for Dhala's well-being. Although he tried to bolt upright to help, all he managed was a muffled groan.

"Askari?" came the startled response.

He stared at Dhala's blood-drenched hands and legs. "What have you done?" Before Dhala could answer, Askari's plates shifted and his skin returned to its normal appearance. The plates caused a tension that he normally didn't notice, but this time, he had been stuck for far too long and the ache began to cause new problems. Now that he had regained his unshifted form, the pain made him light-headed.

Once he was certain the effect of his change were over, he eased onto his elbows until his friend was within reach. But when he leaned in to check the severity of the wound Dhala had inflicted on himself, he was surprised to find them partially healed. He looked around until he found what he'd been searching for, a bowl of astringent for his wounds. He found a piece of leather and squeezed out most of the liquid. He began to gently dab the moist hide over patches of dried blood to soften them. The muted crimson came off with no trouble under his careful touch. When Askari found no open wounds, he searched again a final time.

Askari dropped to his side, panting from even this slight exertion. But he would get his answers. "Dhala, what's going on? You cut into yourself. You were covered in blood. Now the wound is gone. What are you doing?"

Panic filled Dhala's face, his eyes darting from side to side as if Misiq hid inside the warrens. Desperation seemed to build in Dhala, so Askari gave him time to calm himself.

"You were never to see what I did. I've put Tayi in danger. They might take Jua if they know we have true magic."

"You aren't making any sense. Why would anyone want to hurt either of you? By the Father, I can't imagine anyone threatening Tayi. And no one is taking Jua away. They are all afraid he is a carrier of the plague at worst, and bad luck at best. Now, what makes you so afraid?"

Dhala sighed and shook his head. "We are healers. A line of healers blessed by Voda. We are always the herbalist for the village, but our simple herb cures hide the powerful magic we have to work other cures."

Askari started to ask a question when he was waved into silence. "We helped where we could, but Tayi is telling the truth. We need a green Athru to cure the plague, to wipe it from the basin and beyond. Gyam is the last of the Athru caste living, and he's obviously not a green."

Askari considered. "What did you do? What happened to the cuts you did to yourself?"

There was an extended silence while Dhala studied him. He seethed at the thought that Dhala didn't trust him. "What are you afraid of? When has my word not been good enough? I see one of my best friends slice himself with knives and, before the blood dries, his wounds have healed. I know what I saw. Now tell me what you did to save me." The fear worming its way through his system caused his voice to crack. "You did something. Something dangerous, and you did it to save me. Didn't you?"

There was a shorter wait before Dhala responded. "Yes. Tayi told me how to start. But I fought the battle for you."

Askari tensed as his fears grew and his voice became a whisper. "But you've never done it before. Why did Tayi have you heal me?"

Tayi appeared beside them with a faint scowl on her face, "Because I used my reserve, healing other Chinjoka. I miscalculated. Your injuries were more severe than I thought. Those Twins-damned scales are difficult to read through. I came too close to losing you both. Let's not have a repeat of that performance during my lifetime."

She pulled a gathering basket from the shelves and looked over one shoulder before turning to them. "Tell him what you are, Dhala. If you can't trust Askari, then we are not long for this world anyway."

She left, and the two men stared after her for several heartbeats before he turned to Dhala. "Tell me."

Dhala took a deep breath and let the air ease out through his nostrils. "First, I haven't been keeping it from you. Tayi said the gift is passed down her family lines, and no one knows of it. The gifted healing is hidden inside the herbal healing. She says, for most patients, only the herbs are needed. The gift can drain the healer so it's used only as a last resort."

Askari considered him but continued, determined to get answers to all his questions. "Why do you cut yourself? The bleeding must weaken you. But it heals so quickly." He gave Dhala a quizzical look. "What are you leaving out?"

"Let me tell you at my speed. Sprinting ahead won't serve any purpose."

Askari chuckled at his friend, but grabbed his side when the pain lanced through him from his still-healing injuries. "Please, no laughing. It hurts too much."

Dhala shot him a slight smirk before continuing. "Our healing comes from Voda, the Twin who controls the waters. He guides our hands to cut the symbols in our flesh needed. Once the healing is done, the token disappears." He caught the light on his leg, and the blue scar was obvious. "Usually."

"How does it work? Does it take away from your magic if you tell me what you do?"

Dhala appeared confused and shrugged. "I guess it isn't forbidden. Otherwise, Mother would have told me not to share with you. Right?"

Askari wrinkled his face and shrugged. *Maybe some humor will help Dhala get to the point.*

Dhala rolled his eyes, causing Askari to chuckle. "Making faces got you out of trouble when we were fledglings. But it doesn't work now." When Askari remained silent, Dhala cocked his head and looked at Askari. "Is there a reason the piwa would be important to you?"

He studied Dhala. "I suppose if you have to trust me, I have to trust you. Piwa is my soul rider. Why? How did you know?"

"The glyph takes me to another world. Familiar, and yet very different. I can…" Dhala stumbled for words. "I can fly over it. Somehow, I knew that the valley I flew over was you. There were piwa, many piwas. But they were taller than me and could talk. Not to my ears but inside my head. They were battling creatures I'd never seen before."

Askari watched his friend to decide if this was a story for the fledgling or a new truth. He wasn't certain what to think of his words. But he trusted Dhala. "If the piwas did most of the work, what did you do?"

"There is a river, like the one at the bottom of the cliffs, but different. There were high piwa dams on either side, coated with the heavy mud from the river bottom. But it had holes in it. The small ones did little harm to you. But others were great rents, and the waters rushed through them."

"But the piwa are good at repairing their dams. And if these were huge—" Askari shrugged his arms.

"The creatures they fought. Long dark things. They kept the piwas away. One of the piwa told me the dark things killed several of them who tried to repair the breaks."

"What did you do?"

"I used the methods of sky warfare I'd seen Gyam and Choro perform. I hit the first attacker at the end of a full dive. The other, I caught by its head and lifted it into the air. But that was all I accomplished. After killing two of them, they withdrew, and the piwas rushed in to repair the dams."

Askari lay back, exhausted by the slight effort he'd exerted. But as he settled into his bedding, he glanced at Dhala. "It was hard to breathe. My chest felt full, and I thought I was drowning. The river was where I was bleeding into my chest. You couldn't see because my plates kept you out. But today, my plates shifted back, and I could feel the difference. What did you do?"

Dhala looked uncomfortable as he shook his head. "I can't explain it. Things felt wrong, and I—" He shrugged again. "I fixed them. That is the best explanation I have."

The conversation faded like a wisp of smoke when Tayi walked in. "Enough talking. Askari needs rest, and you promised Jua you would take him fishing. If you don't do it soon, both of you can sleep on the grasslands until you do."

DHALA STUDIED THE draining wound from the viewpoint of a healer. He prodded it while keeping a watch on Askari's face to see if he was causing pain. When the only response was a slight flinch, he knew he didn't need to use the healing gift. This could be cured with more routine methods. He met his mother's gaze.

"It only needs drained and an herbal paste. The others are closing and the redness is gone," Dhala said.

His mother scrutinized his work, checking Askari in minute detail before nodding in agreement. "You can move. But you cannot call your plate. It will rip open your wounds and you will be under our care again, only I would be your healer and I will not be as cautious as my son has been. Do you understand?"

He grinned, his gaze darting between them. "So I can get out of this bed? The hata did a lot of damage, but these last few days have driven me insane."

"They were necessary." She finished with a note of steel.

Askari looked sheepish. "Yes, it was necessary. Otherwise, I'd do things that would reopen my wounds. You are right, Tayi."

She glanced at him and cocked an eyebrow. "Child, don't try the patience of the person who once cleaned your backside. And I do not mean when you were a fledgling."

Dhala chuckled as Askari flushed crimson, but silenced himself when she shifted her focus to him. "You will help him too. He needs to walk to stretch the scars so they will not rip when he calls his plate."

She waved Dhala to silence when he started to disagree. "It won't harm either of you. A handful of days, much walking. It will give both of you a chance to recover. Take Jua. Take Gyam. I don't care. But Askari needs to move about."

Dhala only smiled. His mother needed time alone. Too many were underfoot for her comfort. That meant Dhala needed to drain the pocket of infection so Askari's body could begin its work, and they would start their journey as soon as possible. He opened his case and took out an iron blade shorter than his smallest finger. He wasn't calling the healing gift of the Saat. His action was much more routine. With a few swift cuts, he drained the gathering infection, and cleaned and dressed the small incision. Satisfied with his work, he helped Askari stand.

They had only moved a step or two past the doorway when Gyam and Jua appeared beside them. Gyam immediately tried to assist Askari. He stopped and glared at them all.

"Stop it! I'm not an invalid, and I swear to the Twins the next person who tries to help me will find themselves seated on the ground. Tayi gave me specific instructions, and I'll follow them. You're welcome to stay close to save me from whatever you think might attack. But no one's going to carry me. My legs function without any problems."

The other three dropped their gazes to avoid Askari's glare and followed a half step behind. But Jua refused to leave his fishing spear behind, and after a short distance, he was again jabbing at imagined fish much larger than the one he'd taken.

Chapter Seven

ENA MOVED CLOSER to the last of the White Cliffs assigned to him. He'd learned early in his exploration the dangers of the country he traveled through. The loose stones shifted with each step, and the midday sun made him feel as exposed as an osa leg roasting over festival fires. The face of these cliffs was devoid of any type of vegetation. If he fell, nothing existed to stop him until he landed on the jagged piles of broken rock clustered along the foot of the cliffs. The reflection of sun from the glaring white stone made his vision more difficult, but on this part of the cliff face, he'd noticed a rough trail that moved down the formation in a series of switchbacks to end at the edge of the forest several spans from the cliffs. Even though the Misiq were skilled climbers, this descent had the makings of a suicide mission. He considered his predicament and reached a decision. His battle form was best for this trek. Four legs would traverse this path better than two, and he had yet to explore any of the lands to the east of the bluffs. The narrow path might be his best method for scouting the western forest of the Chinjoka.

After checking the situation again, he was comfortable with his decision and started his change. His body became malleable under the forces of the Great Ones who gave him the ability to shift. It happened rapidly, as always, with his long tail coming to life. Once the last of his fur settled into place, he gave his body a shake that ended with a healthy flick of his tail. He loped forward and began his trip down the treacherous trail.

He placed each paw with great care, the path moving beneath each step. After making it to the first switchback, a thin sheet of rock shot sideways, destroying his grip, and broke each paw's hold. With every muscle tense, he studied the path to find an escape.

As he surveyed the area trapping him, he chastised himself for falling for the mistake of a cub. For a span in any direction the path was damaged, if not obliterated, by a rockslide in its recent past. But wind and rain had shaped a trigger for disaster. As he continued to study the situation, he noted several large boulders that would be part of the next rockslide too.

He drew in the scent from around him, assessing if this might be something left as a trap by the Chinjoka, but he detected nothing more sinister than the environment taking advantage of a natural weakness. The hazard confronting him was no less potentially fatal for the fact it was natural. Each change of his weight resulted in more instability beneath him. Once he realized his choices were limited, he moved up the cliff a fingerwidth at a time. His tail twitched over his back like a restless animal. But when he eased the least stable of his feet forward, thin sheets of slate shot from under him.

He froze in place as rock careened down the cliff face. As it gathered more debris from its path below him, he thought the minor rockslide would leave him untouched, but a loud crack sounded from higher up the cliff and the boulders began rolling toward him. Ena's muscles coiled as he tried to escape the growing monster. He jumped as far as he could, but those few spans to safety seemed a world away.

His chest filled with the billowing clouds of dust surrounding him. Each lunge of his muscular body kept him just above the morass threatening to bury him. One of the large boulders broke free, and Ena tumbled away from its path. The lacerations left bloody prints each time Ena's feet touched the ground. Pounded by a barrage of loose stone, he struggled to escape again, but realized to his horror he was losing his battle form.

In a heartbeat, he reverted to his two-legged presence as rocks hammered him. The landslide swept him along, and he tumbled downward. Pain filled him while the cliffs tried to rip him apart, and his arm was wrenched free of its shoulder socket in one horrendous twist. No longer in control, he was part of the mass moving down the mountain.

Ena came to a stop a few spans lower, caught in a pile of rock and boulder that had him in their deadly grip. Agony washed over him in a rapid succession of waves, making it impossible for Ena to gather coherent thought. His body screamed in protest when he tried to pull himself from the rubble. But his slight movement set more of the hillside into motion. Then the mountain released a boulder as tall as Ena. He fought to escape the shower of rock.

The boulder hit his leg, and the torment that shot through him was more than he could bear. He made a last try at pulling himself free, but his senses failed and his world went black.

ASKARI STRETCHED, EAGER for action. Any action. They had spent the last days traveling through the shortgrass swales, far from the river that formed the boundaries of the basin the Chinjoka considered home. But away from the water, the lands became more arid and the plant life limited to those tolerant of the drier conditions. At least today he'd convinced Dhala they should make their way to the White Cliffs and the cutleaf forest that grew for many spans from its base. Even if they hurried, it would be a sun cycle to make the round trip, and if they scaled the cliff, it would take longer.

At Askari's current speed, the trip would be extended further. He'd managed to leave behind all his would-be rescuers with the exception of Dhala. Tayi had asked Gyam and Jua to work in her gardens. He thought she'd felt sorry for him since his friends had hovered over him while he prepared for this trip. At least Dhala didn't hover...as much.

The sun filtered through the dense leaves, nearing midday when they reached the cliff base. They had each kept their peace during today's walk, and Askari found little need to break the restful silence. They paused and studied the network of paths winding their way up the steep slope. Excited by the upcoming climb, Askari's heart beat faster. Once he calmed himself, he turned to Dhala.

"We have to climb. When else would we find a time to explore the White Cliffs?"

"Askari..."

He motioned at the extensive rock face before them. "No. You know I'm right. You want to climb them as much as I do. Admit it."

Dhala fidgeted from foot to foot as he chewed his bottom lip. "Yes, okay. It is a challenge that appeals to me. It is a challenge any Chinjoka would relish. We are the people of the high cliffs. Who would be better prepared than you and me?"

Askari glanced at Dhala. "I have been forced to stay in bed for what seems a moon. I'd like to feel the challenge of climbing the White Cliffs."

Dhala hesitated for a moment and motioned toward the paths. "Make your choice. I will follow."

With a shrug, Askari picked a path and began his slow ascent.

The path he'd chosen was one to test the skills even of the Chinjoka. The narrow trail had been formed over the cycles by the small sharp hooves of herds of osa, and honed by the generations of rain and wind, requiring their complete concentration. Askari tested the slight change in the trail they followed as they made their way through the scattering of white boulders. The rock making up the path fractured at the slightest pressure, and a misstep would send them crashing downward. But the risk was part of the reason he'd chosen this path. It created the challenge Askari ached for after so many sun cycles of being forced to stay immobile. He placed each step with care, sensing the slight shift each time. He slid his hands along the cliff face, checking for vegetation clinging to available cracks that might be used for handholds, but nothing seemed to exist in this part of the climb.

"How are you feeling?"

Askari braced against a convenient head-high rock and turned to Dhala, trying to give his best Tayi scowl. "Like my mother is hovering behind me. That's how I feel." He spun to climb farther, and his feet slid toward the edge.

Dhala snorted. "You fall from these cliffs and there won't be enough pieces left for your piwa to patch back together."

Askari kept silent and focused on the climb. But Dhala's warning continued to echo through him. He moved with deliberation and greater care.

The blazing sun was well past midday when the path widened, and they found a place to relax. Askari was grateful for the break because, while he would never tell Dhala, his legs were shaking from exertion. As they settled onto the ground, Dhala offered him a hand, which he accepted.

They both caught their breath before speaking. Askari leaned downward to discover there were times even Chinjoka were subject to vertigo. This was one. Dhala knelt against the cliff and pulled food packets from the carrier he'd filled that morning. Askari squatted beside him. His stomach growled by the time the food was divided between them. He picked up a morsel and popped it into his mouth, and ate with great care, enjoying the flavors that were always a delightful element of Tayi's cooking. Once he'd swallowed, he grinned at Dhala.

"If you cooked as well as your mother, you might catch Gyam."

Dhala scowled at his friend. "Gyam will eat anything. He eats the hata liver raw after the hunt."

Askari broke into laughter. "Just because he likes his meat a little less cooked doesn't make him an animal. Others like their meat that way too. Some people find the liver a treat."

"For the Athru and Onija, maybe. We Saat do not eat our meat raw."

"We need the fresh meat to change. But you already know that."

Dhala snorted and returned to his meal, ignoring Askari. With an unrepentant grin, Askari focused on the delicious food in front of him. Soon they were down to bits and scraps, which they both gleaned from the rawhide surface of the packet.

With a sigh, Askari sat back and smiled at Dhala. "Yes. Yes indeed. If you cooked this— Ouch!" Askari yelped.

Dhala glared at him and held another rock.

Askari held his hands up in surrender. "All right, I got your message. No more teasing. I thought it was funny."

"It is not funny. What if our roles were reversed and there was someone you found attractive?"

"It's never happened, so I can't say."

Dhala studied him with a brow cocked. "No one? At all?"

"No. Not—that way." Askari sensed the heat rise to his face. An unfamiliar experience. When Dhala was quiet for too long, he glanced toward him. Dhala had a solemn expression. The look fired frustration in Askari.

"That's why I never told you. I don't need a lover for my life to be good."

"Is there no one?"

"The ones our age I don't find attractive. The Chinjoka are so...plain."

Dhala chuckled. "Good to hear I am so unappealing. It eases my mind."

"How nasty. I can't imagine being with you. Or Gyam. Just. So. I don't know. Unsavory. Like a brother."

Askari braced himself for backlash, but when none came, he contemplated what he had told Dhala, and why. It wasn't as if his feelings came from some recent unsettling event. The more Askari thought about what he had said, the more they sounded true. This wasn't a situation they'd never shared before. They'd climbed before; that was why he chose to scale the cliffs. He welcomed the distraction. He didn't want to think about how close he'd come to dying from the goring by the hata. The Twins watched too closely, but there was nothing he could do to change his history.

Not finding a connection with any of the other Chinjoka was an issue he'd never been able to fix. It worried him. His doubts grew since the day he blooded himself with his first game, which had been a piwa too. He had been every bit as excited about his kill as Jua.

"Askari, come here."

He moved to Dhala's side. He glanced around, but saw nothing. His friend stood frozen, continuing to stare at the hillside below them.

"Down there." Dhala motioned. "Near the bottom of that rockslide."

He stared, trying to see what Dhala detected. *There! What was that? Something moved.* He turned his head, trying to capture the sound of whatever he was looking at. He struggled to identify what the landslide trapped. Then it came. An almost inaudible rumbling. It was hard to take in what his senses told him.

"By the Twins, someone's trapped." He started down the slope when Dhala grabbed his arm and brought him to a stop. He glared at Dhala. "They may be dying. Why are you stopping me?"

"What if it is a Misiq?"

Askari started to argue, but saw hair the color of grasses at late summer exposed in the afternoon light. He nodded without taking his eyes off the spot of unusual color. *Dhala may be right. I need to be careful.*

He crawled down the loose rocks. It wasn't a great distance from the path they had been following, but a waist-high boulder had started the slide. As they moved to its resting place, the victim of the avalanche came into view. There was no doubt now; the ear tufts alone were enough to mark this person as Misiq.

Askari sniffed the surrounding air. Him. Definitely a him.

"What are we going to do now? Are you going to give him mercy?" Dhala lifted a brow as he asked.

Askari shook his head. "No, we'll save him."

Dhala's jaw dropped, and worked up and down several times before he stopped with his lips tight against each other.

Askari glared until he knew his wishes were clear. He had succeeded when the tension escaped from Dhala to be replaced by a look of resignation.

"How do you plan to do this without one of us being killed either by the rockslide or the Misiq, oh great Onija?"

Askari frowned at him before moving closer to the pinned man. If the Misiq was awake, this rescue would become many times more difficult and dangerous. A conscious Misiq would likely be searching for ways to kill them, which was the goal of all Misiq. It appeared to be a racial objective at this point. But from where they sat, he first needed to find out if the Misiq was alive. The rockslide could easily have killed him.

"Wait," Dhala said.

Askari turned to find Dhala rummaging through the carriers each of them had brought. Askari was becoming impatient when Dhala lifted a coiled length of rope from one pack.

He held it up with a smile of satisfaction. "I thought she would make sure we had rope before sending us to explore the White Cliffs." He fastened the rope around Askari's waist. Once Dhala was satisfied the rope was secure, he coiled the rest around his arm and nodded toward Askari. "Go carefully. But I can help if it begins to slide again."

Askari waited until he was certain Dhala was prepared before easing himself toward the immobile Misiq. Once he was within touching distance, he studied the injured man. He saw no signs he was faking unconsciousness to trap Askari. When he could see no indications of life, he leaned in and pressed his fingers against the Misiq's throat and breathed a sigh of relief when he felt a pulse, not as strong as he would have liked, but still it existed.

Satisfied the Misiq was alive but unconscious, he scanned the surrounding area until he found a stout branch close to his height. He returned to the boulder, untied the safety rope, and motioned Dhala closer. Dhala made his way down the cliff carefully, skidding on his backside at times, until he stood beside Askari.

"I'll put this under the rock and lift it. Once I do, pull him out. Try not to make the injury worse."

Dhala scowled. "You are telling the healer not to injure the patient?"

"You know what I mean. I hope I can shift the rock that's pinning him."

Dhala moved without argument so he could pull out the Misiq once he was free. When he was in position, Dhala made a quick nod.

Askari rammed the branch in an opening and shoved forward. He braced his feet and dug into the mix of powder and gravel where he stood. His muscles bulged as he strained against the weight. The wood gave out a soft groan, and the rock shifted slightly. He lasted a few moments before letting the branch drop. He stepped away to glare at the immobile stone. He gasped for air as Dhala stepped away.

"It barely moved."

"I know. I was the one pushing. Do you have any ideas?"

"What if we push it downhill, both of us going the same direction?"

Askari nodded in agreement and went to the same side of the boulder. He braced and looked over at Dhala. "Ready?"

At Dhala's nod, they pressed forward. The weight didn't shift, and Askari threw more muscle into the effort. Out of energy, he only sensed a tiny movement in the rock. From the expression on Dhala's face, the Saat sensed the same nonexistent level of accomplishment. As he was reaching the limits of his strength, the boulder shifted. The pair focused on putting what strength remained into freeing the man. It lifted only a palm span and would go no farther in spite of their efforts. A moment later, they reached the limit of their strength and lowered the rock back to where it was resting. Askari contemplated the problem, but as he did, a groan came from the trapped man. He turned to Dhala.

"Can you hold it alone? Just for a few heartbeats."

Dhala looked over the situation before nodding. "Yes. But only hold it. Let me change my grip."

Askari wedged himself against the rock and nodded. Dhala braced his hands on the rough surface, dug his feet into the changing gravel, and shoved.

The boulder lifted the hand span again, and after adjustment, he motioned toward Askari. "Got it."

Askari eased away from the boulder and waited to be certain Dhala could support the weight. Askari glanced around, lunging forward to grab another stout branch. He shoved it under the white mass and pushed the branch while they strained against the weight. Then it shifted, the rocks sliding deeper into the mesh of gravel and grinding to a halt.

Askari's branch wedged under a group of head-sized stones. He glared at it in frustration.

"By the Father! We have to move it, or he'll die," Askari said as he shoved down on the branch.

His push caused the boulder to rock back before coming to settle again. He became hopeful as he studied the situation. "Dhala, here. Help me push down on this."

He moved to one side with each of them pressing downward. The boulder rocked as they pushed on the log until it was tightly pinned against the ground.

"Got it?" Askari asked. After a nod from Dhala, he jumped to the side. He took the Misiq by an arm and leg and tried to pull him free. He struggled for several moments and stopped.

"What's wrong?" Dhala asked.

"His foot. It's trapped. Can you hold him a little longer? I'll dig him out."

"I have it. But hurry!"

The sound of sand and pebbles moving around them filled the air as Dhala strained to keep the thick branch against the ground. Once the opening was large enough for Askari to wriggle inside, he moved forward. He used his hands to dig until he found the Misiq's ankle. Askari tugged once and found it tightly wedged. He focused on freeing the foot, and dirt flew from around them like a mkali creating a new burrow. Progress was slow, and the foot was no less pinned. He knew Dhala must be tiring, and Askari was ready to crawl out and give him a break when the footing changed and the limb slipped free. Askari shot from the tiny cave, grabbed the man's arms, and heaved. The trapped foot refused to move again. Askari joined Dhala in his efforts to shove the boulder, but they didn't budge the monolith. Their next attempts yielded the same results.

Dhala shook as Askari readied for his final try. "Hurry, Askari. I cannot hold this for much longer."

Askari coiled his muscles, took a deep breath, and pulled with all his might. For a moment nothing happened, and Askari worried they would fail. His world changed, and the Misiq broke free and landed on top of Askari. A moment later, Dhala dropped the boulder with a yell.

Askari grinned. "He's free. You can let it down now."

Dhala chuckled and shook his head. "You have an amazing ability for stating the obvious."

Askari glanced up and frowned. "I'd appreciate help. I don't want him waking up and opening me with those claws."

Dhala glanced at the Misiq's fingertips, which had morphed into sharp claws while they struggled to free him. The deadly weapons at the tips of his fingers would open either of them without a problem. Dhala leaned down and helped Askari crawl free.

Askari and Dhala studied the victim. He was large and muscular, like Askari. His yellow hair was pulled into a tight braid, and he wore the traditional knee-length kilt Askari associated with the Misiq. This one was well-constructed in shades of green, which he was fairly certain served as a reliable camouflage. His muscular legs were covered with a plush coating of hair a few shades lighter than his braid. Askari's pulse sped up as he noticed the hair continued over his chest and down his stomach, unlike the bare-skinned Chinjoka. He found the unique marking...desirable.

"Askari. We need to reach the top of the cliffs. It would be good to get that accomplished before he wakes."

Askari saw where they were. The original path was close, but the loose rocks made the possibility of another avalanche high. Askari looked at the slope again and decided.

"We have to get to the trail. We can't leave him."

Dhala sighed. "And how do you see this happening?"

He glanced around and spotted the rope they'd used as a safety line. He snatched it from the ground and coiled it around one shoulder before turning to Dhala with a tight smile. "With this."

Dhala checked the avalanche area. As he did, a few rocks came loose of the lower slide and tumbled down the cliffs. Seeming to have chosen, he held out his hand.

"Give me the rope. I can tie it so it doesn't cause more damage to the Misiq."

Askari nodded and tossed him the tight coil of braided rawhide. Dhala squatted beside the unconscious man, laced the rope under the Misiq's arms, and tied it against his chest. They moved the man using the outer edge of the path where a sprinkling of vegetation helped stabilize the ground, making their task safer. Not safe, but many hazards fewer than the alternatives. They pulled the man up with agonizing slowness to avoid starting another avalanche that would trap all three of them. Askari's concern was heightened since he'd insisted the other end of the rope be tied around his own waist. He had no doubt this Misiq weighed enough to cause the both of them to pitch off the cliff.

They reached the pathway, and relief washed over Askari. He untied the rope from his waist and pulled it taut before glancing at Dhala. "Grab the rope. Move carefully. If the rockslide starts again, we'll all end up buried at the bottom of these cliffs."

Dhala seemed ready to comment, but instead, his lips formed a tight line and he took the rope in his hands. Together, they pulled the unconscious man over the final few treacherous spans of the landslide. Fingerwidth by fingerwidth, they moved him closer to the broken path. They paused several times when the rocks moved, but Askari breathed a sigh of relief once they pulled him onto the crude path.

Dhala untied the rope from around the man's broad chest, coiled it tightly, and tossed it into his carrying pack. He and Dhala exchanged a glance before Askari surveyed the route ahead.

"We are close to the top. Let's see how we can help. But we need to get him off this cliff before we all end up broken among the rocks."

Dhala frowned at Askari. "He would have killed us if he'd found us injured and helpless."

Askari studied the Misiq. "Rescuing him was the right thing. The Twins want this man alive."

Dhala studied him for a moment and dropped his gaze. "All right. If you are that certain about it, I will help. It doesn't have to be the will of the gods for me to help my friend. But if he awakens and turns on us…"

"I agree, we should be prepared. Before we make decisions, we need to find out how much damage he has sustained."

Askari was going to pull him by the arm when Dhala stopped him. "Wait. We don't know how severe the injuries are. We shouldn't pull him any farther by his arms, or we might cause permanent damage."

"Then I'll carry him. Let's go."

"But what if he…"

Askari stared at the injured man until his emotions created a single message, and then nodded in confirmation. With a quirk of his lips, he turned to Dhala. "Can I change?"

Dhala twisted his mouth and stepped closer. He ran through a check of each point of injury, and Askari sensed nothing more than Dhala's skilled touch. But when he ended the inspection, his face was less severe.

"The injuries are more healed than I'd feared. I think it's safe for you to call your plates."

Askari focused on triggering the change. At first, there was nothing, but then the familiar and delicious shifting began. His skin tightened and thickened as it did each time he called on Pilea to bless him again with his natural armor. A few deep breaths later, the placement of each muscle was sharply defined. But if someone touched any of the large scales, it would be as if Askari had slid iron plates in strategic locations to protect his body. A short time later, something inside him formed the iron-hard plates across his thick torso.

When he turned to the injured man, his muscles coiled and stretched under the rigid plates as he positioned himself. Askari squatted and ran one arm behind the Misiq's head and the other at the top of his thighs. As he pulled the injured man against his torso, he caught the scent of exotic spice.

Askari ignored the unfamiliar sensation flowing through him and lifted the man to his chest as he stood. He surveyed the area and spotted a cluster of trees a short distance from the cliff's edge. Askari moved to a small opening in the trees and worked to lower himself and the Misiq into the litter of leaves. He stared at the still form before turning to Dhala.

"What now?"

Dhala pursed his lips as he surveyed the man. He knelt within reach, paused, and touched him. Cautiously at first, but with increasing surety, he checked the man's life points. He ran fingers over the Misiq's head to check for injuries. From there, he moved to what appeared to be the most serious injury.

As he probed the muscular shifter, he caused the first sounds to emerge, a soft groan. Dhala stopped to make certain his patient wasn't awakening, and once the Misiq remained unmoving, he continued. He finished a short time later, moved a safe distance away, and squatted to watch his patient.

"Well?" Askari asked.

"The shoulder is dislocated. He has a sizable knot on his head too. It's probably the reason he's not awake."

"Can you heal him?"

"You want me to use my limited resources to heal a Misiq? You know if I do, I would not be able to help if Jua or Gyam were hurt?"

"Cut the healing mark into my leg then."

Dhala started to disagree, but grew thoughtful as he watched Askari. "I'm uncertain what would happen if I cut the mark into your flesh."

"Will he live if we do nothing?"

"Maybe. But he likely will be crippled."

"The Misiq drown people who are less than perfect as sacrifices to their gods. I can't leave him for that fate." Askari glared at him before saying, "I accept the risks. I want him saved."

"Lie here." Dhala motioned to the spot beside the Misiq as he retrieved his now-familiar pouch from the pack. Askari lay beside the golden-haired man and bared his thigh. Dhala knelt between them and sat unmoving. Askari was becoming concerned when Dhala finally moved with quiet efficiency. He made a series of short quick cuts into Askari's leg. He clenched his teeth against the pain, which reminded Askari more of being burned with a firebrand rather than a simple cut.

Dhala paused, and the burning slowed until the sensation shifted. Askari had the sensation of being filled with snowmelt. This time, he couldn't contain his reactions. He shivered uncontrollably. Time lost meaning as the sensation of being buried in ice overwhelmed him. Askari had reached the limits of his endurance when in a quick reversal, the cold receded.

Askari tried to calm the panic pouring into his system. And with each deep breath, he beat the cold into submission. He looked at his friend, and a slow smile spread across his face.

"Well, we lived through it. We've done things that were more fun, though."

Dhala stared at him with no sign of relief. "I'm not doing that again. I had no control. I was afraid you would die."

"But I didn't. Did it help?"

Dhala stared at their patient. "We should know soon. I worked on the injury to his head. There's no bleeding, and the swelling has decreased."

A soft groan escaped from their patient as he moved. His eyes fluttered open, and Askari looked into an unusually light amber pair of eyes.

As soon as their gazes locked, the slit pupils dilated and his gaze darted to the limits of their rotation. In the next instant, he lunged and tried to escape. But he pushed away with his injured arm and collapsed on the ground with a sharp gasp.

"Be still! I spent a great deal of our healing work getting you better. Don't ruin my work," Dhala said.

The Misiq went quiet, looking first at Dhala and then Askari. Once their eyes met, his gaze seemed to lock on Askari. The silence became tense, but still no one spoke. Askari resettled his balance, and the man moved again, this time spinning to confront them.

"What plan you, flyer?"

The intonation was different, and the word choices were sometimes odd. Askari noted the injured man's voice contained a low hum, but he was easy enough to follow. "We found you trapped by a rockslide on the White Cliffs. A boulder pinned your leg. We dug you loose and carried you to the plateau. Dhala cured your head wound, but we think your shoulder is dislocated. You might have a broken leg too."

"Torture to please your gods I will not allow." He tried to lunge and grabbed at the sheathed knife strapped around Dhala's thigh. Askari threw himself backward and kept the knife safe. The effort did the Misiq little good, leaving him on the ground, writhing in pain, with his jaw clenched.

"That was foolish. Why would we cure you to sacrifice you to the gods? Besides, our gods don't ask for sacrifice," Askari said.

He and Dhala dodged away as the Misiq tried to shift. His hands and feet reshaped into huge paws, and a tail snaked its way from the base of his back. Tawny fur struggled to sprout over his bare skin. But the reshaping of his body came to a halt in less time than it took to begin. With a strangled cry, the Misiq fell to the ground, gasping as he returned to his two-legged form. When Askari decided it was safe, he walked to the Misiq and squatted at his side. This time, he kept a safe distance between them.

"Are you ready to accept our help?" Askari asked. "Otherwise, we'll leave you here, and you can fare for yourself."

"Care for myself I can."

"How far can you travel with a broken leg and a dislocated shoulder? Can you make it back to your pack?"

Dhala moved closer, having remained silent. He glanced at Askari. "Change out of your armor. He will see he can trust us."

Askari considered Dhala's suggestion as a possible next step. Dropping his armor would leave him almost as helpless as Dhala. But he decided his friend was right. It was the only way to convince the Misiq. He sent a familiar release flowing through him, and the slight tension he experienced while in change slipped away. A moment later, he shook himself to help relax. Once his skin regained its normal tone and texture, he looked at the Misiq and made a sweeping motion across his body.

"No plates. I'm defenseless. Would you stop trying to either kill us or run away? If we don't finish the healing, you will have permanent damage from the injuries. The leg needs set, and the shoulder must be put back into place. Neither is painless."

The Misiq studied them for several heartbeats before he slumped to the ground with a grimace. "I can go no further. I must find a trust in enemies of my people."

"If we were your enemies, we would not be trying to heal you. We would have left you to die."

"Why did you not?"

Dhala looked at Askari, his face a blank mask, and didn't utter a word. Askari rolled his eyes before turning to the man. "I felt we should save you."

"Only a feeling?"

Askari scowled, becoming frustrated with the questions. "If it offends you that much, I can cut your throat now. Would that fulfill your wish?"

The Misiq chewed his lip as he glanced from Dhala to Askari. The silence held for several moments before he spoke. "What must I do?"

The tension drained from Dhala and Askari. Dhala cocked his head and met his gaze. "I need to check your shoulder again. I think it should be first. Then we can decide what needs to be done with the leg."

There was a nod, and Dhala stepped forward to begin his examination. A few flickers of pain shot across the Misiq's expressive face, but otherwise, he was quiet through the entire process. Dhala wasn't being gentle, but it was no worse than Askari had seen him do with other Chinjoka.

When they separated, he had a look of satisfaction etched across his face. "Your shoulder seems not to have any injuries that can't be healed. I think if we put it in place, you will have full function." He met the man's eyes with conviction. "We should repair the injury now."

The Misiq ran his tongue along dry lips. "Your names?"

"What? What difference does that make?" Askari said.

The Misiq gave him a look Askari would have reserved for an inexperienced fledgling. "Power resides in a name. By giving your names, you will have less power over me."

Askari exchanged glances with Dhala. As far as they were concerned, there was no power in a name. It was just a...well, name. Other than to get his attention. It was better than "hey, you, big one." But if the Misiq believed names had power, then maybe they could play this to their advantage.

"We rescued you, and you tried to kill us. You need to tell us your name."

Panic flashed across the Misiq's face, but Askari scowled. The injured man sank back and gasped in pain. But only a short time passed before he answered. "Ena. My name is Ena."

Askari's reaction was far beyond what he expected. He couldn't say why, even if someone held a knife to his throat. But Ena looked so crestfallen that he empathized with his pain. The sensation wasn't one he relished.

"Thank you, Ena, for sharing your name with us. I'm Askari and this is Dhala. We're both Chinjoka."

Ena twitched his mouth upward. "Yes, clear it is that you be flyers. I do not understand why you gave me your names, but I will let you finish."

Dhala was about to make a comment that wouldn't be helpful, so Askari plunged into the conversation. "What should we do first? The day is half-gone."

"The dislocation needs to be addressed first. It may be the most painful. Get behind him and let him lean against your chest. I need his arm to the side."

Askari moved behind Ena and scooted underneath. As they slid over each other, the pleasant sensation he'd experienced while carrying Ena resurfaced. Confusion aside, he stepped into the position Dhala dictated. He braced Ena as Dhala maneuvered into position, took the injured arm in his hands, and braced his foot against Ena's armpit. Dhala nodded.

He readied himself in case there was a reaction to the pain, but other than tightening muscles, Ena remained still. Dhala increased the tension until it was enough to make Askari cringe. He gradually increased the force he was putting on the arm, but it fought being put into place. Time stopped for Askari as Ena dripped sweat from the pain. The beautiful eyes, which had drawn in Askari, fluttered shut and his jaw clenched. Askari was ready to ask Dhala to stop when Ena's shoulder changed position and slipped into its socket. Ena whimpered and shuddered in Askari's arms.

"Let him go. It should be in place."

Askari released Ena and sensed his own curious hesitation. Ena moved slowly, flexing his arm slightly. He stared at the two of them. "Better it is. Much better. I can move now."

Dhala cautioned him. "It needs to be bound into place to protect it. We also need to splint your leg. Do you need time to rest?"

Ena studied his leg, bruised and distended, and looked at Dhala. "How bad is it?"

Dhala shrugged. "The bone didn't come through the skin, and it doesn't look crushed. If we set it, you should be back to normal in a moon or so."

Ena smiled at Dhala. "The Misiq fast healing are. Put it as it should be, and I will walk on it in a day."

Dhala shook his head, but then turned to Askari. "Find a few stout branches. And see if we have something in the packs to use for lacing them tight against his leg."

Askari searched the area and located a few thick pieces of wood that would serve as support. He dug through the pack, found a length of braided leather, and returned. He walked behind Dhala and studied the leg carefully. Dhala glanced back to Askari with a satisfied look on his face.

"You will pull on his foot until everything is aligned again. Once the bones are in place, I'll bind the leg to keep it from shifting. Do you understand?"

With a nod, Askari wrapped his hands around Ena's thick foot. He noted the pseudo-claws he had instead of toenails, but he put them out of his thoughts to focus on his task. A word from Dhala jarred him back to his job.

"Begin."

Askari applied tension, and increased the force he exerted.

"Easy."

He slowed but kept the pressure steady. Askari noticed a soft grinding feeling beneath his hands, and he wanted to pull away from the sensation. But he kept his face as blank as the cliffs they'd been climbing. He focused. There was a stout snap, and a loud groan erupted from Ena. The sound filled Askari with dread.

"Stop. Hold it in place."

Askari was glad to stop. He hated to cause someone pain. It was outside his being to make someone suffer. He could kill an attacking enemy, but he was no torturer. Dhala bound the leg with deft movements. Ena remained still through Dhala's administration.

"Done. Set it down with care."

Askari cradled the man's foot and eased it to the ground. He studied Ena and Dhala. He hadn't dealt with the pain or worked the healing, but he was exhausted. Dhala teetered on the edge of collapse. Askari had to find the reserves to take care of everyone.

A chilled wind swept across them, and he realized they would not be traveling that night. They needed shelter and food. He moved toward a dense thicket of dwarfed evergreens and pulled his knife from its sheath. Most of the tree's bases were no thicker than a finger, and Askari gathered enough to create a shelter from the high-altitude cold.

The sun neared the horizon when Askari finished making their shelter. Dhala had a small fire going in front of the refuge so heat would reflect into it.

Askari squatted beside Ena. "We need to move you into the shelter. I can help if you'll allow it."

Ena studied him before nodding. He moved so Askari could reach his uninjured arm. He leaned in, wrapped his arm around Ena's torso, and lifted him to his feet. They made their way to the mouth of the shelter, and Askari helped him onto the cushion of boughs. He knelt beside the fire and picked one of the large leaves Dhala had found. Using it as a platter, he filled it with food they'd brought. Part of him was still uneasy about what they were doing, even if the idea had been his.

Dhala nodded with a soft chuckle. "Feed the man, Askari. I put a lot of effort into healing him. Do not deprive him of food."

He balanced the platter on two hands and carried it to Ena. The Misiq accepted the ration with a shake of his head. "Why did you work so hard to save me? No Misiq would do the same. It's more likely they would have put a knife to your throat."

Askari was tiring of this entire discussion. "Because the Chinjoka gods bade me to save you. That's why. They want you alive for a reason. I don't understand why the gods do what they do, but we will help you and let you return to your people. Later, if you find a Chinjoka at your mercy, then the choice of what to do is yours."

Ena looked disturbed but went silent as he accepted the food from Askari. They stared at each other as Ena ate. A moment later, something bumped Askari's shoulder. He glanced over to see Dhala holding out an almost identical collection of food to him. Silence ruled over the scene once Dhala prepared his own plate and joined the other two. As he ate, it occurred to Askari that Ena needed the shelter more than he and Dhala. Askari might be working from divine intervention, but the Twins had little tolerance for stupidity. He didn't plan to fall into the category that would cause their displeasure.

Askari finished his meal and dropped the leaf he'd used as a platter into their small fire. The pleasant scent that resulted didn't surprise him. That was a detail Dhala would have considered. As the other two followed his example, the scent became stronger. He changed his gaze to Dhala, who shrugged.

"It will keep the biters away, crawling or flying. It will make it more comfortable for those of us not sleeping in the shelter."

Ena looked at each of them. His face never changed from its emotionless expression. But the general sensations traveling from him left Askari with the contentment of a full belly more than any level of danger.

Ena motioned toward the tiny refuge. "Use the shelter you can. Nothing will happen."

Askari considered the options before responding. "You've already said you would have cut our throats. I think we would feel more secure sleeping outside."

"Took my knife you did. I am healing. And you have my name. What could I do?"

Dhala looked up and sighed. "Ena, I've seen your talons. You told us you heal quickly, and we do not have your tradition with names so we don't understand the significance. We will sleep with less concern if we are not sharing the same shelter."

Ena studied them and dropped his gaze. "Very well, no offense."

"Good. Because I intended none. We are just..." Askari said.

"I understand."

ASKARI SAT BESIDE the low-burning fire. He hadn't slept, and now the night was slipping away. He dropped a few more twigs into the flames and heard a rustling from the shelter. Ena crawled across the space separating them to rest beside Askari. He acknowledged Ena's presence with a nod but continued to stare into the flames.

A whisper of a breeze stirred around them, and the scent of burning wood and Ena filled his senses. The sensations left him uncertain. He wanted this moment. But could he trust a man whose people wanted to wipe out the Chinjoka? Ena was exotic. Different than anyone he had experienced in his life. Their gazes met, and Askari lost himself in Ena's features. From the wild amber eyes, the cleft in his upper lip, to the tufts of hair topping each ear, Askari found himself drawn to the Misiq.

"I am healing. I believe I will journey to my home in another day. You should know I realize I have not been an appreciative recipient of your kindness. Grateful you rescued and healed me."

Askari nodded as he considered Ena's words. With a sigh, he spoke. "It makes no sense. Our people are enemies. We should be enemies."

"Ruling Council tells us the Chinjoka healers infested the Misiq with this disease to us."

Startled at the accusation, Askari stared at Ena until the tension became palpable before he replied. When he did, he tried to keep the emotion from his voice. "We've lost two villages; only one remains. We are a dying people. Why would we send this to anyone?"

Ena sighed and dropped his gaze. "I've lost many close friends and family. The pain and anger can make the reasonable unreasonable."

"The plague is too horrible to use against anyone. Dhala is a healer; if he were awake, I'm sure he would tell you none of the Chinjoka healers sent this disease to anyone."

"Dhala is awake. And I can guarantee no healer sent the sickness to your people. We have tried to cure it but had no success. I hoped your healers might have a cure. But it would seem that was a false hope."

"The Misiq do not have healers. With little delay, do we heal. The ill or infirm are returned to the gods so they can be reborn."

Askari felt revulsion at the implications. When he glanced at Dhala, he saw similar raw emotions.

"Children? Even from illness?" Dhala asked.

Ena cocked his head. "We heal quicker when we change. Those who cannot change, given back to be reborn are. Any who can't heal with speed are given to the gods. The Council is clear. It applies to everyone, regardless."

"And now that you've seen the benefit of healing?" Dhala asked.

Ena nodded, his face a mask. "Much is there to be considered. But I am only a warrior. The Ruling Council is guided from the Great Ones."

Dhala seemed finished discussing the Misiq. He moved beside Ena to examine the shoulder they had put in place the day before. One of Dhala's brows rose as he dug into the injury. Askari was amazed the inspection seemed to cause Ena little pain.

When Dhala moved to examine his leg, the results were similar. After an in-depth examination, Dhala rocked back on his heels and looked at them both. "The shoulder seems almost healed. The leg is probably tender, but the bone is growing together." He steadied his gaze on the Misiq. "You heal fast. You weren't exaggerating. I don't think you need anything from us. I would recommend a day before you begin your travels back to make certain everything is as it should be. You will be well enough to begin your journey tomorrow."

Askari's heart skipped a beat at the thought of more time with Ena. But he wasn't certain if his company would be welcome. He turned to the Misiq. "I can work with you today to let your healing progress." Askari looked somewhat hesitant. "If you would find that helpful."

Their gazes met, and Ena's muscles rippled down his body. He waited a time before answering. "I believe correct you are. Rest today would allow my healing to progress."

Dhala studied the pair but then nodded and gave Askari a considered look. "I believe it would be good for you to work with Ena today, Askari."

He lifted his eyebrows almost to his hairline. "And what are you going to do while I am helping Ena?"

Dhala smiled at his friend. "First, I will search for healing herbs unique to this area. I didn't harvest here on my mother's gathering exposition. Otherwise, I will be watchful of any others of Ena's band coming to search for him. At least that way, he can justify being absent for longer than they expected."

Askari nodded, adding nothing further to the conversation. Ena looked between the two of them, but his expression disclosed nothing. "It would not be harmful for me to move my shoulder and leg. Faster they will heal if I am using them." He turned to Askari. "We can climb through the hills. They will try my healing."

"Go then. I will prepare a meal for when you return," Dhala said.

Askari gathered the supplies they needed. Ena stood, took a step, and disclosed a pronounced limp. Askari bit into his lip in concern.

The Misiq glanced over and smiled at Askari. "We won't move quick today. More severe were the injuries than I thought."

Askari nodded in acceptance and motioned for him to go ahead. As they disappeared around the first turn in the path, he glanced at Dhala and winked.

They traveled hesitantly at first, but considering the injuries Ena suffered from just the previous day, they were moving as fast as a hata in stampede. The limp stayed pronounced, but he dealt with the pain without comment. At first, they traveled along the cliff's edge. But after traveling a handful of spans from their camp, Ena turned to him.

"Into the interior hills we should travel. The rugged terrain will make my body to heal with greater speed."

Askari gave him a considered look but shrugged. "I don't know your healing ability. It looks like you are just recovering from a serious injury. But then I remember the severity of your damage and I think you're healing at an amazing speed. If you want to use a more challenging path, then to the rough lands we go."

As the sun reached its apex, the trails took a toll even on Askari, and Ena's mobility was deteriorating. He studied Ena and motioned to a small clearing where they could rest. "I think we should eat and regain our strength before going back to Dhala and the camp. I'm tired, so I'm certain you are struggling as well."

He could tell Ena was about to argue before the fight drained from him. "That might be a good idea. Perhaps I overestimate my healing."

Askari pulled his carrier from his back and gave Ena a palm-sized piece of dried meat then took one for himself. As they ate in silence, Askari noticed a scent that drew him even more than the delicious aroma of Tayi's food. But the aroma was not related to their meal. Instead, it had everything to do with the sensation that bubbled up inside him when he scented Ena.

The smells invading his system were musk, spice, and maleness. He'd never sensed anything similar from a Chinjoka. His body responded in ways he'd never experienced before, but he also did not understand how to deal with these feelings. Without speaking, he reached into the pack and brought out two of Tayi's pocket pies. He handed one to Ena and bit into the other. Ena's first bite was tentative, but soon, he was devouring the food.

Askari understood. The flavors were like nothing else. Filled with tender hata, vegetables, and spices, it all combined to make one of the best foods Askari had ever eaten. His stomach sounded a contented rumble as he licked the last of the juices from his fingers. He glanced upward to find Ena watching him.

"What?"

"Not what I expected you are. Not the evil people described to us."

"Believe me. We have suffered the carnage resulting from the plague. We would never spread it."

Ena popped the final bite into his mouth and studied Askari before turning away. His allure became almost unbearable for Askari. He leaned in, the scent drawing him nearer. He moved close enough to see drops of sweat gather and roll down Ena's neck. Askari found himself attracted to the Misiq. He was beginning to understand the feelings building inside him.

As he struggled to solve the puzzle, he realized Ena had turned back to him, and they were less than a fingerspan away from each other.

"Askari?" Ena asked in a whisper.

The two froze as Askari's struggle intensified. He moved until their lips touched. The crackle of desire flowing through him was strong. He lifted his hand and ran his fingertips across the rough texture of Ena's face. With his hand entwined with Ena's hair, he pulled them tighter against each other. He caught Ena's lip between his teeth and growled as his hunger for Ena grew. He felt his crotch tightening as he stiffened from their contact. Ena was returning his caress, and his musk grew with each moment. The two pressed against each other as their desire built. Ena slipped his hands down Askari's chest, and Askari's lust built as he'd never experienced before. As the sensations washed over him, Askari broke the cycle he was trapped inside.

Reality crashed around him, and he realized he was acting like a fledgling in heat. *This is an enemy who, only yesterday, said that he would have killed us. Now I'm acting as if we have known each other for seasons.* His hands were a blur as he put everything back into the carrier.

Fortunately, no packs of sikari prowled above the cliff, because his thoughts leapt and dodged like an osa newborn. It was Askari's good fortune that Ena said nothing as they made their way back to camp. Once they arrived, he gave Ena to Dhala's care while he focused on whatever task would keep him as far as possible from Ena. He needed the time to puzzle out what these new emotions and desires meant.

With the last of the light fading, Dhala dished up food and handed each of them a filled leaf. Askari ate without sharing his thoughts. He finished and found himself with another sleepless night unfolding.

At the dark gray of predawn, Ena joined him at the fireside. They sat unmoving, each wrapped in their own thoughts. Askari wasn't even certain where his questions originated. Ena leaned close and touched the back of Askari's hand.

"To go back it is time. My fighters might be concerned at my absence, and..." He considered Askari as if reading his thoughts before he continued. "From your lands I would keep them. So I will begin my journey."

Askari sensed Dhala's presence and was glad his friend had joined them.

Ena rose and studied the two of them again before giving them a smile. "Grateful I am for the healing. Head wounds are sometimes problematic. They oftentimes don't heal as well as others. The change to my battle form will also help the healing."

Askari wrinkled his forehead as he considered Ena. "Why didn't you change forms yesterday? You might have escaped or even overpowered us."

There was a deep-throated chuckle from Ena. "Fierce are the plated warriors of the flyers. I don't think I could overcome two plated ones even in my battle form. Reason two? Few reserves remained to change then change again. Likely I would have lost myself."

Askari considered correcting the assumption Ena made in assuming Dhala was also of the Onija caste but decided that information didn't need to be shared. He didn't know how much the Misiq knew about the Chinjoka shape changers, and he would correct nothing that made his people seem more formidable.

"Again, my thanks. I am in your debt," Ena said.

A knot formed in Askari's stomach at the same time a lump grew in his throat. He did no more than nod as the golden-haired man walked a few spans from them before turning.

He lifted his hand and rasped out, "Safe journeys."

Ena's form changed as easily as Dhala shaped clay. His face lengthened, and the tuft of hair already crowning his ears became more dominant. Fingers shortened and thickened, the nails changing to sharp claws that retracted into his morphed fingers. His skin covered with a dense tan fur, and his cuspids stretched past his lower jaw. A tail as thick as Askari's wrist extended from the base of his spine to curl in an arc and flick back and forth behind him.

Ena looked at them before stretching and running his tongue over his fangs. Askari noticed the slight cleft he enjoyed in his human form became much more defined. Ena sounded a coughing roar and walked away. The first movement still showed a definite limp in a hind leg, but with each step, it lessened until Askari no longer detected it. With that, Ena lunged forward and disappeared into the alpine forest without a backward glance.

Askari stood staring at the spot where Ena disappeared. His emotions were in a confusing twist of longing, attraction, and relief.

"Gyam's change is more elegant."

Askari found Dhala with his arms crossed, glaring. When Dhala met his gaze, Askari laughed.

"What?" Dhala asked.

"You aren't the most objective when it comes to Gyam."

Dhala raised an eyebrow as his lips twisted to one side. "Where you have no bias?"

"What do you mean?" Askari said with a defensive note.

"I have watched you, my friend. You have never looked at anyone, of any caste, as you do Ena."

Askari relived the kiss he had exchanged with Ena and the impact it'd had on him. He ran his tongue over his lips as he stared at the forest where Ena had disappeared without a sound, but his alluring scent remained.

Chapter Eight

DHALA LOOKED OVER the shroud of heavy morning fog covering the basin for as far as he could see. He was still trying to reconcile Ena's rescue and his feelings about saving one of their enemies. The experience had shaken his beliefs. Askari asked him to keep silent. But it took no effort for his mother to read him. He tried to deflect her questions but surrendered after a time and told her everything.

First, she insisted on seeing the glyph on Askari's leg. He'd been angry at Dhala for telling his mother, but her sharp questioning gave them both a clear impression of how serious their choice to use Askari as the energy source had been. But the symbol had healed, even if it was a deep-blue permanent scar.

Soft footfalls sounded, and he sensed his mother moving to his side. They stood without speaking until the tension wore on Dhala. He turned and lifted an eyebrow. "You have something you want from me?"

A slight quirk came to her lips, but she nodded in agreement. "Your healing ability is growing. You're trying things even I have never done, like using someone else's life force in your workings. Someone could have died. It's time you found a soul rider to aid you, to act as your mentor."

Dhala stiffened. As a knot formed in his stomach, he considered her request. This was a serious task. People had died calling a soul rider. He calmed himself. "A soul rider? I've heard stories..."

"And they no doubt painted it in a better light than the truth of the danger. You are right. Some potentially skilled healers have lost themselves in their search for a soul rider."

"Then why?"

She shook her head as she considered him. "You are a strong healer, perhaps stronger than myself. But how close did you come to losing yourself in Askari's healing?"

"It was a near thing. Is the search worth the risk?"

"If I told you I had no concerns, I would be lying. But it will be a worthwhile trip. Look at it as an honor. Only the strongest healers need a rider. They help you in ways you cannot imagine. It will only take a few days." His mother turned and held out a filled waterskin. "Remember, only water once you begin. Nothing more."

"Now? I should begin my quest now?"

She sighed. "Yes. Before we both lose the resolve. Because while as one of the last Saat healers you need this, your mother wants to tell you to stay here where it is safe."

He fought down the impulse to roll his eyes and sigh. Instead, he repositioned the weight of the waterskin and nodded. "Yes, Mother. I will leave at once and take nothing other than water. I will go where Voda directs me to find my soul rider."

She looked at him and shared a solemn expression. He hadn't been as successful at hiding his emotions as he'd hoped. "You believe this a useless trip to satisfy an old woman. We'll talk again when you return. You can tell me then how your opinion changed."

Dhala found himself embarrassed that he was so transparent to her. But rather than deny her charges, he leaned in, kissed her cheek, and turned to leave. He half hoped she would stop him. She remained silent as he left the warren entrance and disappeared from sight.

He walked past the village without hesitation, knowing he must travel to the far edges of their lands for what he needed. He trekked along the river's edge, moving farther and farther upstream and nearer to the plateaus, and ultimately the mountains, somewhere he would be assured of privacy. He might wait for days before his rider showed itself.

Dhala drifted without thought through his journey. The sun was well on its arc through the sky when he stepped into cold water and realized his path had deviated from what he had expected. He'd assumed he should go to the high cliffs but, instead, could hear the distant roar of the Mother Falls as the stream plunged from the cliffs. The freshets from the falls created a series of small caves over the generations. Their entrances were also well-hidden in the thickets of trees found only there where the Mother Falls met their needs. Not all Chinjoka knew of these tiny shelters at the junction of water and broken cliffs. But the forces guiding him had sent him in this direction. It was closer to the village than he'd thought he would need to travel, but hidden. They would serve his purpose well.

So he stood, opening himself to the wills of the gods. But nothing more than a slight breeze twisted its way through the forest he found surrounding him. The winds whistled through the bluffs above, but it had little relevance. A cutleaf tree showing out-of-season colors of the harvest season seemed caught in a sudden turbulence Dhala couldn't feel. But its frantic movements drew him closer until he stood under it. His foot splashed as he stepped into a stream he hadn't seen. He pushed aside the underbrush, glad he'd worn his hata-hide leggings to protect his skin from the well-armed plants. Even with the protection, he was still bleeding from numerous scratches by the time he passed through the dense undergrowth.

He had discovered the entrance to a cave a little shorter than himself and several times as deep. Dhala studied the shelter, deciding it would work for his purposes. He ducked inside and settled himself in place. He was likely to be there for several days, and this was better than on a cliff exposed to the high mountain winds. After a long drink from the waterskin, he crossed his legs under him and settled in to wait.

DHALA RAN HIS tongue over his cracked lips. After three sun cycles huddled in the cave, he couldn't seem to drink enough to slake his thirst. He had drained the waterskin long ago and now drank from the spring trickling at the back of his cave. His meditative position had deteriorated until Dhala considered it a victory to be seated upright. He wasn't certain how much longer he could endure, but he refused to leave before his soul rider appeared. Even if that meant he left on his Long Flight.

He pushed himself against the wall when a scratching sound came from the mouth of the cave. He used his remaining energy to turn to see what had joined him. A mkali stood on its back legs contemplating him. This was a large specimen, much larger than his fist. Lethargic and uncaring, he sat as the first animal he had seen studied him.

The animal ran a short distance forward before chattering loudly. It seemed to scold him thoroughly for some transgression. Dhala's world skewed until the entire scene was so impossible he laughed.

The animal stopped, became silent, and stared at Dhala. When it seemed satisfied, it jumped at him and bit into his forearm.

Dhala lunged away and grabbed his now-bleeding arm, but the fog of hunger had vanished. "You little monster!" Dhala croaked. "I'd roast you for dinner, you miniature assassin, if I thought I could catch you."

It stared at him, growing larger with each pulse of Dhala's heart. It grew three times its initial size, and the intelligence of the animal was clear.

"I choose you, Chinjoka."

Dhala's heart sank. His soul rider was a tiny morsel of food that wasn't even worth the bites a hunter would take to harvest it for a meal. Again the gods seemed to find his life worth little more than something relinquished to humorous stories told around the snow-season fires.

"You believe I am not a worthy rider."

Dhala took a deep breath. He refused to chance offending the little being. It might not be the sikari soul rider he'd hoped for, but it was something. "No, soul rider. Being chosen was an honor."

"It was not a question, child. I am your soul rider. Your thoughts are mine to know."

A chill ran through Dhala at the realization he would share himself with another being. He hadn't considered the consequences of a rider until this moment. Now he was sharing his life.

"My apologies, rider. It was not my intent—"

The animal met his gaze and dashed in as if he would inflict a second bite. But the mkali stopped when Dhala did not react to his rush. He studied Dhala for a moment before the animal's eyes closed and he lifted his face skyward. Time slipped by unnoticed as the animal stood without moving. Suddenly, Dhala's world changed drastically.

A new voice filled Dhala. These were not the firm tones of his new soul rider. This voice tasted of summer winds, a dark horizon filled with skyfire, the floods of late in the fire season. This voice resonated with power. Dhala found it achingly familiar, and he hoped he was wrong.

"Why do you find your soul rider lacking, fledgling?"

The scent of a summer storm left a metallic tang on the back of his tongue. The voice crackled like a cleansing fire of summer, and Dhala fought to control the wash of fear and apprehension that overwhelmed him before he replied.

"No, Lord Voda. I am certain they are the right choice for me. It was just unexpected."

He could sense his nearness. He looked toward the cave entrance as a figure reminiscent of Gyam stepped into the cavern. As he moved closer, he could see the deep water swirled in his eyes. Dhala cringed. One did not challenge the soul rider choices made by Voda. The Healing Twin was no more tolerant of foolishness than his sister, and questioning one's choice of soul rider fell directly into the realm of fools.

He spoke again, the rumble of gathering world-changing storms punctuating every word. "You thought a sikari would be more honorable for you? With their great size and snapping teeth, they would be more proper for your fierce personality?"

"I'm sorry, Lord. I am grateful for my rider. Thinking of the sikari as a soul rider was foolish."

The next sound shocked Dhala. It could only be Pilea's laughter. The other of the Twins had appeared, and Dhala was terrified that both Twins had manifested during his search for a soul rider. It was not the tinkling sound some Chinjoka women made for laughter. This was a full-throated laugh of one who expresses their feelings in every situation.

She studied Dhala but still seemed to find him humorous. "Everyone sees the sikari loping across the grassland, a pack taking down a hata. That is one view, but we would hope your understanding is more. Do you know which of the Mother's creations the greatest of the sikari packs seek to avoid?"

Dhala kept his tremble below the surface as he replied. "I do not, Goddess."

"The mkali. Your strong sikari give any mkali colony a wide berth. They have killed a maddened wolf that attacks. They are the most feared animals on the grasslands. But it's not just their individual ferocity. Do you know why?"

"No, Goddess."

"It is because they are one. If you attack one mkali, you have attacked them all."

Dhala nodded, taking in the words of the Twin to consider later when the Goddess of Warriors was not chastising him. He felt weak but kept his gaze cast downward.

"Dhala. Fledgling."

He snapped his head upward and met her gaze. "Yes."

"One last thing to contemplate. The mkali seldom agree to be soul riders. With you, they have made an exception." With that, skyfire crackled then faded. In the same instant, a wall of moist fog washed over him to disappear. The second of the Twins had left.

They are gone. You can collect yourself.

Dhala refocused to the mkali. He realized the animal was no longer speaking out loud. Instead, the thoughts were in his mind, displayed in a mix of images and explanation.

"You spoke as clearly as one of the Chinjoka when you first came to me. Why do you only speak to my mind now?"

Newly chosen can speak. But forever after, we will share our thoughts mind to mind.

He considered the animal for a time then cocked his head. "So, are you my consciousness? Will everything be judged?"

Laughter sounded in his head. *I am not here to judge you. Your private thoughts are yours. Unless you ask for assistance. Mostly, I am here to help you become a better healer and prepare you.*

There was a pause, but Dhala hadn't asked all his questions. "What do you know that I don't?"

The mkali cocked its head and considered Dhala.

You are asked to return to Gyam. The Father and his children believe you are needed there.

Dhala sat for several moments, trying to find an argument that would make a good reason to disobey the wishes of the gods. Then the mkali spoke to him again.

The choices are yours to make, just as some Chinjoka do not follow the teachings of the Father.

"I will try. But he might not allow me to return. He is the one who asked me to leave."

There was a note of humor in his final response. *Yes, we know.*

Chapter Nine

DHALA PACED AT the bottom of the inner passageway. He had recovered from the ordeal of searching for his soul rider, but during that time, he had avoided the instructions given to him by the mkali. His soul rider had told him to work with Gyam again. The mkali had made the options clear. Going back with Gyam was his choice. The Chinjoka always had their free will. But the Twins suggested he serve as Gyam's caretaker again. There was no choice. Dhala was not a fool.

Gyam wouldn't be calm and receptive. He refused to tell Gyam his return was the will of the gods. Dhala had enjoyed the task before Gyam banned him. He'd been happy doing anything that brought him closer to Gyam. But Gyam blamed him for Choro's death, and his stance hadn't changed in the moon that passed since then. The accusation hurt Dhala, but Gyam had asked him to leave and never return.

He carried the blue mark of his soul rider. No one would know that his rider was the mkali. The animal had sent the image it wanted to Dhala, and he carved the design into his flesh. Each individual was unique. Others only recognized it as a soul rider's mark. But he expected Gyam to see only a mark of a Saat.

"Dhala! I want to see the rider mark again," Jua yelled as he burst from the trail running along the interior of the cliffs.

He sighed, but in truth, he was proud he'd impressed someone. Even if it was only Jua. So he twisted his face into a taciturn visage and turned to the boy.

"Jua, you've seen the mark many times. Are you sure you have to look again?"

The boy didn't hesitate. "Yes, I need to see it again. It's the mark of your soul rider. I will have one. It will be a mark of my honor."

He smiled at the boy and pulled aside his legging for Jua to look at the deep-blue symbol on his leg. The fledgling traced his finger over the intricate lines. The twisting elements of the scar gave Dhala a sense of power. Jua studied it carefully before rocking onto his heels. He looked at Dhala and gave a grin that stretched from ear to ear.

"It's the best one in the village. It's even better than Tayi's."

Dhala lost his careful composure for a moment and grinned. But before he replied, Jua was chattering again.

"You need to talk with Gyam. I told him all about your mark. He wants to see it too. Let's go show him now? He's in his aerie. I talked to him a short time ago."

He panicked. This was not the carefully orchestrated discussion he'd envisioned. When Jua grabbed his hand and tugged him, he let himself be led.

In less time than he might have expected, they reached Gyam's aerie. Dhala stood surveying the space. The remnants of Gyam's life when he was alone. *He's never been good at taking care of himself. It was me who put things away. I've only been gone a moon, and the aerie is a mess. He needs someone. If it isn't me then a different Saat.*

A breeze twisted from the sky portal, bringing Gyam's musky scent to Dhala. As it passed, a bitter smell that remained on the back of his throat was less pleasant than the first. Dhala sighed and shook his head. The gods might have their purpose, but it left Dhala with a hollow sensation.

"Gyam! Gyam, where are you?"

Dhala cringed at Jua's loud call, but he supposed it was the best way to find the person they sought. They waited, and he could tell Jua was about to make a more forceful cry when the stocky Athru appeared from a side storeroom. He held something that commanded his attention.

"I'm here, Jua. You visited moments ago. What do you need?"

As he finished, Gyam turned to face them and froze in place. Dhala wanted to chuckle since the self-confident Gyam looked like a Saat on their first hata hunt who had the misfortune of attracting the herd bull's attention. A moment later, he squeezed out a single word.

"Dhala."

"I brought him, Gyam. I told him you wanted to see the soul rider mark. It's amazing. Best in the village," Jua said.

It amused Dhala when Gyam flushed red and stammered. "Jua. I'm sure I didn't say that. Dhala's mark is personal. I wouldn't want him to think he must show me."

Dhala relaxed as signs materialized of the Gyam he'd grown up with. He turned so Gyam could see the design on his leg. "I don't mind if you want to look at the mark."

Gyam leaned in to study the pattern, and Dhala felt somewhat exposed. The stare left Dhala with the premonition he'd missed something. Gyam lifted his hand with a finger extended, surprising Dhala. He looked like Jua had when he touched it earlier. But this time, it wasn't a fledgling. He'd spent time with this man for seasons. The man Dhala could never have.

But he stopped with his finger so close Dhala sensed the heat. He willed his body not to respond but was having little success. When he thought he needed to move away to keep from embarrassing himself, Gyam dropped his hand. He seemed breathless as he turned to Dhala.

"Congratulations. It's striking. I can't imagine the power such a soul rider would give you." He held out a hand to placate Dhala when he chewed his lip. "I would have never asked. It would be beyond improper."

The tension lessened, and he pushed his leggings and breechcloth into place. But when he turned back, his tension redoubled. Now he had to talk to Gyam about the real reason he needed to speak with him.

"Gyam, we need to talk."

Gyam nodded, seeming more receptive than any time since Choro's death. Another breeze swept through the aerie, and the scent it conjured was anything but pleasant.

Jua glared at Gyam. "It stinks in here. It never smells like this at Tayi's warrens, and she has lots of people coming to be healed. You need to clean everything. It's awful. Like rotten stuff." He glanced around, and his gaze stopped on Dhala. "Have Dhala help. He's good at helping people and putting things in order. He helps Tayi all the time."

Dhala glanced at Gyam to gauge his reaction. To his surprise, it was thoughtful. He took that as a sign for him to begin and a possible way to achieve it without begging.

"That's part of the reason I came. Tayi doesn't need my help much now. Your patrol leaves you little time."

Gyam looked away from Jua and met Dhala's gaze. He studied Dhala until the silence in the room became tense. Jua looked from one of them to the other. But before the fledgling voiced his opinion again, Gyam began.

"I could use the help. Since I'm the only Athru left, I spend most of my day flying patrol." He looked at Jua and grinned. "And you are right, Jua. It smells in here. I'm not good at keeping an aerie."

He turned to Dhala. "I would welcome your help. If you would be willing?"

A lump rose in Dhala's throat at Gyam's words. There was still tension, but Gyam didn't oppose Dhala's help.

He continued without hesitation. "Your room is as you left it. Except—" He seemed flustered for a moment. "The smell might be coming from your room. I tried to keep part of an osa inside since it's cooler."

Dhala curled his lips and stepped to the entry of his room. The stench was unbelievable. He didn't know how Gyam tolerated the smell; it must be almost overpowering when he was in his flyer form with its hypersensitive power of smell. Dhala moved closer, fighting down the gag reflex. It took his eyes a moment to adjust, then the outline of an osa carcass came into view, hanging in the far corner. Something was wrong, beside the horrid stench. But he couldn't quite determine what.

He covered his mouth and nose with his arm and took another step forward. The entire carcass was writhing. He studied it for a moment longer and realized the remains contained thousands of carrion maggots, each burrowing through the putrid flesh.

This realization overwhelmed his gag reflex. He sprinted to the outer ledge and lost his meal down the face of the cliff. The stench seemed to cling to him as his stomach revolted, seizing over and over until nothing remained. Once he'd regained control of his body, he glared at Gyam with righteous anger.

"I've never experienced anything like that in my life. I doubt even the sikari would touch that. You do need help, but it will not be me who provides it again. If you want me to return, then this aerie will have to be cleaned until it smells as pure as the prairie after a driving summer rain."

His face contorted even further. "If you want me to help you again, you will clean my room and do whatever needs to be done to eliminate the stench and the infestation of biters. Yes, that's right, Athru. You must clean up after yourself. You should work quickly too. Cocoons cover the floor and they are hatching. You will have a wonderful infestation of biters in a few days."

Dhala spun on his heel and launched himself down the inner corridor.

GYAM PACED FROM one edge of his aerie to the other. He was anxiously waiting for Jua to return with Dhala. At least that was his hope. It had taken him several days to clean the aerie and rid it of the odor. Perhaps even more important, he'd eliminated the pests. He still had a few itchy bite marks. It had been bad, more atrocious. He'd wrapped the disintegrating carcass in an aged hide and flew it past the far side of the valley, onto the grasslands. Far enough it wouldn't tempt meat eaters closer.

The biters and stench had been worse. He'd scrubbed and cleaned, losing his own meal on more than one occasion. After several failures, he had asked Tayi for suggestions. Gyam wasn't certain that her solution wasn't worse than the original smell. But with a few more purges of his stomach, he'd finished. The aerie smelled of summer grass under a blazing sun.

Jua had pronounced the smells eliminated, and Gyam has sent him to ask Dhala to return. Now he waited. He hoped Jua didn't become sidetracked by someone else's errand or a flight of fancy to which youngsters were sometimes prone. He could have gone looking for Dhala himself, but he'd wanted him to see and smell the transformation.

The soft scrape of feet against the stone steps filtered to him, and his stomach knotted. He wasn't certain how he felt about Dhala. The emotions were complex and involved. One thing he knew with certainty: he missed his friend. He realized that the only Chinjoka who might have helped Choro had died in the first wave of people to succumb to the disease. He had no right to blame either Dhala or Tayi for the death. But he'd been angry. People did foolish things when they were angry.

Jua rushed from the corridor with Dhala in tow and flung himself at Gyam. "Found him. He was in the gardens. I told him it didn't smell bad at all and that he needed to come so he can move back in the aerie."

Dhala's face tinted red, but he didn't argue.

Gyam took control of the conversation and turned to Dhala. "He's right. It took time and a lot of effort, but the aerie is spotless and the smells remaining are pleasant."

Dhala nodded and walked into the space. He paused, inhaled, and smiled at Gyam. "Much better."

Gyam motioned him forward. "Your room is ready for you to live in again."

Dhala cocked a brow at Gyam but moved to the chamber. Gyam and Jua followed him as he scrutinized every fingerlength of the room. He studied and sniffed the area where the carcass had hung. But once he'd examined everything, he turned to them with a smile.

"It looks spotless and—" He inhaled deeply. "—smells wonderful. It's ready for my return." He took a deep breath, and Gyam tensed. "If you're still angry with me, this won't work. I will not be the focus of your rage."

Gyam nodded in acknowledgment. "I know it was no one's fault. You and Tayi did all you could. I hold no ill will toward you." He dropped his gaze to the ground and continued. "I miss my friend, Dhala. I have few enough people who will stand beside me. Please. I would like you in my aerie."

Dhala paused for a moment then smiled and nodded. They grabbed each other in a tight embrace.

Chapter Ten

GYAM TIGHTENED HIS grip on the stone floor to keep under control as Dhala checked the last bit of his skin. The deep-red leather-like hide of his flyer form sometimes had places that needed treatment to keep from rubbing and causing an open wound. He enjoyed Dhala's firm touch as he applied the ointment. He hadn't realized the extent to which he'd missed Dhala's attention until he had it again. The past few sun cycles had proven this to him. He wouldn't let that happen again.

"Open your wing."

He turned and snapped his teeth playfully at Dhala before opening his membrane-covered appendage. Bright sunlight shone through it, bathing the room in red, accentuated by points of crimson as the light reflected from the multitude of iron-hard scales covering Gyam's body and limbs.

Dhala checked Gyam, stopping several times to apply Tayi's ointment. Once Dhala treated any worrisome places, they repeated the procedure on the other side. With wings extended, Dhala went over Gyam's back and limbs. When Dhala moved to check Gyam's chest, he growled.

"I need to check for rough spots. Your skin can dry on the front of your body like it can on your back."

Frustrated at the level of intimacy, Gyam did a barking cough at him and swatted him with his wing.

"Stop it! I know you are naked. By the Twins, I am not enjoying it any more than you. I would want it to be more than the touch of friend to friend. Now, silence yourself, and let me do what I'm supposed to do."

Gyam's heart ached at Dhala's words. It was the first time he'd spoken the sentiment out loud, and the pain was more than Gyam expected. He'd known. Deep down, he had always known, because he felt the same about Dhala. But he'd denied the situation for years. He and his best friend were in love with each other.

He turned and screamed his frustration, his roar echoing through the inner passages until people stopped what they were doing and stared at the aerie. Was it a promise to his lover? He had feelings for Dhala but, until this moment, had been unwilling to consider his attraction. They would find a way. He swore it. By the Twins, they would be together. His frustration grew. *This is not the time.* He walked to the sunlit slab of stone at the front of his aerie. Without a glance backward, he threw himself from the heights, plummeting toward the treetops below him, his wings tucked tight. At the last moment, he snapped them outward and sailed westward.

Once he was past the villages cultivated gardens and the river that traced along the base of the cliffs, he glanced back to find Dhala standing at the sky portal. He turned back toward his goal and began his patrols for this day.

Gyam drifted from thermal to thermal as he made his way across the Chinjoka Basin. He rarely traveled this far on a single trip, but that day, he was in no rush to return. When the sun touched the western rim, little time remained. But he was in a part of the Chinjoka lands that had enough moisture to support the trees of an actual forest.

He moved in a search pattern he'd learned early in his training with Choro. Simple but effective. The disadvantage was that he flew much lower than typical. He had completed the first pass when movement caught his attention. The shapes were somewhat familiar. At first, he thought it was a new sikari pack. With a second pass, he realized it was something much more dangerous. A Misiq battle group. All in animal form, almost unseen as they slipped through the trees.

They were attacking the village. His village.

He changed his flight pattern again, determined to send them to their dens. If he could kill or maim their leader, it might send them scrambling back to their lands. After several high passes, he spotted the leader and targeted it. The Misiq entered a wide meadow, giving Gyam time for at least one dive.

He rode the thermals higher, waiting for the right moment. The tawny shape emerged from the brush. He tucked his wings, dropping like a boulder at his target. The Misiq were halfway across the opening before they realized the danger. The leader reared on its hind leg to rake Gyam from the sky but moved a fraction of a second too slow. Gyam hit with balled feet, his full weight and velocity behind the dive. The Misiq he had targeted was dead before it stopped tumbling.

He spun over, rowing his wings to regain an attack height. One of the Misiq leapt at Gyam, covering the distance between them. He tried to avoid the attack but was too low to do more than a desperate spin to meet the attack with talons extended.

They hit the ground as Gyam's talons buried themselves, slicing through arteries and muscle. But the Misiq's hind legs raked across Gyam's torso. The impact left his body screaming in pain, and he'd broken some of the bones in his chest. Between the wounds from the Misiq's hind legs and damage from their impact, each breath Gyam took felt like an arrow piercing him.

He glanced back while they struggled, horrified to find the other Misiq changing, and they were armed. His time was leaping away.

In a desperate move, he snapped his muzzle open and grabbed the weakening Misiq by the throat. As his awl-sharp teeth sank into flesh, enemy blood washed through his mouth. The Misiq warrior, in a final desperate move, curled upward and clawed at the webbing of Gyam's wings.

To his horror, a Misiq claw penetrated one wing, and it parted like a soft tanned osa hide under an iron blade. He fought for his life, knocked the Misiq aside, and braced for another attack.

The Misiq that had assaulted him lay unmoving, and Gyam glanced to see the others had almost completed their change. Shocked that they didn't attack in their changing form, he had no choice. Injured or not, he must get airborne.

He leapt to his feet, extending his wings before him and pumped downward. The pain in his damaged wing was intense. The opening tore farther with each stroke until it stopped at the bone frame of the wing. He'd cleared the treetops when the first arrow shot past. Gyam rolled to one side, but the damaged wing made the move clumsy and almost fatal as the iron-headed arrow pierced the webbing of the other wing, creating a new weakness.

This was his last chance, and if he fell...well, it would be better if the fall killed him than letting the Misiq find him. He flew, straining for open sky. Pain and blood loss took their toll. He thought the situation was hopeless when a sun-heated thermal rose from the ground.

He risked a glance backward. The Misiq launched a flock of iron-tipped bringers of death at him, but they fell far below. He was out of range. Survival was possible. Then he would deal with the feeling welling up at his first kill of an enemy.

THE WIND RUSHED across Gyam's fevered skin. He could no longer fly, but the hot summer day saved him by letting him climb on a column of warm air, and when he'd reached the heights, he would glide toward the village until he found another thermal. His luck held for span after span across the basin. But then it appeared his good fortune had run out. Several spans from the village, Gyam glided only a short distance above the trees.

He'd decided to try a landing, since there was barely enough of his tattered wings left to slow him. But he was dropping fast enough he would crash if he didn't change tactics. His weakened state hurt the situation. If he became unconscious, there would be little hope for survival. Disoriented, he was unsure of his exact location, but he believed there was a small opening in the brush a few lengths ahead.

Trying to bring his thoughts into focus, he watched for the open space. There were several times when a clearing flickered in and out of sight before he could act. Then a clearing appeared below him. Without thinking, Gyam opened his wings and tried to back-wing to slow himself. The pain from his wings overwhelmed him, and a scream left him that ripped through the air. The ground rushed toward him, his speed too fast for a safe landing. Gyam tried to stop, but he hit the tall brush and his world went black.

JUA CAME RUSHING down the passage, yelling, "Gyam crashed! Into the trees! I saw."

Dhala grabbed the fledgling and tried to calm him. "Jua, what did you see? What're you talking about?"

"Gyam. Gyam crashed. Just down the river. We have to go help!"

He was almost certain the dimming light had confused the boy. But it was easier to check than convince Jua nothing had happened. "All right, if you're certain. We can check."

He trotted after the racing fledgling. By the time they sprinted from the village, Askari loped alongside them.

"What's going on? Gyam is hurt?" Askari asked.

Dhala nodded as they picked up the pace. "Jua says Gyam crashed upriver a short distance. He was insistent. We're going to check."

Askari raced behind Jua. Dhala picked up speed as they came closer and discovered signs Jua was right. He came to a cluster of stunted trees and stopped.

Wrapped in the debris ripped from the grove was Gyam, or what remained of him. The damage was so severe that a horrified sob escaped Dhala. A heartbeat later, Askari stood beside him and showed his anguish at the sight. Dhala slammed down his own emotions and became the dispassionate healer. Gyam's injuries were severe; they needed to move and heal Gyam in his flyer form.

He spun to the expanding group of people who had either seen the crash themselves or followed him and Askari. "Get the carrying skins. He's too injured to change, so we will have to heal him as he is. Watch his talons and teeth. If he struggles, we will need to restrain him. Hurry."

Gyam bled from a dozen serious wounds besides the damage to his wings. To add to his concerns, Dhala couldn't tell how much damage his internal organs had sustained. He worked to heal some of the wounds but feared Gyam wouldn't survive to see the light of another day.

The thick hides arrived, and they got him onto them with little response. Not a good sign. He trotted beside the litter, holding Gyam's hand as they raced to Tayi's warren. He hoped she had been told what had happened and was preparing everything needed.

Tayi waited outside for them and directed the litter carriers where to put him. Then she chased everyone from the room other than Dhala and Askari. She grabbed Askari and moved him as if he were a fledgling.

She caught his eyes with her own and directed her considerable force of will on him. "You will be the energy source again. It will leave you marked worse than you are now. I swore it would never be used a second time, but I see no other solution."

Askari stared at her for a heartbeat before growling in return. "Whatever he needs. The marks are nothing."

"Then stay out of the way until you're needed. We will tell you." She turned to Dhala. "Work on the bleeding. The battles will be short but intense."

He nodded and cut an entire series of glyphs that appeared to him. Once he had finished carving the symbols into himself, he touched the worst of Gyam's wounds and found himself ripped into a battle-torn grassland littered with bodies. He battled the twisted animals attacking Gyam's defenders. In this war, Dhala wielded a long-bladed spear, which he used to deadly effect. Soon the tide of battle turned in Gyam's favor and Dhala flew into the reddening sky, and out.

Once he found himself in his own body, he relieved the pressure on the wound and found, to his relief, the bleeding had stopped. The wounds were closing.

Dhala moved into Gyam again, fighting the battle and healing bone and tissue. He plunged into each one with whatever weapon he'd been given, finding each one perfect for the task at hand. Dhala swayed, trying to remain standing as a line of fresh glyphs traveled down his thigh, blood coating his legs. He warmed with satisfaction to discover his mother had been just as successful. But the most difficult healing remained, the tattered webbing of his wing.

Dhala looked at his mother, who braced herself against the wall, even more exhausted than he was. But they had no choice. "We need to treat his wing. It will never heal as it is."

She nodded and turned away, exhaustion making every movement she made seem many times slower than Dhala had ever seen. But she returned with an awl and a basket of fine sinew thread. She pulled together the edges of the webbing, punctured the skin, worked the thread through, and tied a knot. She was already halfway through the second stitch when she gave Dhala instructions.

"Use the energy from Askari. I will sew it together, but you will have to battle for the healing. If you become fatigued, stop. We are all close to the point of exhaustion. Gyam will live. He would not thank us if we die trying to heal him."

He will also not be pleased if he cannot fly. Dhala turned to Askari, who simply exposed his leg and nodded. Dhala cut the glyph in his skin and plunged into the battle to heal Gyam.

He again was flying. This time over a familiar landscape, devastated and under attack from the same vicious animals. They were destroying anything living as they moved up the valley. Behind them was a land more damaged than by any summer wildfire.

He spotted a small group and dove toward them. Flipping into a back-wing at the last moment, he sank his talons into the neck of one animal. He flapped his wings in desperation until he'd gained a lethal altitude and dropped his prey onto its pack mates. There was a howl of fury followed by sudden yelps of pain.

Gyam's own resources were able to help in the fight at a diminished level. The sound of battle rang from behind them. He fought for Gyam, the last chance of the Chinjoka.

Dhala continued his passages across this strange landscape, attacking the forces of destruction when he could. His judgment slipped as battle garnered him more than a few minor wounds. But the combinations of battles left him exhausted. When he surveyed the battlefield, he feared the retreat by the other forces was only a ruse. Then he realized another regiment of the animals had arrived. They destroyed a large section of what had been undamaged lands.

A battle cry arose from deep inside Dhala, a side he'd never seen. With that, he dove at the animals. His wings snapped open, and his muscles tightened as the wings strained. His finger length talons sliced flesh like iron blades. He ripped through their battle lines, leaving behind a swath of dead and dying. He hit open air, flipped toward them, and began a second run.

The return path proved more difficult as the creatures armed themselves with clubs and rocks. But still he cut a lethal swath through the gray-skinned brutes. His responses were slowing as reserves dwindled. He tried to bank and come around again. He had almost completed the maneuver when a rock the size of his head smashed between his shoulder blades.

His vision sparked more than he'd seen with a greenwood fire as pain filled him. He had to escape. He couldn't help Gyam any longer. He pumped his leathery wings once and plummeted to the ground. His damaged and overtaxed wing muscles cramped and refused to lift him again.

The animals bounded toward him, and he rolled to one knee. They narrowed the distance to a few spans, and Dhala searched for a weapon. Something to make his death cost the creatures many lives. He focused only on the foremost animal, wanting it to pay.

One of the lean creatures let out an ear-shattering shriek and rolled to the side, clawing itself. A heartbeat later, another was rolling on the ground trying to fight...something. A handful of attackers fell back an instant later, and a defender the size of his fist dove toward one creature.

Can it be? Soul rider?

A small blur shot over his shoulder and onto the face of the lead attacker. It sank its teeth into the animal's nose and tore flesh. The creature slung its head, frantic to rid itself of the ferocious mkali attached to its face. Instead of knocking it free, it seemed to create a furor in the small attacker. Somehow, it crawled up its eye, bit by bit, and, when close enough, buried its claws in the vulnerable organ.

The creature went mad with pain, running its face along the ground to dislodge the ferocious mkali biting it again. The furred warrior lost its grip and was rolling across the rocky ground.

Dhala braced himself, ready to fight off the now-freed creature. But the animal that had been killing Gyam turned into dust, disappearing with the next breeze. The same scenario played out repeatedly in the battle surrounding him. A few ran, tucking their scaled tails behind them. But most just disappeared.

Dhala sat down hard, wings tucked against his back. He stared at the horde of little warriors. He had no difficulty believing they were congratulating each other on a successful battle campaign. Then the mkali who helped save him walked closer, scampered on top of his knee, and plopped down. He looked from side to side, crossed his front legs over his stomach, and sighed.

"That was a good battle, two-foot. Your flyer form is formidable. In the history of the mkali, no story exists of one of your kind killing so many of the eaters."

Dhala tried to work out the details, forgetting for a moment he was not in the Chinjoka Basin but fighting for Gyam's life, or at least his flight. He looked back, but the landscape seemed to hold its breath. He pushed himself upward, but the mkali crawled onto his chest.

"No, you are finished. You will return to your own body."

"Or what will you do?" Dhala asked, rebellious toward the mkali giving him orders.

It turned to him, leaned until he was a fingerwidth from his nose, and clicked his teeth once.

Dhala surrendered. "All right, I'll go."

The mkali nodded and crawled off Dhala. He stood, no longer exhausted, and unfurled his wings. He spread them wide, testing for failure. But they seemed undamaged if somewhat fatigued. Knowing this was his only chance, he flapped his wings. Slowly at first but with increasing strength, he rose from the ground.

He pumped into the blue sky above this place that had no description in his world. Then the opening formed above him, and his entire focus was finding his way home.

GYAM CRINGED TO see how many blue marks covered Dhala's leg. His...love's hands touched his wings, and this world faded away.

The next time Gyam awoke, it was Askari sitting beside him. He tried to rise upright, but the effort sent him into a coughing fit that left him gasping. Once he returned to his bedding, Askari held out a bowl of water that Gyam cradled in his shaking hands.

Hands? No wings? How did I change?

He strained to ask the same question of Askari, but Askari motioned Gyam into silence. "You shifted while being healed. Tayi doesn't know what triggered it. But one minute, you were all red skin, teeth, and claws, and the next moment, you had two legs and were as naked as a new fledgling."

Then Gyam remembered Dhala cutting himself. As he started to tell Askari, Dhala brought him a bowl of broth. But Gyam knocked it away, shattering it on the stone wall.

"You lied! You're more than an herbal healer. Choro died because of you. You could have healed everyone. But instead you kept your ability a secret. I can't believe you claimed to love me. Traitor! Murderer!"

Dhala shot Gyam a glare filled with the devastation of the accusations aimed at he and his mother. "This is why we kept them secret! Because of thinking like yours. And hiding it did not keep us from using our abilities. We. Cannot. Cure. Plague."

"I saw your legs. They're covered with healer's marks. You've been protecting yourself and leaving the rest of us to save ourselves. Admit it! This once, be honest."

Gyam's head snapped to the side as Askari's fist smashed into his jaw. When his vision returned and the ringing left his head, Askari was glaring at him.

"I thought you were smarter than you are. Or you're still suffering from your injuries. Dhala almost died saving you. He repaired your wing because he knew how important flight is to you. He also healed me after the hata gored me. Now you call him a coward and traitor! Your brain is too small for your mouth."

Gyam started to talk, his mouth working, but he didn't know what to do. Askari began again. He pulled his legging to one side to see several dark marks. "These are to help you too. Dhala used energy from me. So if you want to hate everyone who cares about you, add me to your list."

He kept his silence, scanning the room, trying to think. Then Gyam's gaze came to rest on Tayi and, from her expression, knew in a short time he'd insulted everyone he cared about. With that, he slumped against the bedding.

"Askari is right. I am stupid. You all cared enough to save me, and I repay you with insults. I'm shamed by my behavior." He spoke to Dhala as if they were alone. "I care about you deeply. We will be together."

Dhala smiled and sat beside him. "I know we will. We will break tradition. But you cannot keep withdrawing your trust."

Tayi smiled at the pair. "You won't be the first. There are ways for lovers."

Gyam joined Dhala and considered Tayi for a moment, trying to unravel the mystery of her words. Dhala broke the contest of wills first and asked the question they had for the Athru "How did you get so injured? What happened?"

Gyam bolted upright, his gaze darting around the room. "Misiq. A troop of Misiq. They were in the far valley, near the White Cliffs. And they are hunting us." He stared at each of them. "They have not attacked us for several seasons, and now it appears that time was all in preparation. We must ready ourselves to meet the attackers."

Chapter Eleven

LOOKOUTS DOTTED THE high reaches. They had already sealed and reinforced the lower warrens. Gyam scanned the valley again, his eyes whirling red gems as he observed every level he had the ability to perceive. The Misiq were close, but he wasn't completely healed and Tayi had made it clear that he was not to take any chances of reopening an injury. So for now, he watched.

"We're ready. They will be sorry they attacked the Chinjoka," Jua said.

Gyam grinned at the boy. "Yes, Jua. We're ready. All the warrens are closed to the invaders should they get this far. The Misiq won't take us by surprise. You did your duty to make sure everyone knew."

The fledgling gave a single definitive nod then turned to watch. Gyam reached over and ruffled his hair.

"Gyam! I'm watching. That gets hair all in my eyes."

He nodded and stepped behind the child, and untied his own hair from its typical tail and used his fingers to comb it straight. Jua was trying to ignore him, but curiosity was getting the better of his concentration. Gyam moved his fingers quickly, and a moment later, he was wrapping a leather strip around the bottom of the braid he'd created for Jua. The braid impressed him when it reached Jua's waist.

"There. Now you have a warrior's braid. You won't have to worry about it getting in your eyes."

The boy nodded, tears filling the corners of his eyes. He scrubbed the back of his hand over them as he returned to sentinel duty. The little warrior he'd just created practiced the hata spear patterns Askari was training him to use while keeping an eye on the lands in front of the aerie.

With a soft scrape, Dhala stepped into the room. Their eyes met, but then Dhala raised his brow as he nodded toward Jua. Gyam moved beside him and spoke in low tones. "I think he's earned his warrior braid. You wouldn't get him to change it again now."

Dhala tilted his head and smirked at Gyam. "He's young enough. He might lose his braid to the Athru and fly with you."

Gyam made a dismissive sound and changed subjects. "I need to search for the Misiq. We have to locate them. If they somehow surprise us, the Chinjoka will be no more. If they attack, it will not matter if I am not healed."

"You are still recovering. We can watch for the Misiq."

"We need to know where they are. The hata meat is dried and in caches, and our gardens are full of the summer harvest. What if the Misiq destroy them? They should be here by now. They almost captured me."

"They almost killed you." Dhala stopped in midstep and stared at Gyam. "They think you're dead. They may have one or two scouts close to the village, but the rest of their encampment is far away so we aren't alerted. Then it would be—" He turned to Gyam. "It would be a massacre. They want no one to survive. They think we're—" Dhala froze, realizing he came too close to giving away Askari and Ena's secret.

"They think we're what?"

"That we're their inferiors," he shot back.

The muscles in Gyam's jaw tightened, and a look of determination filled his face. "I need to check. I will soar as high as possible, gliding so I'm mistaken for an eagle. I promise not to attack, but we need information."

Dhala's lips twisted. "High. So very high. Promise me."

He smiled at Dhala in a way that was difficult to decipher. But he nodded. "I promise." He turned to Jua. "Young warrior. I need you to run an errand for me. Find Tayi and ask if she has more bandage wrap."

The boy turned and scowled at Gyam. "You don't want me here because you are about to change. I can keep a secret. You don't need to send me away."

Gyam squatted, so they were face-to-face. "I must fly. But I am not trying to hide anything from you. I promise, next time you can stay."

"You mean it?"

"Yes, on my warrior's honor."

Jua nodded, laid his spear over his shoulder, and started down the passageway stairs. His footsteps receded, and Dhala turned to Gyam. He cupped Dhala's head in one hand and pressed the other tight against the small of his back.

He pressed his lips against Dhala's, and it was as if bolts of skyfire struck him. Gyam lost track of time as the kiss stretched further, but when they parted, he gasped for air as if he'd run from the White Cliffs. He was uncertain what to say.

"I will return, and we will discuss our future. We will work out all the problems I let my mind create."

Dhala nodded but didn't hesitate to watch Gyam undress, appearing to enjoy the sight before him. Gyam chuckled at his smirk and kissed him again.

"I will return soon. A few spans in either direction should be enough to see if they're close."

"Maybe they returned to their lands."

Gyam shook his head. "No. They will not stop until they wipe us out." He focused for a moment and started the change. It always began with his hands, the knifelike talons growing from his fingers. A tingle flowed through him, and he found himself armed with ten knives. The process was quick and painless. Wings pressing through the skin from between his shoulder blades were always an interesting sensation, and cutting them free of the membrane they grew from was painless too. His mouth and jaw were past human speech at this point. As he stretched and tested each part of him, including his scarred wings, he remembered killing the Misiq before tucking the guilt away to deal with later. And he would do so again.

Satisfied he was ready, he folded his wings against his back and walked to the opening. He swiveled his head toward Dhala and winked. Then he plunged from the rocks, sorting the scents only this form could discern. It had been too long since his last flight.

He pulled out of the dive early, not wanting to damage his newly healed wounds. The early-afternoon heat brought a series of thermals that made keeping his promise to Dhala easy. He rode the first column of air until it cooled. From these heights, the heat from any Misiq could be detected, and he would look like a dot. His vision would be greater than anyone on the ground.

After flying a complex search pattern and finding nothing, he covered the grounds farther from the village cliffs. The mixture of brush and grasslands below him were empty of life. As Gyam made another pass, it was that very absence of life that gave him the clue he needed. The great herds of hata had made their spring passage, but stragglers always traveled days behind the main herd. And osa should be in small family groups spread across the basin and into the grass-covered plateaus. The grass was still the tender green of early spring, and every plant eater should be eating their fill of the grasses. As he crossed near Mother Falls, he saw no other life moving. Even the chime-like calls of the birds normally found in the tops of the cutleaf tree were absent.

Something was frightening the animals. He knew it had to be the Misiq. How the animals of the basin knew to hide from them, when Gyam couldn't sense them, was a mystery. It was up to Gyam to discover why they were acting as they were.

DHALA SCRATCHED AT the back of his hands while he surveyed the valley stretched out in front of him. Nothing could be spotted across the green tapestry spreading as far as he could see. Gyam concerned him, and he was becoming anxious as he waited for the flyer's return. It was his hope that Gyam had the intelligence to honor his promise and stay well out of range of the Misiq bows. He recalled their parting kiss, and the tightening in his crotch was something he would enjoy exploring with Gyam. He also considered Gyam's promise to work past the issues so they could join with each other.

The burning itch worsened and drew Dhala's attention back to the present. He lifted his hands and was shocked to find he'd shredded the skin, but there was no blood. It was as if his skin was shedding.

"What's wrong?"

He hid his hands and turned to Askari. "Nothing. Just trying to see if Gyam was staying high enough. Lost in my own thoughts, I guess."

Askari lifted a brow and stared at Dhala. "Jua said you were doing yucky stuff with Gyam."

He flushed, his gaze snapping to Askari's grinning face. "We didn't do anything—wrong."

Askari's laughter left no doubt about what he thought of the pair's discovery by the fledgling. When the chuckling continued, Dhala folded his arms over his chest and glared at his friend. "We sent him down. He must have snuck back up to see what we were doing. And it was a kiss. Nothing like he described, I'm certain."

"I'm not so sure about that. He demonstrated. It was impressive."

The heat of embarrassment crawled up Dhala's neck as he tried to recall the private moment, frustrated that he wasn't keeping their secrets for only the two of them. "No. I don't. No! It wasn't anything as dramatic as Jua indicated."

"Well, he described it something like this." He wrapped his arms around himself and writhed, moaning. His embarrassment deepened when Askari continued his reenactment with his tongue piercing the air like a bull spear during a hunt.

"No, nothing like that. Just. Just a kiss."

"Just a kiss? From the person you've wanted since you hit puberty. Not a life-changing event at all?"

The itch on Dhala's hands spread over his forearms, and the urge to scratch became stronger with each breath. The sensation of something crawling across him was overwhelming. He pulled his arms to the front and raked his nails over them, and turned to Askari as he dug into his skin, shredding it.

Askari grabbed Dhala's wrists, keeping him from causing any more damage to his skin. "What are you doing? You're ripping up your arms."

"Something's wrong. Nothing's ever itched like this. I don't know what caused it." Dhala stopped and stared at Askari. "I need to go to Tayi. This is something serious."

Askari considered Dhala's arms and hands. "We don't need Tayi. I know what it is. How long has it been going on?"

Dhala shrugged. "I'm not sure. A sun cycle or so? It wasn't much when it first started. But since Gyam left, it has worsened."

"Since he kissed you?" Askari asked with a smirk.

Dhala's face burned like a summer grassfire. "Well, we kissed before he left, so I suppose that was correct. But I don't see..."

Askari got the distant look he sometimes had when he was working through a problem. Then he muttered to himself, "That's what it has to be. I can't think of anything else. Yes. There must be some stored in the aerie. Where would it be, though?"

Askari sprinted into Gyam's sleeping chamber. Dhala was so surprised at Askari pillaging the room that his discomfort was forgotten. Dhala moved to the doorway, still absently scratching.

"What are you looking for?"

"Skin stuff. I have some. But Gyam must have ointment too. He'd need it with all the changes."

He spun to Dhala. "You must put it on him. For the dry spots he gets in his flyer form."

"Oh, the rub." He moved to the storage on one side of his sleeping chamber and brought out a bowl with a sealed lid, which he handed to Askari. He opened the lid and sniffed. After a moment, he ran his fingers through the thick substance and smeared a layer over Dhala's arm.

The ointment spreading across his skin startled Dhala. His panic heightened with each passing moment. He tugged to win his way free of Askari's grip. "Stop! That's the medicine Tayi made for Gyam."

Askari waved him into silence. "It's the same we all use. Be still."

Dhala fidgeted but let Askari smear the ointment over his hands and arms. A heartbeat later, he breathed a sigh of relief. It was working. The itch vanished as the light-green cream covered his skin. Then Askari's words came to him.

"What do you mean we all use this? It's Gyam's."

Askari smeared another thick layer over the clawed areas, and Dhala's skin seemed to absorb the ointment as soon as it was applied. It disappeared, and a small pattern became discernible. He glanced at Askari and turned to stare in disbelief.

"It can't. I'm too old. I'm Saat. My mother is Saat. My father—"

"The man whose life force made you was Athru."

They spun to find Dhala's mother behind them. "Choro's essence created you. But whatever your lineage, you're changing."

Dhala stared at her with his mouth hanging open as he tried to bring his thoughts together. She walked closer and took his arm in her hands. She studied it before she looked at him. "You're changing. The itch is from your skin becoming plated. The change is not complete. You will learn control. These are all things that take time. But I will make more ointment to relieve the itch. It will make it more comfortable as the plates grow."

Being hit by the largest hata bull on the grasslands would have been no more world-changing for Dhala. "So. I am Onija? I am no longer Saat?"

His mother and Askari exchanged a significant look before turning to him. "You are changing," she said. "We don't know where it might stop or why it waited so long to begin. You are many seasons past the typical age."

Panic welled inside Dhala. "What about..." He glanced to the open blue sky.

Askari cocked an eyebrow as Dhala's mother pursed her lips. "Gyam is more unyielding than the thickest rawhide container. Worry about taking care of yourself during the time your plates develop." She handed him the container Askari had been holding and shooed him to the sleeping chamber. "Go, put it on the rest of your body. The itch will spread across your skin as the Twins decide what type of Chinjoka you will be."

Dhala tilted his head and walked to where he could have privacy to put on the ointment. He stopped to see looks of concern on both his friend's and mother's faces. He scratched at his hip while he waited to see if they said anything further.

After a moment, his mother smiled and shook her head. "Go. Or you will feel as if biters cover you."

He made a quick nod before disappearing into the darkened recesses.

Chapter Twelve

GYAM BANKED AS he skimmed along the hills marking the northern boundaries of the Chinjoka lands. He had set out to discover the Misiq and how they were hiding from him, but he was reaching the limit of his endurance. After considering traveling home, he decided the warm day made his search more effortless than he would have experienced any other way. True forests filled the western reaches of the basin. They were also the logical entry for the Misiq from their homelands to the far west. Small canyons littering the area would also need scrutiny, but they would be the last of his search. He took care that nothing escaped his notice.

He brought his taloned forefeet and hindlegs tight against his body as he made several strong strokes with his enormous wings. Occasionally, there was a reflective glimmer from one of the multitude of scales covering him, each no larger than the pad of his thumb. They offered protection, nothing compared to the large, thick plates Askari sported, but still protection. But he had been happy to have them when he crashed. He doubted that he would have survived if not for the protection they had offered. Gyam swung his head from side to side, taking advantage of the long powerful neck of this form to scan for invaders.

He made a wide arc over the dense forests, finding nothing, and spotted a place on the nearby cliffs where it was possible to land and study the area. They had to be there. The forests were the logical place for them to hide. But he hadn't been able to find them. Besides, if he could tell Dhala he had stopped for a rest, it would satisfy the man's protective nature. He glided close to the ledge before back-winging and landing on the protrusion of stone with almost no sound. Gyam spread his wings in the delicious sun as he flattened across the exposed surface, enjoying the warmth that soaked into his body.

He lay for several moments, drifting, smiling at the thought of his shared moment with Dhala. He was no longer willing to be separated from Dhala because they were from different castes. Choro had never spoken of intimacies outside the Athru caste being forbidden. Although tradition and the opinions of others had made the choice challenging for Gyam. But he would no longer hide his attraction to Dhala. A glint of light from deep in the trees brought his attention back to his task. He focused on its source and recognized its light signature. It was the reflection of a Misiq long knife.

He shifted his vision and found the heat aura of the invader. Gyam followed it until the red-tinted form blinked from sight. He swept the area without locating another. His frustration and concern built until he was at the point of leaving to report the little information he had, but then it happened again, another heat ghost appeared, moved a short distance, and vanished.

They'd created underground dens! Hidden in the forested part of the valley, the Misiq band waited for the best opportunity to attack. He considered his options before deciding to fly over the subterranean shelters and see what he could discover. Gyam stood and moved to the edge of the outcropping before launching himself. He rose to a height above the range of their composite bows and used the thermals to circle the area.

Now that he knew what he searched for, he spotted the openings. Once he'd found the first one, others revealed themselves. Their locations were well hidden, with each thicket and cluster of greenery hiding another entry. But the numbers of Misiq he found were too small to pose a serious threat to his people. What he was seeing didn't ring true for Gyam. He needed to locate the leader of this group and was well aware they were also the heaviest guarded.

Perhaps I can get close enough to overhear their plans. There is more I'm missing.

He identified a massive cutleaf tree that would serve his plans to listen to their conversation. With the sun at his back, he glided into the thigh-thick upper branches and landed with only the lightest of creaks. He slipped deep into the thick foliage and froze, using all his senses to be sure he'd landed undetected. To his relief, no one had raised an alarm.

Soft voices drifted from below him. While he strained to understand, he got only the occasional word. Dhala would beat him senseless if he ever found out he was this close to the Misiq, but the village needed more information. He reached downward, sank talons of one forepaw into the mottled bark of the tree and eased his weight to the next lower branch. With great care, he repeated the process until Gyam was as low as he felt was safe. He pressed against the trunk of the tree and listened again. Two voices were now faint, but clear.

"The regiment is coming?"

"Yes, they should arrive before dusk." There was an unholy glee in the tone. "Tomorrow, we will wipe out the vermin. We will rid ourselves of the ones who carry this sickness."

Cold dread spread through Gyam at those few words. These were the scouts. They were living in underground dens. He was surprised they hadn't tried the tactic before. Traditionally, their homes were groups of underground tunnels. But the dens he had found explained how the figures he'd spotted kept disappearing. The dens had taken time, but he'd been watching. The burrows were new, or Gyam would've seen them before. The truth unfolded for him. Somehow, they'd constructed an outpost and had a system of runners in place to pass information between the scouts and the main body of warriors. Gyam's talons dug into the tree's soft wood as his anger built. His mind cleared, and he knew he must return to warn his people.

He climbed until the branches were too small to support his weight. He crouched to launch himself when an arrow cut a thin line along his cheek and buried itself into the tree behind him. With an echoing scream of pain and anger, he flung himself toward the open sky as he struggled to get beyond the tangle of branches. He pitched earthward for a moment as he broke free. Arrows flew past as he pumped harder, lengthening his distance from the Misiq. He flew in a pattern of confusion Choro had taught him when he was first learning the skills of the Athru long ago. He blessed the elder's determination that he reach a level of perfection even though Gyam had found the training to be tedious and demanding. Now he was sending the master praises as he dodged arrow after arrow. Their sharp iron tips carved a few shallow cuts even with his scales when he misjudged, but Gyam avoided anything more severe.

He pressed harder, determined he would get his critical information to Askari and the other warriors. He beat his wings furiously, diving when he sensed an arrow coming close. It missed by a fingerbreadth, and Gyam thanked the Twins.

The arrows seemed more erratic. He hoped he was at the limit of their reach when pain slammed into him. Gyam gasped and threw himself sideways as the agony burned through every nerve in his body. He blocked the torment that washed over him as best he could. The embedded shaft was deep in his shoulder and sent new levels of agony with each wing beat. Gyam thanked the Father when other arrows fell far below him.

He climbed to his limits before beginning a long series of glides to return to the village.

ASKARI FOUGHT THE urge to pace as they waited for Gyam's return. The light was growing dim and soon Gyam wouldn't be able to see well enough to land.

"He's coming!" Jua cried.

Askari didn't care what impression he might give and dashed to stand beside Dhala. At first, he saw nothing. Then a dark speck appeared. A few heartbeats later, he discerned the tiny figure. From its unstable flight, it was in trouble. Gyam was not flying with his usual strength. The distress became more gut-wrenching. Worse yet, it was clear he planned to land in the aerie. Normally, this wouldn't have concerned Askari, but Gyam was flying so erratically that Askari wasn't sure he had the control to glide through the sky portal.

Askari paused and pulled the change onto him. His plates hardened and his muscles thickened. He checked the quality of his shift before moving beside Dhala. Their eyes met, and by silent agreement, they turned to meet the struggling Gyam, who would be upon them in an instant.

Askari braced himself for impact, and before he could plan any further, he was tumbling backward in a mix of muscle, plate, and talon. The impact against the inner wall knocked the air from him. They lay still to recover, then separated with groans and gasps as injuries screamed out. But in a short time, they pulled away from Gyam, who changed to his two-legged form.

Dhala went to him while Gyam struggled to catch his breath. A moment passed before Dhala relaxed and turned to Askari.

"Nothing fatal. The arrow hit Gyam's shoulder and missed any organs. We need to remove it soon. I don't know if the Misiq use any poisons. The wood of the shaft is unfamiliar, and sometimes wood itself is toxic."

Dhala knelt beside Gyam and studied the protruding shaft again. After more scrutiny, he began his work. "We need to remove the arrowhead. Help me roll him to his side."

"They are coming. A large force. They blame us for the plague and intend to wipe us from the Father's realm," Gyam managed to gasp out.

Both Askari and Dhala started. But then Dhala cocked an eyebrow and glanced at Gyam's face. "We'll deal with that later. I studied the shaft of the arrow again and still don't recognize the wood. Even though I can detect no reaction, it needs to come out now." Then he glared at Gyam. "Then we will also discuss how an Athru flying the thermals appears to have been dodging arrows."

Gyam twisted his lips but said nothing.

They positioned Gyam on his side. Dhala studied the wound again.

"I'll remove the arrow, and it will be painful. It's no doubt a war shaft, and the barbed heads bury themselves in the flesh and stay in place." He focused on Askari. "You may need to help hold him still."

Askari nodded and moved to keep Gyam immobile. He looked down, and Gyam held out his hand. "You won't need to hold me down, but I'd like a hand to squeeze. A plated one is even better."

Askari chuckled, took his hand, and patted the back of it. "I'd be a lot more worried about what Dhala will do. You should never anger a healer. They know too well how you're put together."

Dhala found two pieces of hollow reed that were wider than the arrowhead. He cleaned them and slid them along the arrow's shaft. His expression changed when he reached the iron head and worked a reed on either side, sandwiching the arrowhead between them. Gyam found himself drenched in sweat as he dealt with the pain.

"I'm ready to remove it. You can't move, or the head might come loose."

Gyam nodded and tightened his grip on Askari. He understood why Gyam asked to use him. Askari was still in his plated form, and even two-footed, Gyam's grip might damage a Saat. He grinned at the knowledge that Dhala could now withstand the force of Gyam's grip, although this time, he would be busy saving Gyam.

Askari watched as Dhala worked the arrow from Gyam's body. Fingerwidth by fingerwidth, he pulled it out. Gyam shifted once, and Dhala froze and admonished him.

"You cannot move. If the head dislodges, you might die from the infection."

Gyam nodded through clenched teeth. Dhala gave him time to prepare before refocusing on the task. Askari gripped tightly, holding his breath. The tools shifted in Dhala's hands, and Gyam bit back a cry. Dhala made several attempts, each one bringing new gasps of pain from Gyam, before Dhala slumped, his lips twisted in a scowl.

"What's wrong?" Askari said.

"The barbs are embedded. I can't get it to move."

Askari considered the problem and glanced at Dhala. "What about the tiny knives you use. Could you cut it free?"

Dhala considered Askari's suggestion and nodded. Without a word, he pulled one of the glyph knives from its case, a long slender blade. He slipped the knife along the arrow shaft and, with a studied expression, made a few quick motions with the blade. Sweat ran from Gyam's face, but he didn't move. After easing the blade from the wound, Dhala grasped the bundle and guided the arrow again. Askari returned Gyam's tight grip. Time crept past until Dhala pulled the intact arrow and the reeds from the wound. He peered at the injury and sat back with a satisfied smile. He showed the iron head to Askari, who sagged with relief. Gyam watched as Dhala set aside the tools he'd used.

"Askari. Askari!"

Startled to the present, Askari looked down at Gyam. He smiled at the ashen color to his friend's face. "You can let go now. Dhala's finished."

"Oh. Sorry." Gyam released his iron grip.

Once Gyam released his hand, Askari shook it and grimaced. "You have a strong grip, my friend. I wouldn't want it turned against me. I still owe the Misiq a taste of my hata spear, but you'll recover."

Gyam nodded then grimaced as Dhala stitched the front wound shut. From the expression Gyam wore, Dhala was not being as gentle as one might hope.

Once they finished, Gyam rose to his feet and motioned to Askari. "Gather everyone and tell them to arm themselves. We will need every spear and bow in this village to save the Chinjoka."

ASKARI SLIPPED THROUGH the tall grass and thick brush of midbasin. The Chinjoka force comprised the entire Onija caste, with some of the Saat. The rest of his people were at the village, armed with bows capable of downing a charging hata. If the Misiq thought they would be an easy conquest, they were wrong.

He'd strapped a small round shield to his arm. No one would scoff at an extra shield even if one had plating. His precious hata spear he held tight with his other hand. The iron blade was as long as his two hands together. With a counterweight of an iron brace on the opposite end, it was a formidable weapon. He had given Tayi his bow. She was a skilled archer and would make the Misiq pay if they attacked the village.

He stopped and crouched after hearing rustling in the brush ahead. There were no battle cries from the Chinjoka, so they had not encountered the enemy. Askari felt more than heard the next movement, and three Misiq in battle form appeared. They paced back and forth, smelling the air and watching him. Their tails twitching behind them gave away their excitement. He shifted his balance, and three sets of tufted ears turned toward him.

The three Misiq lunged at him, teeth bared and claws extended. Askari's plating responded, thickening and hardening. His face guards extended into ridges on his brow and down the bridge of his nose. With a bellowed war cry, Askari swung the spear in a lethal swath. The long blade opened the lead Misiq's gut. It crumpled to the ground in front of Askari.

The two remaining Misiq leapt at him as Misiq archers added themselves into the small battleground. Askari had no choice but to trust his plate to deflect the arrows while he dealt with the two attacking close at hand. He spun the spear in his hand and slashed at the closest attacker. His aim was true, and the blade buried itself into the leaping figure. The Misiq died in midstride. But in the moment it took for him to free his weapon, two arrows hit him, and the other battle-form Misiq leapt on his back. His plating deflected the arrows but left Askari bruised. Those same plates kept the Misiq's teeth from sinking into the back of his neck and severing his spine.

The archers released two more arrows, and he spun. While not a complete success, he got one arrow embedded in the Misiq trying to claw through his back plating. It roared with pain and loosened for a moment. Askari felt the change and dropped to a knee. The momentum sent the attacker over one shoulder to land hard in front of Askari. He drove his knife deep into the Misiq's chest. As it died, the Misiq raked his claws over Askari's arms and torso, leaving more damage.

Another arrow hit him in a plate protecting his chest and drove the breath from him for an instant. The pain was intense, and he sagged under the attack. He grabbed the whip sword coiled around his chest. It unfurled with the hiss of a nyoka. He snapped his hand backward then his arm forward with as much force as possible, aiming at the archer.

The thin steel blade left a deep gash across the Misiq's chest. The blade in Askari's hands was a living thing that fought against the Misiq. The soldier grabbed his chest and crumpled to the ground. With another call to attack, the whip sword bit deeply into the Misiq's throat, ensuring he would not battle against the Chinjoka again.

Askari scanned the area, holding tight to the spear shaft as he struggled to control the pain coursing through his body. He stumbled, struggling to stay upright as an arrow hit him from the side again. This archer was the largest Misiq he'd ever seen, and the bow he held matched its owner in size and girth. Askari's armor didn't repel this arrow. It broke a plate and cut into his side. He struggled to stand as the man drew the bowstring to his cheek, grinned, and released.

The arrow leapt from the bow, and Askari projected its path as the shaft arched then straightened. An instant later, it hit the already damaged plate, breaking it and driving the iron head into his chest.

The impact threw Askari backward. He landed with a groan, sprawled across the ground. The Misiq warrior stalked toward him, stopped a short distance away, and drew his bow. Desperate for a way to save himself, he realized his numbing hand still gripped the haft of his spear. He slammed down on his overwhelming pain for a fragment of a heartbeat and rolled to one side, disrupting the Misiq's shot. As the archer took aim again, Askari grabbed the spear in one hand, twisted in a motion that sent pain ripping through him, and hurled the spear at the Misiq.

Askari fell backward, gasping with the searing pain. The part of his mind not dealing with the agony waited for the arrow to pierce his heart. Once the pain receded and he still lived, he knew his attempt at self-preservation must have been successful. Pushing himself upward, he saw that somehow his cast spear had embedded itself in his opponent's neck. The thick leather armor that covered the rest of his body had failed in that one thin spot.

He sat still, knowing the battle had begun. Screams of pain, growls, and shouts of victory filled the air. There was movement nearby, but Askari was in no condition to fight again. If he tried, he wouldn't survive. He glanced at his spear and decided the group was too close. There was not enough time. He held his short blade in one hand and his whip sword in the other.

I don't need more weapons. I need to disappear.

He rolled to his hands and knees, crawling into the deepest grasses to hide from the Misiq who were close enough to hear. He pressed his back against a cluster of dense shrubs, settled into the most comfortable position he could manage, and waited.

THE MISIQ EXPRESSED their anger as they found the bodies of the ones who'd attacked him. The howls of Misiq in battle form, trying to find his scent, filled him. His grip tightened on his knife, willing his damaged plates to heal.

"That enough is. Fight has moved to the White Cliffs. There we are needed."

"But, Ena—"

"Now! Question me not. I will check here for survivors."

The name and the deep rumbling voice sent a shiver through Askari. *Is that my Ena? It matches my memory. How could it be?* Then he realized the others were moving farther away. The sounds of their passage became fainter until they faded. The snap of a twig had him clenching his knife.

"Askari?" came the soft whisper.

Askari wanted to run, toward Ena or away—he wasn't certain which. But the Misiq had sensed him. His heart pounded out of his chest with a mixture of fear, excitement, and apprehension.

But instead, he sat without moving and whispered, "Ena?"

A face that had been occupying his dreams appeared in front of him. The same remarkable amber eyes, the tufts of hair protruding from the tops of his elongated ears, the endearing demarcation in his upper lip: it was the Ena he remembered. Askari had dreamed their reunion in many ways. None of which included him being close to helpless and Ena leading Misiq who hunted him.

"Yes, me it is. It had to be you. Distinct is your scent."

Askari smiled and nodded. "Yes, I'm so glad you were leading the patrol." He cocked his head as he continued. "You sent the others away. Was it to keep them from finding me?"

He nodded and made a vague motion in the direction he'd sent the others. "Scented you as soon as we entered the forest opening. Some of the ones with me were in battle form. Much more astute are our senses in that state. They would've found you in a few heartbeats. I didn't want to choose between them...and you."

Askari wanted to ask which choice Ena would have made, but didn't dare. He ran his tongue over his parched lips. He formed the question that concerned him more than any others. "They are gone, and you have found me. What happens now?"

Ena closed the distance between them and squatted beside Askari. He studied him from the top of his head to his toes and examined the arrow shaft embedded in his chest plate, but paused before he touched the shaft.

"We need to take this out. Some Misiq poison their arrow shafts. This warrior, I know. He enjoys the giving of pain. But I need to find out if the arrow is stopping the bleeding. If it is, then the task becomes more difficult."

Askari met Ena's gaze, and they stood unwavering, judging each other. The time stretched on too long before Askari nodded permission.

Ena evaluated and tested the deadly missile with his fingertips. There were a few twitches across Ena's face, but nothing Askari could decipher. He finished his survey, turned to Askari, and gripped the shaft. Before he could stop Ena, the arrow was yanked free and discarded. The pain had Askari curled like a newborn, gasping to control the wave of agony. Once the white-hot pain lessened, it surprised him when he turned to Ena and found his face contorted with concern.

"Why? I thought..."

Realization flashed from Ena. "No. No, you understand not. I not trying to harm you. The arrowhead was only slightly past your protective plate. If you'd tensed, the barbs might not free. I hoped by removing it as fast as possible, it would come out intact. The archer who made that arrow fastens his arrowheads tight. It came out with little resistance, and no damage was done."

Ena studied the open wound. Then he changed his gaze to Askari. "Not healing. Is there other damage?"

He stared at Ena, wondering why he thought the injury wasn't healing as it should. Then it occurred to Askari. Ena had healed at a miraculous rate when he and Dhala saved him from the rockslide. Afterward, they'd agreed their grasp of time hadn't been correct. But perhaps he *had* healed that quickly. He shrugged.

"We don't heal as you do. That's why healers like Dhala are so important to us."

Ena stared at Askari and, after a short time, shook his head. "If that is your belief, then it must be so. It sounds doubtful." He paused again before continuing. "Hidden you need until your people find you. Is there some place close?"

Askari sifted through his memories, but then sighed. "Nothing good. But the grass and brush are thick here. Osa hide without difficulty. Only the flyers can hunt them in this cover."

"These osa, they are the small-hooved animals with the curved horns?"

He nodded. "Yes, they are plentiful through the basin."

Ena grunted and motioned around them. "If it can hide them that well, then we can hide you here too. But we have to move you away from this battle site. You are too easy to track by your scent. Is there a stream close by? That would help mask your smell."

Askari thought again, trying to determine how far they were from running water. After a moment, he was confident of his answer. "A few leagues to the east is a major feeder stream to Father River. It's too wide to jump over, shallow, and not too rocky. It should be easy to cross."

"Sounds perfect."

He offered his hand to Askari, who reached up and used the aid to regain his feet. When Ena moved to place Askari across his shoulders, he became confused and stepped away.

"What are you doing? I can walk."

"Scent trail you can stop making also?"

Askari lifted a brow. "No, I suppose not."

"Then I will carry you. Eliminate your scent it will not, but help it will. At least to the stream. From there, perhaps you can walk on your own."

Askari sighed. "All right. I guess I don't have much choice."

Ena moved close again. Taking Askari by one arm, he pulled him across his shoulders then grabbed a leg just at the knee to help stabilize his load. Ena made several small adjustments until he seemed satisfied. Almost as an afterthought, Ena picked up Askari's spear.

As they moved, Ena's familiar odors gathered around Askari. They smelled of sharp spice, grass curing in the midsummer, and musk. Askari found the combination drew him to the big Misiq. His body responded as it had when he and Dhala had helped Ena.

They moved upstream for several leagues, the sounds of battle becoming more distant. At last, Ena paused at the lower part of a quick, shallow rapids. He scanned the area surrounding them then eased his way to a wide expanse of rocks that extended to the edge of a sand-plum thicket. Animal runways littered the head-high thicket, yielding pathways through the otherwise impassable brush. It extended to the tall grass where the two mingled. Askari could fend off a determined force inside the thicket. The interlaced branchlets would even make it difficult to reach him with an arrow. It was the perfect shelter.

Ena eased him to the ground before the largest of the entryways; the trail generations of osa used to make their way through the thicket. Not only for safe travel, but also as a source of food as they fed on the ripe fruit. Once Askari was in a defensible spot, Ena untied the hata spear from his back and slipped it beside Askari.

Their eyes met, and Askari found it hard to swallow. He lost himself in Ena's amber eyes and, without thinking, lifted his hand to caress Ena's face. His body responded with waves of pleasure Askari had experienced only with Ena. He froze as their scents mixed, which added to his confusion. His arms shook as Ena moved closer.

Askari felt like an osa caught on the high prairie by a pack of sikari. Fire and heat flooded his body as their lips touched. Ena pressed harder, lips tight against his. Time stopped, and the world around them fell silent as they moved, his skin burning at the touch.

They broke the kiss only with hesitation. Askari was bound by Ena's gaze. They leaned close again, embracing, the stiff hairs on Ena's cheek setting Askari's face on fire.

A scream sounded nearby, and both shook themselves from the moment. Ena ran his tongue over his lips, the cleft moving in a way Askari found attractive. But the battle moved closer.

Askari sighed as Ena caressed his cheek. But then his hand dropped, and he shot Askari a determined look. "Crawl in as deep as possible. You have your long-bladed spear. I will lead the Misiq warriors in the other direction." He reached down and touched Askari again. "Keep yourself safe. I must see you again."

Askari nodded, at a loss for words.

Ena smiled as he shimmered, changing into battle form. He stepped forward and opened his teeth-filled maw. Askari had doubts, but then Ena's tongue caught him on the jawline and swabbed a wet path across his cheek. With that, he spun and bounded across the rocks to disappear down the stream.

By the Twins, a Misiq just licked me.

DHALA CROUCHED LOW and surveyed the landscape before him. They'd intercepted the first forerunners of the Misiq close to the middle of the verdant basin. Rain swept with enough frequency to support the tall grass. A fingercount of hata could be hidden a span from him in any direction and he wouldn't know. The head-high thatch of grass could easily conceal more battle-form Misiq than he wanted to consider.

His knuckles were white from the tight grip he had on his short bow made of hata horn layers. The longbow like Askari's was more effective, but this was his bow, one Choro had given him when he reached adulthood. It had a familiarity he needed.

It had shocked Dhala when Askari assigned him as one of the rear scouts. Few of the Saat were sent out to aid the Onija in repelling the Misiq attack. But as he considered the situation, having him on the front lines kept his newly emerging scales out of everyone's scrutiny. Askari had been little assistance on how to deal with the developing patches once he had told Dhala about the ointment that kept him from clawing the new skin. Askari's only other observation was to point out how small Dhala's scales were in comparison to the ones that marked Askari as part of the Onija caste. Dhala's scales were less than the tip of his finger.

He tried to remember what Gyam's skin looked like before and after he had adapted his flyer form, but he couldn't recall the details. One thought comforted him. Once the scales finished forming, he would have control over them the same as Askari had over his plates. In addition to the revelation of Dhala growing scales was the relationship between him and Gyam, which was no more stable than the sinking mud found in places along Father River. He didn't want to stress their fragile connection by peppering Gyam with questions about how the changes happened in the Athru caste. He wondered how Gyam would take this new revelation anyway. But Dhala's focus had to stay on the attacking Misiq.

He scrambled to another cluster of brush and scanned the surrounding terrain. They had repelled the first Misiq wave. The sight of his mother standing on the outer rock shelf of Gyam's aerie, holding Askari's bow with a filled quiver beside her, would forever be burned into his memories. The bow was as tall as her, but she handled the weapon with no difficulty.

A snap sounded behind him, sending him scuttling deeper into the thicket of grass and thornbrush. The thick speech of the Misiq came closer. He was in their path. He dropped to his stomach and opened his senses to the area surrounding him. The head-high foliage restricted his vision, but he could tell this was a large group of Misiq—and it surrounded him.

They moved through the grasslands on either side. He hoped they were moving at a fast enough pace that they would go past without noticing his presence. Dhala breathed easier as they disappeared into the foliage opposite him. He adjusted his position and drove a sharp thorn into his stomach. A soft grunt of pain escaped from him, and the last Misiq stopped and turned to his fellow.

"What?"

"Did you hear that?"

The Misiq strained to hear the sound again. Dhala held his breath, hoping they would decide it was nothing and move to rejoin the others. As they strained to detect anything out of the ordinary, a four-legged Misiq in battle form appeared beside them.

"Heard something I did. Test for the scent. Quick we must be."

The animal snorted and bobbed its head before moving along their back trail. Dhala positioned himself so he could use his bow, ready to take as many Misiq with him on the Long Flight as possible. But as the Misiq searched, something seemed familiar. But was he willing to risk everything on his intuition?

The fierce form moved closer until Dhala could smell its scent and hear the soft crunch of its footsteps on the dried dirt. It lowered itself, peering inside Dhala's shelter, and their eyes met. Dhala froze, wondering if he had been as wrong as it seemed at that moment. But the Misiq passed with no movement from either of them. The four-legged Misiq crawled backward and turned to pad up to the warriors ahead of them. It met the gaze of the others and let out a barking cough.

"Ena! Silence. You will control your battle form or the Ruling Council will decide your fate."

Without a backward look, Ena trotted to catch up with the main formation. The other two shook their heads and turned to follow. Soon they moved beyond his hearing, and Dhala crawled from his hiding spot.

Dhala scanned the surrounding area again, the heat of the day beating down. He thought about Ena's movements. They were more than random animal sounds and motions. The noise of battle continued around him. High above, he occasionally spotted Gyam as a dark dot in the sky. At random intervals, he would drop into a dive Dhala was certain didn't end well for one of the Misiq.

It occurred to him that Ena traveled toward the part of the valley assigned to Askari's battle group. His stomach knotted, and he turned to intercept Askari's group. But as he moved closer, the sounds of battle moved in the opposite direction from his goal.

He paused several times to listen. He took cover once when a handful of Misiq warriors passed a few spans away from him. Dhala waited until the sound of their steps faded then started again to his goal. The sense of urgency grew as his thoughts drifted toward darker scenarios of what might have happened to Askari.

He crossed a stream that ran from above the White Cliffs. This was one of Askari's favorite hunting grounds. He knew the area, including the best places for an injured Chinjoka to hide.

He rushed across the stream and continued his search. Dhala moved with great care even though the battle raged far to the west. As that thought occurred to him, low voices drifted from the river. He flattened himself under an overhanging of branches and waited.

"What doing we? Upseeri is wasting time sending us to look for survivors. The Chinjoka who attacked are dying somewhere in the deep brush."

The other motioned him. "Quiet! If any live, they now know we are searching for them. And if you are foolish enough to challenge Upseeri, don't look for aid."

Dhala watched them, hoping they would pass him by and let him continue to search for his friend. They moved without making a sound past his hiding place. Then the Twins deserted Dhala, and the breeze that drifted up the stream changed directions and blew from Dhala to the two Misiq.

They tensed and turned to see Dhala as clearly as if they all scaled the bare White Cliffs. Dhala had no choice. He rose to his knees, drew the bowstring, and released the first arrow. A heartbeat later, the arrow was buried to its white fletching in one of the Misiq's chest. The rush of battle filled him as he nocked another arrow and swung to the second attacker who had disappeared into the brush.

Dhala released the arrow, hoping his guess was correct. It sliced through the foliage the Misiq had vanished into, and a scream of pain filled the surrounding area. Dhala slipped another arrow into his bow as he crossed the water and ran to the spot where the warrior disappeared. If it changed to battle form, it would be an even more vicious opponent. There was a snap of a twig breaking. Dhala drew the bow to cover the spot—and found nothing.

Dhala scanned the area for the escaping Misiq. He even tried his newly expanded ability to detect scents but found nothing. He debated how long to search when the wind shifted again. This time, the source of the strong scent was Askari.

He crossed the stream, racing up its length. The smells became stronger as he came to a rock outcropping. He checked their surroundings then studied the brush that edged the rocks. He inhaled again and only detected Askari. Abandoning caution, he called.

"Askari?"

There was a soft rustling in the thicket, and Dhala called again. "Askari, are you here? It's Dhala."

"Dhala?"

He spun in time to see Askari crawl from a game trail that ran like a leafy maze through the dense thicket. He still had his hata spear too, pulling it along as he cleared the entry. Askari moved beyond the thicket's edge and stood with the aid of his spear. Their eyes met, and the beginnings of a smile appeared on Dhala's face.

"Well, your injury is not as bad as I'd thought."

Askari's chuckle became a cough that had Dhala grimacing. "I'd be glad to trade your tiny-itchy scales for the cracked plates I have. One of the Trickster-damned Misiq monsters was drawing a bow heavier than any we used in the hata hunts. It seems it will break Onija plating."

Dhala glanced around them. "And where is this brute now?"

Askari smiled and twisted the spear so its head glistened in the sun. "It seems a hata spear can take down many opponents."

Dhala swallowed hard, remembering the Misiq he had dispatched just a short time before. The knot forming in his chest had to be forced down. He turned to Askari.

"There were Misiq scouts, a little farther downstream." He paused to gather his thoughts before continuing. "I took care of one, but the other may have changed forms and escaped. Can you walk? The Misiq are close and we need to move to a safer location."

Dhala stood waiting, ready to help his friend as he took his first tentative step. As Askari moved, a small hiss escaped from between his clenched teeth. He stood for a moment, then slid another leg forward, balanced carefully, then took another step. Using the spear to help steady himself, he worked his way down the stream and toward the Chinjoka village.

Dhala darted under his arm and tried to take some of the weight from his injury, but Askari motioned him away. "My legs are fine. I can travel. The cracked and broken plates are the most painful."

Dhala inspected him, paying closest attention to the chest wound that still seeped blood. "The chest wound is the worst, but it's closing. The other damaged plates are still intact, although they couldn't withstand another direct arrow hit. I can't do a full healing now. We are too exposed. But I have ointments Tayi sent."

Askari nodded, and Dhala shed his pack and dug into its contents. He found the sealed container he had been searching for. Without asking for permission, he coated each injury. He dealt with the chest wound last. Dhala studied it again and pulled a small rawhide envelope from the pack. He flipped it open, reached in, and pulled out a tiny awl and coil of fine sinew.

With deft fingers, he put in a few small stitches, pulling the edges of the skin back to cover the injury. Once he finished, he replaced everything to its proper place in the healing kit. Having accomplished that task, he looked to Askari.

"How does that feel?"

Askari moved back and forth, testing his body. After a few steps, he nodded toward Dhala. "Better. Much better."

"Good. It won't last beyond the sun's disappearance, but it will at least keep the pain to a minimum. It's also the strongest healing we have other than to battle inside you."

"Good, we need to move. Otherwise, it will be too late. I've heard Gyam's battle scream too often. I think they are focused on him. That must not happen."

THE FURY FILLING Gyam fueled his continued attacks against the largest Misiq groups. In spite of the odds against the Chinjoka, his attacks kept the Misiq from gaining the needed momentum to win the battle. He stayed well beyond the range of their bows for the most part, but when he dove, the descent was so fast he was only a ruddy-colored blur. With each dive, he had taken out at least one of the Misiq warriors. His method had been simple, but it worked. Drop from the sky and hammer them with balled talons, or snatch Misiq warriors from the ground and carry them to great heights before dropping them. The result left them hiding under dense trees that would prevent his attacks.

The din of battle grew around him with fierce engagements spread across many leagues. He noted the Misiq yielded under the pressure of his attacks. This forced them into the areas of thicker forests, making Gyam's dives more difficult. When an archer stepped into a small opening to find an open shot, predator's fury filled Gyam as he tucked into a dive.

Curled until he resembled the blade of Askari's precious hata spear, he sliced through the air with the hunger that sustained him all day. As he raced toward the ground, he realized he would crash through the top branches of the huge trees the Misiq used as shelter. He wound his way through the thick branches but kept his focus on his quarry. When he burst through the lowest limbs and found himself in an open area, he had an instant of satisfaction. This would be an easy kill.

The hunter dropped his bow and ran. Something wasn't right. He didn't look frightened. In fact, the Misiq had a fierce smile across its face.

A trap!

Gyam tucked his wings and regained some of his momentum as he slammed into his victim. Gyam's impact knocked the air from the Misiq he hit. When they slammed into the ground together, the sound changed to a breathless scream. Gyam thrust his head outward and bellowed in defiance.

He leapt upward and rowed for the opening between the giant trees. Misiq appeared on either side, whipping weighted nets around their heads. They launched them at Gyam. He roared in frustration as he searched for another escape from their well-planned trap. He slowed to thread his way through the lower branches when one net tangled with his hind leg. Gyam screamed in frustration and anger. He reached forward and grabbed one branch ahead of him, sinking his talons deep. A second net twisted around him, and Gyam's grasp slipped as more weight came to bear on the nets entangling him. He struggled, trying to escape what would soon be his death.

The twang of a bowstring sounded over the din rising below him, and he braced for its impact. He had nothing to match Askari's thick plates, but he hoped his scales would be of some defense against this attack. He felt the burn of the arrowhead cutting across his skin, but either due to lack of skill from the archer or Gyam's skin being stronger than he feared, the missile wasn't as devastating as he'd expected.

He spotted three Misiq swinging hooked ropes, and bellowed again. A moment later, the thick iron hooks raked across his skin, trying to find purchase. The first one scraped over his back, leaving a shallow, painful furrow as it fell off him. He wasn't as fortunate with the others.

Both wrapped themselves around his hind legs, and soon his lower half was immobilized. Still pounding his wings to escape, he glanced down to see several warriors taking aim with their bows. The first arrow created only a minor wound. But his opportunity to escape was brief.

"Stop your fire! Pull the savage from the trees. He will be an offering to the Angry God, and we will no longer have the threat of the wasting sickness. He is the last of the flyers."

Fear flooded his system. He had no chance. The number of Misiq seemed to grow with each heartbeat. Another net curled around him, followed by yet another. His forelegs screamed in agony as he held on for his life. With a mighty effort, the branch curled to its maximum, and Gyam's talons slipped. First fraction by fraction then a fingerspan at a time, he lost his grip. He released, deciding his death would cost them dearly when a host of hooks filled the surrounding air.

Trees broke and shattered as he crashed full force into the ground. He gasped for air as he tried to move. They surrounded him from every angle. A vicious strike to his head sent his world spinning to black.

Chapter Thirteen

DHALA'S BLOOD RAN cold at Gyam's first scream. He glanced to Askari who sent him with a fierce motion. "Go. Help. They have him. I'll come as I can."

Dhala hurtled over the brush at the edge of the clearing they'd had been moving through. Another cry of frustration and fear ripped through the air, driving Dhala to even greater speeds. *They can't be far. I have to find him.*

He parted the air with his narrowing body, his enlarged nostrils filling the new capacity of his lungs. Angry cries came from Gyam as Dhala lunged forward and landed on all four of his powerful limbs. The shock of impact rushed through him from talon to tooth. At this point, he had one focus: saving his mate.

He flooded the area surrounding him with his sense of place, and found the pieces that did not fit and were foreign to the Chinjoka Basin— Misiq. He leapt at the closest with a snarl and opened his throat with a swipe of his taloned foreclaw. A scream came to Dhala, pulling him in a new direction. He was a rampaging Athru in flyer form and someone was causing his mate pain. Moving on instinct, he cleared the trees in a single jump with powerful wings of bone, sinew, and corded muscle. He scanned the area, his spinning green eyes raking the forest around them. He spotted his target. Gyam. Bound and helpless in a clearing almost too small to accommodate him.

One of the Misiq moved to Gyam's side and lifted an enormous iron dagger above Gyam's beating heart. There was nothing remaining but animalistic fury as Dhala dove at the Misiq. Emerald eyes whirled as the man's arm tensed to raise the knife above Gyam. The Misiq paused, and Dhala's new vision saw a single bead of sweat run down his cheek.

He drove the dagger downward with all his strength.

Dhala was primal fury. The Misiq attacking Gyam would pay. Dhala became a primal beast. And he had just seen his mate killed. He would have his revenge. With a scream heard through the entire basin, he plunged into a killing rage.

He targeted the Misiq who had killed Gyam, and what he saw made him falter. Gyam had moved, and the Misiq prepared a second attempt with the sacrificial dagger. The knife descended again but slipped to one side. As the Misiq lifted the knife a third time, Dhala slammed into him with talons extended, the full force of his dive behind him.

The impact drove the man across the opening and against a massive tree trunk. A trail of blood ran from his mouth as he crumpled into a heap at the base of the tree. Dhala raced back, mantling over Gyam as he trumpeted his victory. Then he became a blur, slashing the rope holding Gyam's jaws bound. In a series of movements almost invisible to the eye, he freed Gyam.

He stood, calling to his mate as he guarded him against the remaining warriors. With the fire of first change on Dhala, he was quicker even than the Misiq in battle form. A few archers fired, but Dhala deflected them with his newly grown wings. The attack seemed to change when Dhala spun to find a Misiq whose bow was at full draw. Dhala swung his wings to cover them, knowing he couldn't deflect this attack from the less well-protected parts of his anatomy.

The archer spasmed, releasing his arrow into the sky. He fell to his knees and pitched forward. Dhala snapped his gaze from the dying figure to a shadowed form at the dark edge of the trees. Amber rippled through its eyes before it disappeared into the thick underbrush.

A weak moan came from behind him, and Dhala chanced a quick glance. He was shocked to discover Gyam, lying limp, naked, and unconscious on the ground. The attack had caused him to shift back to his two-legged form. Cuts and bruises covered his body with blood trickling from the more severe. There were two deeper injuries over his chest where the knife had slid across plated skin. In the heartbeats it took to make judgment, the Misiq regrouped and launched a renewed attack. An arrow zipped past Dhala's guard and cut a shallow wound into his shoulder. He roared again as he released his animal and lunged at the closest of the attackers. As he did, others tried to recapture Gyam from his protection. He stormed back, rearing to his hind legs, rending the air with his talons as he beat back each wave of attackers.

Several of the Misiq spun the grappling hooks they had used on Gyam. The first arced toward them, and Dhala batted it down with a wing. Several others shot upward when the archers released arrows each time he left an opening. The skies above him beckoned, and he was desperate for escape. But Gyam moaned and moved his body. Dhala fought down his animal instincts, knowing he would never desert Gyam. He spread his wings around them and screamed his challenge. An archer sighted on them, and Dhala focused, hoping he could deflect another arrow. He twitched and flung his wing up to create a shield.

The attack didn't skid away with minimal effect; the heavy-shafted war arrow burst through the webbing of his wings and hit Dhala in the shoulder. He recoiled in pain from the violent attack. The archer drew again on them, but he froze, his eyes growing. A heartbeat later, an enormous spear shot into the clearing. There was time for only a squeak before the mighty iron head buried itself in his chest. He looked at the weapon protruding from his body before collapsing.

Dhala spun. There was only a single person who could throw a hata spear with such deadly effect. He spotted Askari as another arrow shot toward him. *By the Twins, they won't take me. Not now.*

He jumped into the skies, flew a few lengths from the ground, did a quick wing over, and fell from the sky toward their enemies. He balled his fore- and hind-claws as he hit the Misiq. By the time his momentum dropped, he had injured several invaders. As he again winged skyward, he got a glimpse of Askari raging across the battlefield. He'd gotten a bow and was releasing a deadly rain into the Misiq. When they moved too close, he used the thick bow as a club.

The surrounding air echoed with an animal's call like none he'd experienced before. It was part howl, part hiss with a blood-chilling cry of one of the great eagles. The Misiq froze for an instant then disappeared into the forest. A scream punctuated the final arrow released by Askari.

Dhala's cry frightened most of the Misiq into retreat. They crouched low, studying the area to see if any of the invaders were hiding. Dhala flexed his claws, the fire of battle still raging. He scented Gyam and knew he still lived. The injury was serious, but he was alive. He felt a presence and turned his head to find Askari smiling at him and well out of his reach.

"A green. I should have known you'd be a green."

He started to roar a challenge but realized Askari was right. Scales covered his body. They were every imaginable shade of green, from the deep rich color of the evergreen forest in midsummer to the pale yellow-green of the first growth of spring. The shades of life covered him. When he turned again to Askari, the only noise he made was a soft murmur.

Askari moved closer, running his hand over Dhala's shoulder and made a low whistle. "I never would have believed a network of such tiny scales would deflect arrows so well."

Dhala held out his punctured wing as proof he hadn't emerged unscathed. Askari inspected it with careful attention, but then he turned to Dhala with a smile.

"It would seem the stories of the power of the green Athru are true. Your wounds are almost healed. Change to your two-leg form."

Dhala turned inward and realized he did not understand how to move between forms. Panic flooded him, and he tried to voice his concern. His words came through in a series of sharp barks. Askari looked at him in shock.

"Change. You just...change. I call them out, and I have plates."

Sound rolled over them from behind Askari, and they both focused on the forest closest to the village. A moment later, a force of Chinjoka burst into the clearing. He had no problem identifying the leader of the group, his mother.

Relief filled Dhala as he spotted her, bow still clenched in her fist. She and several others ran to them.

She checked his wounds, but after finishing her inspection, she stepped back with a nod. "Your injuries are healing faster than typical."

She walked to Gyam and gently probed his injuries. After a moment, she motioned toward the Chinjoka who came with her. "He needs healing that can't be done here. We're moving him to the village."

She met Dhala's gaze, and he made a tiny sigh.

"Guard us from the Misiq. Gyam is the only one who can teach you to move between forms. If he dies..."

Dhala's gut twisted at the thought, both of Gyam dying and being forever in the flyer form. After a moment, Askari asked a question that nagged them both. "If he can't change, what happens?"

"It hasn't happened in living memories, only in cold-time stories told by the elders." She gave Dhala a sad smile. "Life doesn't end well for an Athru stuck in flyer form."

Her expression hardened, and she barked out a few orders. "Get Gyam on the hata skin. Everyone grab where you can and we will make this as painless as possible."

She motioned to Dhala in his flyer form. "Dhala has transcended into Athru caste and has shown his flyer form. He will fly over us and watch for Misiq. Use care. Gyam's injuries are severe."

A low murmur traveled through the group. All Dhala picked out from the chatter was a whispered "green Athru," and he refused to press that idea any further. He studied the Chinjoka as they moved Gyam to the soft skin, spread out around its edge, grabbed a piece of the hide, and walked toward the village at a fast clip.

Dhala waited a moment before leaping into the skies and pounding his wings until he reached a height where he could see for leagues in any direction. With the fire of battle burning low, Dhala was more clumsy and fatigued than at any point during the confrontation with the Misiq. But he refused to fail at this task.

With a few snaps of his jaws at imagined enemies, he rose above the treetops. He scanned the area closely but worried how he would spot a Misiq hidden beneath the trees. Then he remembered Gyam talking about being able to see the heat coming from living beings. With a target, he winged higher and searched for the telltale heat shadows of Misiq.

ASKARI LIFTED GYAM with one arm while dribbling water into his mouth with the other. There was a choking sound, and most of the water bubbled out. The fire gaze of the midday heat beat down on the rocks outside the cave, but in its dim recesses, the breeze was a cool whisper over his skin. They had been able to move Gyam to Tayi's warren where she had her healing supplies.

The wounds from the battle with the Misiq the day before still seeped blood and left Askari stiff and with limited mobility. He picked up the bowl of wash Tayi had made as a treatment for Gyam's numerous cuts and scrapes. As he carefully cleaned each injury, Askari considered the man he was helping to treat. Gyam hadn't awakened since the Misiq tried to sacrifice him. Before he was able to do any more to help Tayi, he was interrupted by a sound like a length of metal pulled over stone. He glanced toward its source, and in the darkest corner of the room, swirling green gems glowed, which served as Dhala's eyes.

Dhala had moved there and become an intractable shadow. He wanted to help with Gyam's healing, but none of them could work out the details of either shifting to his two-footed form or healing Gyam. Askari sensed Dhala's emotions to a much larger extent than he ever had with Gyam. He knew the dejection was growing with each passing fingerwidth the sun moved.

Tayi knelt beside Gyam and checked for the heartbeat along his neck and inner thigh before moving to survey the myriad of injuries he had sustained. She moved back with a shake of her head.

"He's very weak. I can barely detect his heartbeat." She looked into the deep shadows where Dhala kept making slight whimpering sounds. "Try. It's taking you both if something isn't done soon."

Dhala's bugle sounded of doubt, so unlike his battlefield scream of triumph, it would seem to be from a different Athru. He was afraid, Askari could tell. Dhala looked first at his mother, then Askari. Ready for direction, guidance.

"I have no idea. Do what you did before. You changed to the flyer form while you ran toward Gyam. Maybe somehow you can reverse the change. You can try to heal Gyam while in your flyer form. It might not work, but you have to try everything."

Askari felt the burn of Dhala's gaze, followed by a calm that washed over him. Hope became one of a mix of emotions Askari felt. He was afraid he would lose both his friends.

Dhala moved to Gyam's side and spread his wings. The length of webbing and bone filled the room before they curled around Gyam's body. Dhala made a gurgling sound as he laid his muzzle across Gyam's torso before using his wings to cover them both. A deep rumble from Dhala reverberated through the stone floor. Askari studied the pair mounded on the floor; tension moved in ripples down Dhala's back as he tried to heal Gyam.

Time stretched out as the invisible war carried on between Dhala and the forces inside Gyam. At times, Dhala would snap or whine as the battle continued unseen to Askari. Tayi walked past with a new level of frequency, but there was no sign of an end.

The sun had moved a significant distance since Dhala began his attempt, but Askari saw no change. Tayi entered the room and stopped to study them. A moment passed before she gazed at Askari.

"I do not know how Dhala is progressing. When he healed you, it did not take this long. I am worried."

Askari stared at the twitching form of his friend, unable to determine his state either. He lifted his head and met Tayi's gaze. "What can we do? Is there some way we can help?"

"We will have to separate them. But since they are joined in a healing, I'm uncertain what it will do to either of them. Dhala might lose all humanity and become an animal we would have to destroy. Gyam would die. But they are running out of time."

Askari nodded as he struggled to absorb the information. He glanced out the now-cleared doorway to the sight of the sun touching the tips of the trees. As he stared at the orb that was the Fire Twin manifested, he turned to Tayi.

"After the sun goes down. Give them that much time."

With a slight hesitancy, she nodded. "Yes, we can wait that long." She glared at him. "If we lose the last of the Athru…"

Askari dropped his gaze to the scene before them. "I know. The Misiq press us harder with each attack. Gyam saved us, and Dhala rescued him."

He sat, waiting. Askari refused to track the path of the sun. He could tell enough from the shadows lengthening. Tayi walked past them several times, but Askari focused on his friends too much for him to take more than a passing notice.

Before he'd realized the day had disappeared, Tayi lit the fire and had a small blaze inside the warren. She started a brand from the central fire and moved around the room igniting the hata oil lamps. Steeling himself against the coming event, he stared after her. She set the final lamp to burning before kneeling beside Dhala. She checked his pulse and leveled a concerned expression at him.

"We have to separate them. Otherwise, we will lose at least one of them," she told Askari.

He reached to Dhala's forearm, and it was as if he'd touched stone. Cold and unforgiving. He tried to pry them apart, but there was no yielding. It was as if iron encased Gyam, keeping everything out and in. Tayi and Askari became more forceful as fear filled them like a dry streambed during a summer flash flood. Strain as they would, they had no results. He even prodded at Dhala's injuries, hoping the pain would break through the spell…but nothing.

A faint gasp made him realize they had an observer. He glanced to the edge of the flickering light to see Jua holding a filled waterskin.

The fledgling swallowed hard as they turned to him. "Are they dead? Are Dhala and Gyam gone?"

"No, Jua. Dhala is trying to help Gyam, but we're worried."

The child shot forward and launched himself toward the bound pair. Askari tried to intercept the youngling, but nothing broke the fledgling's determination to reach Dhala and Gyam. He crawled on top of Dhala's form and held on as if his life depended upon it. Tears rolled down his face, dropping onto his two heroes. Askari gave him a few moments but then reached for him. Tayi grabbed his wrist, stopping him from touching Jua.

"Look," she said.

He paused, seeing nothing at first. Then a pattern of scales no larger than the tip of a finger appeared on Jua. The pattern undulated across his small back as Askari stared. "Is that—"

She held up a hand to stop him. "I'm uncertain. But give him a moment. He could not exert any more force than we did."

They waited, giving Jua time. There was a low moan. In the next instant, Dhala's wings slid apart, and there was a louder gasp that sounded like scraping of iron against stone. Askari turned toward the other two. He gnawed at his lip as the huge form in front of him stumbled to one side. He shot to Dhala's side and lent support.

"Easy, Dhala. You're weak. Rest and I will get you some food."

Dhala sank to the floor, and Askari dashed to one side for food. He returned with a hindquarter of an osa, which had been hanging high above the fire pit. Dhala swayed back and forth, staring at the piece of meat for a moment before recognizing it. When he did, he grabbed it in his talons, ripped off chunks of meat, and swallowed them.

"Askari. Help me."

He spun to find Tayi kneeling beside Gyam. Gyam's eyes were open and staring around the room. Tayi held a bowl of water to his lips. A sip sent him into a coughing fit, but when he stopped a moment later, he seemed more aware. With Tayi's insistence, he sipped again from the bowl. He swallowed, and his face twisted.

"Twins, Tayi! That tastes awful!"

They chuckled at his protests. He looked between them and became more frantic. He locked gazes with Askari. "Where is Dhala? Before I passed out, I had a vision. He was Athru and saved me. I don't understand what that means."

Askari laughed. He motioned to Dhala, who had been splintering the bone and devouring the marrow from the hindquarter. The Chinjoka in flyer form stepped into the light where Gyam could see him. Gyam's mouth dropped open, and he stared at the vision standing before him.

"Dhala?" Gyam whispered.

The huge creature nodded as its eyes slowly swirled.

Askari motioned to Dhala. "He changed right in front of me. Then attacked the Misiq who were trying to kill you. If it weren't for him, you would have died. You still sustained serious injuries, though. He's been healing you all day."

Jua moved to the side of the room but didn't leave. He looked protective of his friends.

"Jua helped too. Just now."

Gyam reached over and patted his shoulder. "That was very brave of you. You did well."

He turned to Dhala and nodded. "Thank you for coming to my rescue. But you should change. Flyer form is too dangerous to support for long."

"That's the problem. None of us can make the change happen. He became this form because the Misiq were about to kill you," Askari said.

"Oh," Gyam said. Then a moment later, "Oh!"

He stood and made his way in front of Dhala, who dipped his head low enough that they were staring into each other's eyes. A quirky smile appeared once Gyam studied Dhala. "Were you so afraid I wouldn't honor my pledge, that you became Athru?"

Dhala bugled, the sound reverberating around them. Gyam covered his ears for a moment and motioned for Dhala to calm himself. "I know. I know. You were happy with your role as Saat. I was teasing...teasing someone I hope to come to know better. Let me check your shifting. Sometimes, our skin gets damaged in the first few changes."

Dhala followed instructions and stood still while Gyam inspected him. Gently at first, but with building vigor. Askari became concerned when Gyam took far too long.

"Is something wrong?"

He paused for a moment. "Not a problem. It's just..."

"What? The last days were not easy for any of us. If Dhala has a problem, we need to know. Now," Askari said.

Gyam started but shook his head. "His scales are hard. Much harder and thicker than mine. He might be able to deflect arrows."

"He did, when he came in to save you."

Gyam nodded then seemed to realize. He looked at Dhala and smiled. "You shouldn't have any trouble. A tough set of plates never hurt anyone."

Askari detected a vein of fear pulsing through Dhala. But Gyam glanced around the room. "Everyone here can know the secret. I never understood why this was hidden. It almost died with me."

He stepped close and placed his hands on either side of Dhala's muzzle. He looked into the faceted eyes, and their spinning slowed. "Listen, Dhala. Change is easy. It is more a matter of timing than anything else. Go down and inside like you do when you heal, but do it inside yourself. As soon as the darkness of the healing lands overtakes you, you will see a bright star in the eastern sky. Will yourself to that star. Go with the pull you feel. Once the motion begins, relax and you will come back to us."

He stepped away with a confident smile. Dhala met the gaze of each person in the room. It was as if he were wishing them well and saying goodbye. Askari moved forward to comfort Dhala when he curled his wings against his body and tucked his head against one wing.

Askari watched with trepidation. His concern built when the time seemed to crawl with nothing changing. His heart pounded, and he scented fear coming from the others too. Gyam watched Dhala with concern.

"Is he all right? It seems to be taking longer than any change I've seen before. What's wrong?"

Gyam stood silently before meeting Askari's gaze. "He could be waiting, building courage. The first time is frightening."

He studied Gyam. "What else? What are you not telling us?"

Gyam tensed for a moment, but then his muscles relaxed. "He might also be lost. It's possible. At least that was what the older Athru told us."

"Lost? What do you mean, lost?"

"It means he can't find his way."

A tremor passed through Askari. "What happens then?"

Gyam stared at Dhala. "The body will die, and while it lives, there will be no Dhala inside."

A sob echoed through the chamber. They had forgotten Jua remained with them. He came running from the darkness toward Dhala's form, but Askari swept him into his arms.

"Let me go!" Jua screamed. "I helped last time."

Askari held the struggling fledgling as he fought. He only lasted a short time before he dropped his head against Askari's shoulder with sobs wracking his body. The other two stepped beside Askari to comfort Jua.

"Gyam. You give terrible directions. There are three stars."

The group spun to find a shaky Dhala standing where the huddled flyer form had been an instant earlier. He tried to take a step, and only Gyam's swift action kept him from falling. Tayi moved to the other side and helped lower him to the bedding. She darted from the room for a moment then returned with a softly tanned osa skin, which she draped over him.

Gyam appeared at his side with a bowl of soup Tayi had created to help him recover, which they had kept warm by the cooking fire. Askari released Jua, who shot to Dhala's side and curled against him.

"I'm glad you picked the right star," Jua said.

Dhala cupped his face and smiled. "Me too, Jua. Me too."

The fledgling turned to look more closely and inspected Dhala's wounds. Dhala caught Askari's gaze. Once he did, he glanced at Jua and mimed clawing at his skin.

Askari shrugged. Jua's developing scales would wait for another time.

Chapter Fourteen

DHALA WOKE THE next day tired but with a feeling of satisfaction. He still wasn't certain how he'd become a green Athru or how he had saved Gyam, for that matter. But he knew it had not been some kind of sleep vision. He had lived it. When he moved and pain reminded him of the injuries he'd gotten in his rescue of Gyam, his memories were validated. The healing he had somehow performed afterward no doubt accounted for much of the exhaustion he experienced. He moved again, and couldn't suppress a groan. In an instant, a figure materialized at his bedside. Gyam.

"Dhala? Are you awake?"

He eased his eyes open and was glad he had slept deep in Tayi's warrens. Even there, it took him a few seconds of adjustment to the light before he could see clearly. When he did, it was obvious Gyam was concerned. He smiled at the thought of their progress since Choro had left this world. But they still had much to do, and the stampede of recent development had not made any discussions more likely. He realized Gyam waited for his response.

"Yes, I am awake. A little battle worn, but I seem to be recovering faster than normal. Tayi told me the green Athru heal ourselves with great speed."

Gyam moved closer and surveyed him for a considerable length of time before speaking again. "You have several impressive bruises, but otherwise your injuries are healed. Considering the amount of airtime you experienced for a new flyer—well, it is to your advantage that you are a green."

Dhala's heart fluttered at the sight of Gyam's smile.

"I would still be in bed complaining of my injuries."

Dhala chuckled, and could tell his condition had improved even since he had awakened. But Dhala couldn't refrain from commenting. "No, you would be unconscious while mother and I tried to put the pieces back together."

A deepening silence was his only response for a time, then Gyam began to chuckle. "I can't argue with you. I have spent more time in your bed as a patient than as your mate."

Dhala started to correct Gyam's statement when a featherlight touch descended on his shoulder, announcing Tayi had moved beside them. At her touch, he knew what he was about to say did not need to move past anything more than a random thought. But then she surprised him.

"You have not had time to discover each other, not as potential mates. The Misiq will be in hiding today or, better still, in retreat. I want you to find a private place away from the cliffs. Talk to the Twins. Call on the Father. But talk to each other. You are the last Athru. You will have to discover the way of a green flyer without guidance. The two of you must find a way to work together. I wish we had more time for you to accomplish these goals. But all I can give you is this sun cycle. We will be vigilant, but I must ask that you be quick."

Dhala sat up from the bed and locked gazes with Gyam. "Today, we must work out what we are. We should have more time, but we are the last Athru."

Gyam nodded in agreement and, in a sensuous motion, stood beside Dhala and offered a hand to assist him. Their hands intertwined, and Gyam's lifted Dhala with little effort. He glanced around the room and decided they needed only the clothing they wore. He turned to Tayi, but she had given her advice and left to care for others who needed her assistance. The Misiq had not sent anyone on their Long Flight, but several were injured to one degree or another. He turned to find Gyam smiling at him.

"Your mother was never one for wordy goodbyes. I think we have the last of her advice."

Dhala chuckled. "You're no doubt right. North seemed to be the direction we were sent. Let us begin our travels."

They quickly made their way out of the village and north toward the crags and Mother Falls. As they traced the river's path upstream, the trees grew larger and the grass less frequent. The sun had traveled for several fingerwidths when Dhala realized they were in the catacomb where he had found his soul rider. This seemed to be a good location to talk of private matters without any listening ears other than those few animals that made their home there.

He turned to find Gyam had moved close. He lifted his hand and caressed Dhala's cheek, leaving a line of sweet fire that had Dhala gasping for breath. He caught Gyam's face between his hands and pressed their lips together. First gently, but with increasing urgency, the two shared each other in a way that had Dhala tingling. He moved with urgency, wanting more from Gyam. His inexperience surfaced, and in his excitement, he clipped his teeth against Gyam's. The jolt of pain had them flying apart faster than if their tongues had touched a firebrand. Gyam rubbed his front teeth and chuckled.

"A little less frantic maybe? I don't want to explain to your mother why our front teeth are chipped," Gyam said with a smile.

Dhala blushed and tried to calm his breathing. Not an easy task given that he was moving into full mating heat. His desire for Gyam was becoming stronger than the sun during heat moon. Even given that desire, he was certain he was not the lover Gyam deserved. He had been with only one person before. But since he had become developed enough to want intimacies with anyone, Gyam had always been his desire. Now he stumbled like a newborn fledgling.

Gyam curled his strong hands around Dhala's bare torso and pulled him backward against Gyam's chest. The tingle grew and his body responded. A moment later, his cock was as hard as stone, and he was making soft gasps.

Gyam slid his fingers over Dhala's skin, and the sensations intensified with each pass. He slid his hands over Dhala's hard shaft and squeezed. Dhala yelped. "Careful! It might feel like rock, but it is still attached."

With a soft chuckle, Gyam made another attempt, and this time, his touch was gentler.

He leaned closer and traced his tongue along the rim of Dhala's ear and whispered, "Sorry. This is all very exciting to me too. We will both learn. But the feelings you are creating inside me are like nothing I have experienced before. It's difficult to control myself." His expression changed to one of innocence. But Dhala wasn't sure he believed the tale Gyam spun. His resolve weakened when Gyam started stroking his hard length again. Once he started seducing Dhala, it wasn't long before Dhala wanted to think of nothing more than Gyam's touch.

Soon Gyam slipped his hand inside Dhala's breechcloth and caressed his aching cock and balls. The sensations swirling around them filled Dhala's being. Gyam wrapped his hand snuggly around Dhala's cock and began stroking it slowly. A flood of pleasure filled Dhala, and jolts of ecstasy ran through his body. His muscles locked, and the pleasure overcame the swirl of other emotions going through him.

Dhala lost all sense of time when his orgasm began. With each convulsion of his body, he filled with the bliss of reaching his fantasy and being with Gyam. As his body returned to his own control, he was surrounded with the strong scent of sex and the wet sound made each time Gyam slid his hand through the thick essence he had coated them with. As the final shudder left his body, he relaxed against Gyam's solid form. He began to recover but was determined to make Gyam feel amazing too.

He turned in Gyam's arms and kissed him again. He contained his adolescent enthusiasm, and they managed to keep from injuring each other again. He ran his hands over Gyam and enjoyed the leisurely exploration he was able to do now that his lust was satisfied.

He slid his hands across Gyam's chest and was rewarded with a deep groan. Dhala stored the information away for another time. That day, his goal was other, and he intended to explore it thoroughly. With that thought, he pressed lower until he cupped Gyam's muscular butt. It had always intrigued Dhala, and now he could explore it as he saw fit. His primary goal was to bring Gyam pleasure.

With that in mind, he gripped tight and pulled them together until Gyam's hardness pressed against Dhala's flaccid member. He searched for a moment before Dhala located his goal, and Gyam's breechcloth fluttered to the ground at Dhala's feet. Gyam's erection jutted out, and Dhala's ran his tongue over his lips as he enjoyed the sight before him.

He slipped his hand between them and wrapped his fingers around the shaft. While caressing Gyam's back and hips, he began teasing Gyam with long slow strokes. The touch had its desired effect as a soft moan escaped from Gyam. When their eyes met, there was no doubt in the heat of Gyam's gaze. Dhala pulled back Gyam's foreskin and smeared his length with the thick clear liquid it leaked. A rattling gasp was his reward for stimulating one of Gyam's erogenous zones.

He ran his hand through the slick coating on his stomach, grabbed Gyam again, and began stroking. He sensed Gyam move closer to the sweet ecstasy he had experienced a few moments earlier. Their adolescent mimicry of the adults when they were young held no comparison.

His strokes came faster as Gyam gripped his shoulders with frantic enjoyment. Dhala could feel the tremors emanating from Gyam's core. He bit his lip, holding in a cry of pleasure, and the first trail of orgasm landed across Dhala's abdomen. He continued to stroke as stream after stream shot from Gyam's iron-hard cock. With a few soft gasps coming from Gyam, they sank to the plush grass and into each other's arms.

They began to cool, but neither moved to separate from the other. The gentle breeze brought scents that were both familiar and new. The smell of their combined musk was strong and one Dhala enjoyed. They relaxed against each other and drifted into a light slumber.

DHALA WOKE TO the sensation of being watched and grabbed for the knife at his waist, only to remember he was naked and weaponless. He moved toward his clothes but was surprised when a liquid chuckle reminded him of the high-mountain snowmelts during the warm-season moons. He looked toward its source and froze in place.

The ice-blue eyes and the aqua-tinged skin clearly identified the visitor. It was Voda. The last time one of the Twins had manifest themselves to Dhala, it had been to scold him. He hoped the intimacy he and Gyam had shared did not offend the gods. Gyam hadn't moved. He shook the limp form next to him and got no response. Ignoring the manifestation a few spans from him, Dhala began to check Gyam's life points.

"He is well. I choose for him to continue his slumber. You were the one who I wished to converse with. Your life has changed drastically in the past days. We felt it was time to speak with you about the change."

Dhala stayed next to Gyam, protective of the person beside him. But he felt no need to dress in spite of the lithe figure before him. The silence stretched out until Dhala decided to discover the reason for the visit.

"Voda, I stand before you as a child. And like a child, I do not know what grievance you might have against us. The shared intimacies were a common goal between the two of us. It was as much my idea as his. But you said things have changed and we might have questions. I would agree. I know I do not understand what has happened or why, so late in my life, I have transitioned from the caste of no change to the flyers. I have dreamed of being Athru for my entire life. Now that it has happened, I have great concern." He glanced again to Gyam. His chest slowly rose and fell, and Dhala was slightly reassured. He turned back to the Twin of Waters. "Have we caused insult upon the gods? It was not our intent. We are even caste mates now. Gyam believed cross-caste matings were forbidden."

The tinkling laughter filled the air again, and Dhala was drawn into the happy sound. After a moment, the laughter drifted away and Voda met Dhala's stare. Dhala lasted only a second before he was driven to look away.

Then Voda spoke again. "The castes have never been forbidden to intermarry. That is a restriction the Chinjoka brought upon themselves. We wondered at the time why our children would strive to make their lives more difficult. Our goal is never to make life more troublesome. But with free will, we do not take away every obstacle put before you. How you deal with personal hurtles will determine the richness of your life. But I am not here to scold you for intimacies which are not forbidden."

He paused and, after a moment, nodded toward Dhala. "You are the first green Athru in many cycles. You scolded me when you met your soul riders and accused the gods of leaving the Chinjoka to solve the crisis. You now have the resources to heal the sickness that permeates your people." He paused and gazed at Gyam.

An instant later, he lurched from their bedding and took in the scene with wild eyes. He realized he was as bare as Dhala and his face flushed a deep crimson.

Before he could say anything, Dhala rested his hand on Gyam's leg and squeezed gently. "He is not here to punish us. It would seem we have all the ingredients to cure the plague."

Gyam studied them both before turning to Voda. "Dhala in his role as green Athru can cure any new cases of the disease that might occur?"

"No. Dhala as green Athru is only one part of the solution. It will take more than a single flyer to cure the pestilence. But the Father has seen that with your change all the elements needed are in place."

"What else do we need?" Gyam asked.

Voda shook his head sadly. "We do not know the answer to that question. Only that the components are in place."

Dhala looked first at one figure then the other. "No one is sick with the illness at the village. We have time." He turned to Voda with a cocked eyebrow. "Has the disease ended? Is that the cure?"

Voda considered the question until Dhala was squirming with anticipation. Then the first response was a shrug. "Perhaps, perhaps not. The flights of the future are difficult to foretell. I would search for a less fortuitous solution were it me. When the Ancients decide the future, it is seldom that the bones fall as anyone might like. It is a varied thing."

Dhala easily sensed the tension building inside Gyam. He could see no benefit of losing his temper with one of the Twins. Granted, if you were to make that unfortunate choice, far better it be with Voda than Pilea. There was a slight chance the offender would survive if it were Voda. But still, not a good choice.

He squeezed tighter, and when Gyam looked at him, he lifted a brow ever so slightly. Gyam tensed in that instant but took almost the same length of time before uncoiling under Dhala's touch. They both looked back at the Twin to discover he was shifting. A breath or two later, he stood before them, an unheard-of blue flyer. With an economy of wing strokes, he lifted from the ground but then studied the two of them before a voice filled their heads.

"Do not stop sharing yourselves with each other. Explore and learn. The journey can be amazing."

With that declaration, he winged upward and rowed higher with a few strokes of his wings, and disappeared.

The pair remained where they were, nestled into the ground. With a shared look of agreement, they began dressing. As they finished, a breath of air came down from the Mother Falls.

Gyam inhaled deeply. "The Mother's scents are so pleasurable. I always feel rejuvenated when I can sense them like this."

Dhala drew in a breath and held it for a few moments before exhaling. He smiled, pulled Gyam close, and kissed him, careful not to damage his mate. *My mate. That sounds so wonderful. Our mating was Voda blessed. I couldn't ask for more.*

"Yes, and the scents of the Mother vary during the season. The constant change is wonderful."

Dhala clasped his hand against Gyam's waist, and they began their return trip to the village.

Chapter Fifteen

DHALA SAT IN the upper canopy of one of the great cutleaf trees found along the western reaches of the Chinjoka Basin. His talons sank deep into the bark. He hoped to blend with the foliage. He moved high enough that, even in their battle form, the Misiq should not be able to scent him. Dhala still felt the sting of his mother's tongue when he had told her, after a single night's rest, he was able to fly again.

He knew he was much less damaged than Gyam—the Misiq had come close to killing him. Their time together had been helpful, and Dhala healed quickly. When he'd checked the mobility of his chest muscles, he knew the cost of bringing him back from the brink of death, but he still was many days from healed.

But when Dhala worked through familiar exercises, it was as if he hadn't been through a battle earlier. None of them wanted him to go but soon realized, whether they wanted it or not, he was their best chance to see if the Misiq were returning.

Gyam resigned himself to giving Dhala a few short lessons on performing a change and navigating the skies without making himself into a giant green target. The first changes between forms had left Dhala shaking, but he was quick to pick up the intricacies.

Dhala exited from the ledge on Gyam's aerie without too much difficulty. But as the sun warmed the surrounding land, the wind made flying more difficult. With the Onija patrolling closer to the village, Dhala fought the winds until he was high above the valley, soaring to the west, toward the retreating Misiq. The flight lasted a good part of the morning, but when he reached the western forests, he dropped lower and began a series of passes closer to the treetops while still out of arrow range. He neared the foothills to the north of the chalk cliffs when he spotted the Misiq.

The flight had brought him to a tree whose foliage hid him well and gave plenty of opportunity to examine the area surrounding him. At first, he wasn't certain what he was watching. The Athru vision differed from his normal eyesight. Richer and with more depth, it took time for Dhala to become familiar with the subtleties. What he saw through Athru vision was different. Its form was dense, compact, and...mobile. He remembered Gyam talking about the heat shadows visible to his flyer form, and Dhala knew he had found his quarry.

Faint voices rose to him, and he crept lower on the massive trunk. Once he had crawled as low as he dared, he sat and tried to capture the bits of conversation going on below him.

"Ena, why are you avoiding my questions? This isn't a time to argue with your superior. Were there signs of the traitor?"

"And I told you, Upseeri. Unreadable the trail was. A Chinjoka might have shot Tasi. Just because it was a Misiq arrow doesn't mean a Misiq shot it."

A long silence followed and drew Dhala lower yet. With his claws deep in the bark of the tree, he eased down until he could peer through the thin layer of leaves.

Two Misiq were in the forest opening. Their kilts hung to just above their knees and were decorated with heavy embroidery. For a moment, they looked very much alike, but he picked out details and, within a few heartbeats, had no problem working out which of the Misiq was Ena. He craned his neck and let his eyes twirl for a moment before focusing on the pair again. The ear tuffs were as unmistakably Ena's as the deep cleft in his lip.

Dhala would have liked it much better if he didn't have to wonder if it had been Ena who had caused some of the Misiq deaths. The big man turned slightly and glanced upward. Dhala drew away, surprised. No one ever checked the trees, two-legged or four. But Ena scanned the foliage as if he knew Dhala was in them. After a moment of consideration, he scrunched his face and turned to the other Misiq.

"You are always looking for the flyers. That habit will get you killed. There are no creatures in these trees that could cause us trouble," Upseeri said.

"You might be surprised by what hides in the leaves above us. The Chinjoka are not foolish. They would check to see if all of our people left their lands or if we laid traps."

Upseeri glanced at Ena and cocked an eyebrow. "The snares and deadfalls we left will remind the Chinjoka that you do no trivialize the

Misiq." He studied Ena with a harsh expression for a moment before motioning him to move. "Change to your battle form and guard our back trail. We have more surprises to set and don't need one of those flyers finding us." He stopped and studied Ena until Dhala began to question, but then Upseeri continued. "Do you remember their scent when they are in their flyer form?"

A smile grew on Ena's face that left Dhala wondering even more about the Misiq they had saved.

"Well?"

"Yes, Upseeri. Their scent is strongly embedded in me. None will be close without my knowledge."

The older Misiq walked away, shouting orders to others that had been just beyond the trees blocking Dhala from seeing them. Once Upseeri disappeared into the foliage, Ena stopped, turned toward Dhala, and their eyes locked. Dhala felt like trapped prey. He tensed, unsure of what to do. His previous path had taken him far too deep in the tree's branches to allow him to jump into enough clear space to escape through flight, and if he tried to get out by climbing to the crown of the tree, he was certain to make an easy target for the Misiq.

So he remained still, wondering what Ena would do next. He was shocked when the Misiq gave him a slow nod then seemed to melt into himself to reform as a sleek four-legged beast with tawny fur and amber eyes. With one more coughing cry, he turned to the forest and moved to follow Upseeri, but Dhala's world shifted at the sight of several Misiq surrounding Ena. Before he could react, one of the Misiq brought the hilt of the knife used against Gyam down hard on the back of Ena's skull.

Ena shifted back, his body went stiff, and the Misiq standing close let him pitch face-first into the ground. After a moment, another of them kicked him in the side and used his booted foot to roll Ena to his back before glancing up to Upseeri, who had joined the small crowd.

Dhala could see the sardonic expression that filled Upseeri's face, and his blood ran cold. *They know Ena helped.* He had to find Askari and rescue Ena. At least he still lived, but in the next instant, the reason for the reprieve became abundantly clear.

"Bind him well. Put the captive collar tight around his throat so he cannot regain his battle form. At the next rising of the sun, he will be given to the Angry One in the most painful execution seen among the Misiq."

Dhala froze against the tree, uncertain of what just happened. Ena had seen him. He was certain of that. Perhaps in repayment for what he and Askari had done to save him before. But the other Misiq had taken him captive and planned him as a sacrifice to one of their gods the next day.

Dhala shook himself as the heat shadows moved through the foliage away from him, and he realized Misiq surrounded him, many of them in their battle form. He buried his claws deep into the thick trunk, working his way higher with as much speed as he thought was safe.

He reached the thick canopy, clung tight for a few breaths before throwing himself into the open sky. The wind rushed past him as he plummeted toward the hazard-strewn ground.

He waited as long as he could based on Gyam's instruction from this morning. Once his time was short, he snapped his wings open, catching the wind in their outstretched forms. He was tossed upward by the delicious force as his wings filled. A few spans from the ground, his pumping wings caught and began to climb out of the well of green surrounding him. With a few beats, he lifted himself skyward. Miraculously unseen by the Misiq archers, he continued to climb until he was nothing but a dot in the blue sky. Then he began his flight home.

ASKARI PACED THE warren with a ferocity Dhala had seen only a few times in the past. When Dhala described how the other Misiq had knocked Ena unconscious and trussed him like a newly taken osa, Askari grabbed his bow and spear and was several spans toward the west before anyone could move to stop him. It had taken both Dhala and Gyam to restrain him, then a fingerwidth of daylight passed trying to convince him of the illogic of charging in with no plan.

Now he gathered the last of their gear while Gyam tried to talk battle strategy with Askari, who would have none of it. He had a single attack strategy. Anyone who had caused Ena pain was either to be fed several handspans of iron spear tip or serve as a temporary living quiver for his arm-long arrows.

The only reason Askari wasn't racing toward Ena was a solution Tayi remembered from the winter-teaching tales, a carry net. Once the idea was presented, it was quickly acknowledged as the only viable solution, and Dhala began to help his mother in its construction. It hadn't been used in cycles, but the net they worked on would allow them to carry Askari to wherever they held Ena. It gave them little time as the sun moved into the dark portion of its cycle. Gyam had never used the harness before, and Dhala certainly hadn't, but nothing else was going to get the three of them past the cutleaf forest and over the White Cliffs soon enough to save Ena.

The Chinjoka had formed an attack flight, but even if they were able to travel through the night, they couldn't reach Ena before the sun crested. The only chance for Ena's survival was the rescue they planned. With grips for Dhala and Gyam, their weapons and Askari were in the expanse of netting between the two flyers. With the final knots tightened, Tayi gave it a tug to satisfy her concern that something would come loose, but no part of the carrier displayed a weakness.

She turned to Dhala and Gyam. "Change. The group on foot has left. Even now, the sun is waning and you have little time." She grasped Dhala and held him tight for a few heartbeats before releasing him. Without a word, she turned to Gyam and scowled. "Bring my son home safely. In recent memory there have been too many times that I almost lost him." Her expression softened. "Since he is your mate, he is your responsibility. Now, hurry. You need to find this mysterious man of Askari's."

They acknowledged her order and began their change. In a few hammered heartbeats, the two young Chinjoka men were gone, and in their place were two enormous flyers, one in shades of crimson and the other in tones of emerald. Without a sound, they moved to the carrying net spread before the sky portal and took it up in their hind legs. They looked to Askari then to each other.

As they crouched to leap from the cliff, Askari spun to Tayi. "What should I do?"

They leapt into the air as she shouted, "Don't fall off."

They plummeted to the river while struggling to adjust to the additional weight and the fact that they were tied to each other. But their wings flared and they soared westward, even if the net had been a scant number of spans above the ground when they recovered. Once they lifted several spans higher, he chanced a look to see how Askari was adjusting to the carrier.

Dhala didn't think Askari would volunteer to ride inside the net again. His fierce friend looked like his last meal might be lost at any moment. Gyam was also battling the netting and extra weight. But before much longer, both Athru had adapted to the task. Unfortunately, the sun had disappeared in its cycle beneath the world. They were left with a sliver of a moon that kept the trip from being completely impossible. As they came closer to the cutleaf trees, they could see nothing more than a darker shape against an already dark shape.

They gained in altitude to keep a safe distance above the looming forest. Without being able to see obstacles ahead, their pace was far slower than it would have been in the daylight. Then the White Cliffs loomed before them, and they flew harder so they were well above the terrain as they entered Misiq territory.

Now to find the camp—and Ena.

Dhala thought they wouldn't have carried the unconscious Ena for a great distance, not if they wanted to keep him alive for the morning sacrifice. He hoped that was the case. Their only plan now was "save Ena." Not the most detailed plan he had ever worked with.

Askari squirmed in the netting, pulling them to one side. Dhala and Gyam struggled to regain their balance. After they compensated for the sliding weight, Gyam swung his head toward Askari and hissed. Dhala could understand Gyam's frustration. But having just had his lifetime of desire fulfilled, he could understand why Askari would be anxious.

Dhala swung his head back to their line of travel and faltered. The heat ghosts, which he could see faintly in the moonlight, looked like small fires in the dark of a new moon. With the cluster of heat signatures he spotted ahead, he was certain they had found their goal. He glanced toward Gyam and knew he had seen them too. They circled for several revolutions around the Misiq encampment as they searched for a landing site far enough away so they wouldn't be heard and a place where they could leave their equipment to gather it on their retreat. They still needed a plan—any plan would make Dhala much happier.

They started on another survey spot and discovered they were much lower than any of the earlier passes. He could discern the individual Misiq, and he found Ena in the mix. He was more obvious because he was separated from the others. Dhala was confidant Ena would be heavily guarded in preparation for morning. They had little time and needed to develop a plan to free Ena. They also needed to make certain Askari didn't charge off to save Ena and, in the process, get both of them killed.

They retraced their flight, landing in a clearing they had noticed when they passed over it. Fortunately, Dhala and Gyam had much better night vision in their flyer form and were able to alight in the seeming impassable darkness. As soon as the netting touched the ground, Askari scampered to solid ground and lay panting. After a few moments passed, he rose and glared at each of them in turn.

"That was horrifying," Askari said. "What if you dropped me? I would have splattered across half the basin."

Dhala shifted to his two-legged form and dressed from clothing brought in the carrier. He turned and motioned. "Gyam, stay in flyer form. You should be able to sense them before they are close. I doubt they would expect a Chinjoka rescue party for one of their warriors, but we should take care."

He pulled Askari close with Gyam and him. After a glance, Dhala realized he could see more of the surroundings than a short time before. "All right," he said softly. "They are a short distance from here. The sun is beginning its journey through the sky again. There are many times more Misiq than the three of us. The only path I can see is for Gyam and I to deal with the Misiq while Askari frees Ena. Once you are gone from the area, we can escape to the skies. But we cannot hold out long against the massing of their warriors."

"Then we must go now. If we surprise them in the gray of predawn, they will not be able to fight back as readily as they might have been able to do otherwise."

"Then we will fly ahead and wait in the high trees. Once you arrive, we will attack and gain you a distraction. Please, move quickly, Askari."

His request drew him a glare. "Dhala, I know the risks. I don't need for you to tell me again. I will have him out as fast as possible."

Dhala started to add more advice but considered what a mistake that would be and closed his mouth. He carefully chose his next words. He smiled as he realized he sounded like Tayi.

He understood they needed to begin. "The sun comes. If it appears, they are going to harm Ena. We will attack even if you aren't there. If we have no other choice, one of us will carry him off. He will have talon wounds, but that is better than sent on his Long Flight—" He smiled at Askari. "—or whatever the Misiq have for the next life."

"Change. I will be there long before you."

ASKARI SQUATTED LOW in the brush surrounding the Misiq encampment. This was not the carefully planned dens they had constructed to ambush the Chinjoka. They were obviously in retreat from the basin. They would sacrifice Ena as the first rays of the sun broke through the leaves.

Askari refused to let that happen.

He waited, listening with his whole being for the sign Dhala and Gyam had begun their diversion. He had no idea what it would be, though. His impression was he would have no doubts about when the diversion began. So he waited as his surroundings became more distinct with each passing breath. He was questioning his friends' tactics, afraid they had changed the plan and he was alone. Then it began.

Two shrill cries pierced the silence in the clearing, and Askari had no doubt the attack had begun. An instant later, the first dive made contact with a Misiq. The snap of a bone breaking punctuated by the Misiq's death scream was enough to send Askari into action.

He had an idea where Ena was being held and sprinted toward what had been the most heavily guarded of any part of the forest clearing. As he raced to Ena, a Misiq materialized from the mist of early morning. Askari's battle fever was too enraged for a single Misiq to cause him to pause. He spun his hata spear like a giant sword and cleaved the offender from shoulder to sternum. He vaulted the body that crumpled before him, focused only on one task: rescuing Ena.

He sensed as much as felt another Misiq attacker coming from his side. He readied to avoid the attacker when it was hit from above. The rippling green skin readily identified Dhala. His skills were improving quickly. The force he hit with was enough to kill the Misiq instantly. As he ran, Askari shifted into his plate, tossed his bow aside, and grabbed his spear with both hands. He was sure any battles he was involved with would be at close quarters as well as quick and violent.

Askari glanced at the battle surrounding him and knew many of the Misiq were shifting to battle form. Others had realized Dhala and Gyam were a distraction, deadly but still not the purpose of the Chinjoka's mission. Those were racing to intercept Askari. *They know I am here to save the one they consider traitor.*

He spun from the path of a heavy-shafted war arrow. He turned in a tight arc and whipped the spear in a deadly swath ahead of him. The power of his attack left the Misiq in two flailing pieces.

He was nearing the spot where he sensed Ena when Dhala and Gyam landed and formed a wall between him and the Misiq archers. Gyam lashed and tore with talon and wing while Dhala used the tough emerald scales covering him as a way to shield all of them.

Askari knew he had little time. The escape had to happen now. And in the dawn light, he could tell the slumped form was Ena and slid to a halt. Ena was cocooned with ropes keeping him immobile. Askari yanked his short knife from his belt and began sawing at the bindings. He had only been able to free one of the multitudes of ropes when an arrow glanced off his shoulder armor. This had to happen faster than a small knife was capable of doing. His idea was high risk. He needed to tell Ena.

He cut free the gag binding him and tore the fibers from Ena's mouth. Ena spit out the last of the bits with a low snarl. "Free me! Upseeri will pay for what he planned."

"This is a mission to rescue you, not find revenge. There are only the three of us, and the Misiq will overpower us soon. If I don't free you, we will be lost."

"Free me! Bindings you should cut. Vengeance can wait for another day."

"And that is the problem. I can't cut through the ropes. The only chance is to remove them with the hata spear. But if I lack skills..."

"Do it. We die otherwise."

He grabbed his spear and hacked at the material covering Ena. Fortunately, after a few strikes, he could sense where Ena was in the thick bindings. He hewed at the ropes, occasionally nicking Ena, until he was able to slip the iron blade into the binding and slice them off. The final motion of his spear cut the collar binding Ena's throat. Askari could see the ripple of satisfaction as he moved without restriction. The instant Ena was free, Askari threw him over one shoulder and sprinted toward the Chinjoka lands, trusting Dhala and Gyam to keep the Misiq at bay.

He was a handful of spans past the Misiq encampment when the clash with the Misiq changed in tone.

"Discovered I am not in their possession. Let me down. I can move without help."

Askari lowered him from his shoulder and, with hesitancy, released Ena. They glanced back at another outburst of shrill cries. The calls pulled to him. He recognized Dhala's voice as the one screaming. But

Askari had known Dhala's flyer form too short a time to be able to tell if the cry was of loss, victory, or just frustration. He took a step down their back trail and felt a strong hand against his arm plate.

"Fight with you I will if you try to go back. But you have already schooled me for not appreciating the opportunity the three of you provided. Are you about to make the same mistake?"

Askari considered Ena's question. Then another scream of battle filled the air, and he turned to stare down the span of trees behind them. With a sigh, he nodded in agreement. "I won't waste their sacrifice. We need to go back to where we slept last night and get Dhala and Gyam's clothes. Hopefully, they'll arrive in a short time."

Ena nodded. "Travel east. They will wait."

Without a backward glance, Askari ran to where they'd hid the supplies brought in the carrier. He was worried about his friends and the one man he'd ever found attractive. He glanced at the carrier net and considered their trip back to the Chinjoka village. They would make the journey, and it would be with all of them intact, but it would be on his own sweet feet. He never again wanted to be hanging from the talons of his two friends in a net that was more suitable for Jua and his fishing. But he carefully folded it and stowed it away in one of the packs that had been among the equipment in the net with him.

They had traveled a few spans farther when he realized Ena was moving much slower than Askari was, and seemed to be favoring one leg over the other. He stopped and let Ena catch up. When he arrived, Askari studied him for a few moments. "Are you hurt? You would be easy for me to carry."

Ena's expression changed slightly and made Askari wonder.

"What? Something is wrong?"

"I can't keep up this way. I need to change to battle form. The change will heal many of the injuries."

He studied Ena. A trickle of blood was coming from under Ena's kilt and running down his leg. He winced as he moved his weight, and Askari immediately understood.

"Change, please. You never need to ask my permission to be who you are."

Ena looked relieved and began his change. A short time later, he was winding his tail around Askari's legs, and he would have sworn the animal smiled.

"All right, we need to go. Hopefully, they will be waiting." When Askari took off at a lope, Ena had no trouble keeping up with his pace.

The sun was blazing high in the eastern sky when they reached the campsite they had used the previous night to plan their attack to save Ena. He walked about the small opening in the forest, wondering what had happened to the two huge flyers. He was overwhelmed, certain something was wrong. Maybe one of them was injured. He worked himself into a state before Ena released the barking cough he used to get Askari's attention.

He spun around to discover the sight he needed. Dhala and Gyam were skimming the tops of the trees, rapidly coming their direction. As they got closer, he could tell they were dealing with injuries. When they cleared the last line of trees, both Athru dropped lower and spread their wings in an effort to slow themselves.

Dhala touched the ground first. He was still traveling too fast and crumpled into a blue-green ball of wings, legs, and body that rolled across the ground and came to rest at the base of one of the forest giants. No sooner had Dhala stopped his forward motion than Gyam touched down—in a dwarfed pinleaf thicket that lived up to its name as a hundred sharp needles slid under Gyam's scales and punctured the tender skin underneath.

As loud as Gyam was howling and hissing, Askari was sure he would recover. But Dhala wasn't moving. He sprinted to his friend and—stared.

Dhala was a trained healer and a green Athru, making him twice the healer. The only person to help was Tayi, and she was in the village waiting. He wasn't sure what else could be done to help. Ena moved close, his tail flattened behind him. He sniffed Dhala then moved around him carefully, sniffing every few steps. Eventually, he returned to Askari and shocked him when he stuck his nose in Askari's crotch and inhaled deeply. Askari became awash in desire for Ena, and when he looked again, Ena was changing from his four-legged form.

"Askari!"

He spun to find Gyam, changed to his two-legged form, still stuck in the pinleaf thicket. He looked miserable. He glanced again at Dhala and somehow knew Dhala was all right. He trotted over to Gyam, took his hand, and yanked him from the thicket. He was certain it was far from painless. Judging from the scream of agony, he was right. They covered him with such abundance that he looked like he had grown hair. But as miserable as he was, Gyam was awake and talking. Askari couldn't say the same for Dhala.

He turned to check on the man and found Ena kneeling beside the ball of what was once Dhala. He was afraid this would be the last of the Chinjoka healers. Once he was close, Ena turned to look at him.

"He smells like a Misiq in a healing trance. Believe I he will recover."

"He smells like a Misiq?"

"Smells like a *healing* Misiq."

Askari worked his mouth a few times, but no words came out. He paused and gathered his thoughts to ask for more from Ena's description. But before he could put words to thought, Dhala growled softly, looked at Askari, and shifted.

Askari retrieved Dhala's clothes, and by the time he returned with them, Dhala sat with a dazed expression. The healing continued, and soon he was able to stand. He quickly slipped into his breechcloth then turned to a still-complaining Gyam. He examined the spines that covered Gyam. Without consideration, Dhala lifted his palms skyward, and almost instantly they began to glisten. The next thing Askari knew, Dhala ran his hands over Gyam like a flock of birds cleaning the last of the harvest.

After a few passes of his hands, Askari realized with each swipe of Dhala's hands he removed a swath of the sharp points from Gyam's skin. He moved quickly, clearing most of Gyam's body in a few moments. Dhala flicked his hands toward the thicket, spraying the leaves with what he had collected. Once he made a last pass, Askari had to smile at the expression of relief on Gyam's face.

"Better?" Askari asked.

Gyam rolled his shoulder and smiled. "Yes, it is much better." He turned to Dhala just as the green scales disappeared from his hands. "Thank you for the help, Dhala. They felt like someone had coated me with fire."

"Excellent. I'm pleased I was able to help," Dhala said.

Askari took Dhala by the wrist and studied his hands carefully, then looked up at him. "How did you do that? I've never seen that done before. Not even by Tayi."

Dhala shook slightly as if to bring himself from a trance. When he stared at Askari, his expression seemed to relax. "I'm not certain where it came from. I wished for a way to wipe off the barrage of pinleaf spines. After that, it just happened."

Ena handed Gyam his clothing, which he slipped into. As soon as he was dressed, Gyam retrieved the travel food they had stored at the site. Dhala had hung it on a high branch, protecting it from being broken into. He untied the package carefully and separated the food into four piles, giving one to each of the men and keeping one for himself.

Askari picked up a piece of dried meat and began eating. He was hungry enough to consider the mkali, if they weren't such fierce little creatures. Of course, even if he were that foolish, Dhala would never allow them to be hunted again. He'd finished several pieces of the leather-stiff meat when he noticed Ena had already eaten what he'd been given, and when he glanced around, he seemed still in search of food to fill his empty belly. Askari slipped the majority of the food he still had onto Ena's platter. When Ena glanced at Askari, he winked.

Askari was a little surprised Ena developed a sudden bout of nerves and became so shy. Askari slipped into Ena's private space and leaned toward him. He cupped his hand around Ena's face and pressed his lips against Ena's. The tingle that rose spread through his entire body. He pressed harder, raking his teeth over Ena's lip. Their kiss stretched longer, but eventually he sensed Ena pull away from him.

He released his grip and stared into Ena's eyes. He was relieved to see a twinkle in them and a bit of mirth playing at Ena's lips. There was a rustling behind him, and Askari recalled he and Ena were not alone. He found Dhala and Gyam smiling at them. He felt sheepish and grinned. His face still burned with the heat of embarrassment when he started planning for the four of them.

"We should escape the White Cliffs now. The sun is past halfway through the sky. I have no intention of being hauled skyward again, so I thought Ena and I could travel across the basin on foot while you return with the news that we released Ena and are returning. The rescue party could also be told they are no longer needed. We will make our way through the basin and arrive long after the two of you. That will keep Tayi from worry, which she would do if we all made the trek afoot."

Dhala and Gyam exchanged looks and turned to Askari. "We will fly ahead happily. Everyone will be relieved to discover we have succeeded. That will let you make your own speed to the village." Dhala paused as his smile broadened. "You will probably need to stop with great frequency to...rest."

Askari refused to be baited, although he wasn't certain Dhala was far from correct. But instead of rising to Dhala's teasing, he turned to Ena. "I know we need to leave soon, but how quickly will the Misiq be trailing us?"

"They will not. Once the Angry God feasted on my blood, they were returning to the homelands. They lost half in the battle."

Dhala and Gyam listened intently. "The Misiq are leaving our basin?"

"Yes, that was Upseeri's plan when last he gave it out to the troops. The battle with the cliff people costs too many lives."

The Chinjoka exchanged expressions of joy. They had hoped that the battles with the Misiq were ended. The news resulting from this raid was better with each new revelation.

Dhala and Gyam helped pack bags for the other two. The final preparations happened quickly, and soon Ena and Askari were settling packs on their shoulders. Askari exchanged embraces with Dhala and Gyam before watching them change into flyer form and soar to the south. When he could not see them anymore, he turned to Ena and gave him a gentle kiss.

"Ready to go to your new home?"

"With you? Yes, even to the evils of the Chinjoka."

THE DAY WAS one of the best Askari could remember. Having spent it with Ena had left him wanting the man more with each passing moment. He was obsessed with Ena's hard body. They reached a portion of the basin where the trees intermingled with the grasslands. As they moved silently through the brush, Askari heard a familiar rustling sound as the two of them slipped through the knee-high grass.

Askari stopped Ena and motioned to the sound ahead of them. Ena cocked his head, and an instant later, a smile grew across his face. They cast about on the ground, and both came to have a stone in each hand. They separated as they stalked their small quarry. He heard the scratching of many feet through the cover. He glanced at Ena, who nodded. With that exchange, they screamed and plunged into a huge flock of runner birds. The bird's short wings thrummed through the air in every direction.

Askari threw the first rock at one of the larger birds, tossed another rock into his throwing hand, and launched the second missile. By the time he had knocked down his second quarry, the flock was back in the tall grass, running from them in every direction. He gathered his game, careful to break their necks so they did not suffer.

Ena walked beside him with a bird in each hand. Askari noticed each was headless. He glanced up in time to see Ena swallow and lick his lips. Askari choked down his bile before meeting Ena's gaze.

"The heads are delicious," Ena said.

Askari handed Ena his two birds and walked to a rocky outcropping ahead of them. As he walked past, he glanced to Ena. "You get them ready to eat. And yes, at least mine has to be cooked."

Ena chuckled from behind Askari. "I like them cooked also."

After finding a good spot for building a hearth, he gathered his fire-making kit and soon had a small blaze that would easily cook the four birds they had taken. He created a low crackling flame, and by the time the skin was crisp and brown, the fire would be a bed of red coals they would use to finish roasting the meat. Ena arrived with the cleaned carcasses on two spits, ready for cooking.

Ena took charge of the meal and soon the aroma of roasting runner bird filled their surroundings. Askari could almost taste the crispy brown skin on each one. He waited for Ena to finish, but hunger was stretching his ability by the time Ena decreed them ready.

After sliding them onto a flat rock Askari had cleaned to act as a platter, he tossed the grease-soaked sticks into the fire where they cast light as if they were using a hata-tallow lamp. Askari folded his legs under him and began to eat the burning-hot bits of meat.

They ate like starving sikari gnawing on a particularly tasty morsel of osa fawn. Once the final bone had been sucked clean of its marrow and tossed into the fire, Askari began licking the savory juice from his fingers. Ena leaned close, took Askari's finger, and licked it clean. The sensation of Ena's hot tongue brought back the enjoyment of their earlier kisses. He continued to clean each of Askari's fingers, and by the time he'd completed the last one, Askari's body was awash with the heat of lust.

Ena leaned in, pressed his lips against Askari's neck, and whispered, "Your smooth skin sends sparks of life through me."

"I do that for you?"

Ena took Askari's hand in his and pressed it against the hard lump in his kilt. Askari moaned deeply at the feel of Ena's hard cock under his hand. He began squeezing it softly and Ena sighed. After reveling in the sensation filling him, it built to levels that were almost unbearable. But he felt more awkward than he had since he first reached maturity. His hand slowed as he considered his inexperience.

"Wrong what is, Askari?"

He turned to meet Ena's gaze. "I have never shared intimacies. I don't know how to make someone feel the pleasures you have given me."

"You have pleasured yourself. Correct?"

Askari blushed and began to harden. "Yes, I have pleasured myself."

"Then do what you enjoy. I will enjoy also." Ena considered Askari thoughtfully. "Tell me what you want to do most. I will help make your fantasy come true."

Askari's reply came with little hesitation. "Your hair. The hair on your body. I find it very desirable."

Ena ran his fingers over the patch of golden brown hair between his pecs, traveling down his torso, to finally spread thickly around his navel. He smiled at Askari. "You like the way I'm haired, and I like your smooth hairless body. I suppose that makes our pairing good." He took Askari's hand and pushed it over the coarse hair on his torso.

For Askari, the textures under his palms were driving him toward a release, but many times more pleasurable than anything he'd managed alone. He pressed the tips of his fingers under the edge of Ena's kilt and teased at the hair he found there. He glanced toward Ena, who met his questioning gaze with a smile.

"Do what you want. I am enjoying your touch."

With trembling hands, he opened Ena's kilt and let it fall away. His body trembled at the sight of Ena's hard cock straining from the curly forest of gold. His night vision with the low burning fire made it possible to see every detail of Ena's body. He wrapped his fingers around the column of hard flesh and stroked it. As he toyed with Ena's cock, he felt his breechcloth slip to one side and his cock hover over his stomach. Ena's hot breath across his crotch registered an instant before his cock slipped into Ena's mouth and he could think of nothing other than sex. The sensations built, and he fought to keep from spraying his essence into Ena's mouth. Askari trembled and moved toward the point of no return. He wanted to join with Ena in every possible way, but he knew they would be finished soon if Ena kept giving him this kind of pleasure.

"Ena. I— Oh by the Twins," Askari stuttered.

Ena looked up, and a smile crawled across his face. "Are you enjoying?"

"Yes. Oh yes. By everything that is holy, yes. But I will be finished soon unless we change roles. I would like for our first time of shared pleasures to be longer than the blink of an eye."

Ena nodded then the smile grew wider. "Perhaps move somewhere more comfortable than rocks?"

At Ena's words, Askari became aware of the stones under them. It took little time for them to find a spot more conducive to their activities—a thick bed of moss under a trio of trees a few strides away. Once they settled into the spot, Ena lay on his back, legs spread, and with his hands behind his head. The spicy scent Askari associated with Ena filled their new shelter, and Askari's body responded. He pushed his hands along Ena's legs, reaching higher and higher as he enjoyed the textured feel.

By the time he moved to Ena's cock, he was ready to give Ena the kind of pleasure he had gotten. He took the hard shaft in his hand, ran his tongue along the underside, and lapped the clear juice oozing from its tip. The smells and tastes were far beyond anything Askari had experienced before, and when they were combined with the textures of Ena's body—Askari wanted more with each passing beat of his hammering heart.

He lost himself in pleasuring Ena, running his tongue over more and more of Ena. When he rubbed his hand over Ena's nipple, he was rewarded with a hiss followed by a deep sigh. Askari grinned as he continued to explore Ena.

He returned to the spots where he'd gotten the most response. He chewed on Ena's nipple as he caressed the underside of Ena's cockhead. He could feel trembling. Askari thought Ena was going to release, but instead, Ena rolled them so he was on top. He pinned Askari's hard cock into the cleft of his ass and ground his muscular butt up and down Askari's length. Ena began to play with Askari's chest, and Askari tensed against the attention. Ena tossed his head back, his braid swinging through the thickly scented air surrounding them. He slowed as they both gasped with ecstasy.

"Inside me. I want to be mated, our essence intermingled. Would you give me that honor?"

Askari paused for a moment before answering. "Yes, of course I would."

Before Askari could press any further, Ena impaled himself on Askari's shaft. The tight heat engulfed Askari as he sank deep inside his mate. His lust built to a boil as they froze in position, interconnected in the most intimate way possible. Askari raced toward orgasm as Ena rocked on his member. He panted, trying to control his buildup of passion. He struggled to warn Ena, warn him that he would fill him in a short time, but Ena just smiled down at him with understanding.

"Release yourself. It will be the fulfillment of a lifetime for each of us."

Ena's words pressed Askari beyond his final hurtle, and he thrust upward harder and faster as their passion overwhelmed. It took only a few thrusts before he plunged into his orgasm. His muscles tensed into rock, and he trembled before the first wave erupted into Ena. The convulsions came in waves to which Askari lost himself. The feast of pleasure began to slow until, with a mighty breath, the last wave left Ena moving slowly with Askari inside. He leaned down and kissed Askari as his cock softened and slipped out.

"That was amazing. I've never felt anything like this before."

"We're not finished. It is your turn to be pleasured."

Ena smiled and watched as Askari took his hardness between his lips and started licking him again. Askari soon had him hovering on the edge. Ena shook harder with each heartbeat until he tensed and a long shrill cry erupted from his lips.

Ena's cock thickened, twitched, and Askari's mouth was filled. He swallowed as quickly as possible as Ena repeatedly filled him. Out of breath, Askari lifted himself and let the last few emissions pool across his face. With a smile, he licked the last drops of translucent white from his lips.

They held each other gently, their mating bond growing stronger. As the mountain chill cooled them, they moved tightly together. Neither was willing to separate from the other as they drifted to contented sleep.

Chapter Sixteen

GYAM SCOWLED AS Dhala cleaned the main room of the debris left by the steady stream of people who made their way through the aerie. First to make certain no one was injured, but also to marvel at the changes. The first was the Saat who became a green Athru. The greens were uncommon, and their last one had been a first casualty of the sickness. Now Dhala gave them a reason for hope. Gyam scowled to see the adoring expressions on people who a few days earlier wouldn't give Dhala a second glance.

The second object of fascination followed Askari like a shadow: Ena. Gyam wasn't certain which the people surrounding them found more fascinating: Ena in his battle form—which was huge and impressive—or Askari's happiness.

Another winner that evening was Jua. He found a small niche and watched the activities with great intensity. He sometimes sat so still he looked like a carving of one of the Twins. From time to time, someone would bring him a treat or sit to talk. During those times, he had the appearance of a respected elder dispensing knowledge. Fortunately, after this had gone on for a long length of time, Tayi took over and kept the fledgling busy.

Gyam was losing patience with Dhala's insistence on continuing to perform his duties, when Askari walked into the room. "Why are you cleaning, Dhala? You're no longer Gyam's Saat." Askari winked at Dhala. "Let the slob clean up after himself. There was talk among the old women he ran off his last Saat and regretted it later."

Ena walked to Askari's side, watching the good-natured banter with his head cocked. Askari dropped his hand to the back of Ena's neck, holding tightly to his newly discovered mate. The Misiq was enormous. Gyam's flyer form was several times larger but much less densely muscled. Ena'd changed to this form as the aerie filled with inquisitive Chinjoka. He had been uneasy in his two-legged form. It was easy to see from the expression on his face he wished he was anywhere but in this crowd of people—most of whom had thought of him as an enemy only a few fingerspans earlier in the day.

As it became obvious Askari had no idea how to make Ena more at ease, Gyam moved to his other side and spoke softly. "Ena is not happy. He's making the Chinjoka unhappy too. See if he would be more comfortable in his two-legged form."

Askari studied him for a moment before shrugging. "All right, if you'd feel better. I'll talk with him about changing to his two-legged form." Askari glanced around them then grinned. "Let's go to the lusty lover's bedroom. We can use it to change. Hopefully, the results of their noisy morning activity has dried."

The crowd was thinning, and Ena seemed ready to move back to another form. Tayi slipped beside them and smiled.

"Today has been a wonderful day, but I think it's time for you to relax. Jua can stay with me tonight. You do not need a fledgling in your aerie. He can help me in the warrens. The family plot needs tending, and Jua can start that process."

"Ah, Tayi! I want to play with the others," Jua said from the darkened corner where he'd been lurking.

Tayi had been well aware that he was listening in on their conversation and let him know it. "Fledgling, you are too young for some things, and you might not like finding out things you do not need to know. You will come with me, and we can get some things done over the next few days." She winked at Dhala and Gyam as she herded Jua to the inner pathway.

The four of them smiled as Tayi led the last visitor away. As their footsteps faded, Askari turned to Ena. "You can change now, love. Everyone is gone, and I can feel that you are itching to leave your four-legged form behind."

Ena let out a low growl and began to shift. Not surprisingly, it was the reverse of his previous change. His claws drew inside as his paws elongated, returning to wide hands and long fingers. His face and body flowed like clay at the hands of a master forming thick legs and muscular arms. The final changes were his teeth's transformation from the sharp fangs they were, then his ears found their home, complete with the thick tufts of hair on their tips. His kilt had reappeared from—somewhere—as his genitals reformed in their correct location.

Askari ran his hand through the coarse copper-colored hair that spread down the center of his torso. He leaned in, kissed Ena along his jawline, and slipped the tips of his fingers inside the back of his kilt.

Gyam cleared his throat, and Askari turned to him with a satisfied smile. "Yes, Gyam? Did you need to speak to me of something? Because Ena and I are going to be busy for a very long, satisfying time."

Heat flashed across Gyam's body as his friend licked up the side of Ena's neck, eliciting a low growl.

Gyam waved his hands, halfway between laughter and embarrassment. Then Dhala wrapped his set of delicate hands around Gyam's chest. He glanced back to find Dhala smiling at him.

"If we stay, we're going to be watching these two in a frantic bout of mating. I believe we need to be gone before that happens."

Gyam let Dhala lead him to the sky portal, where they stood in the cooling breeze and looked at the basin spread before them. Dhala kissed him again, then Dhala's breechcloth slithered into a pile at his feet as his mate transformed into his Athru body and launched himself into the afternoon sky. The sun played across his emerald-green scales in patterns that heightened Gyam's desire.

He glanced back into the aerie to find Askari and Ena intertwined and their moans of pleasure filling the air. He turned quickly, dropped his breechcloth beside Dhala's, and soon was sharing the afternoon sky with the only other Athru who remained. They played like fledglings, riding the thermals until the air cooled then diving after each other. Their juvenile activities belayed the serious side effect of improving their skills. After a considerable amount of flying, they spotted a family group of osa and tried for a meal. But they were too winded and the osa's lead doe was too smart. She had them traveling in the deepest thickets where, even in their best flying shape, they would have been challenged to take any from her group.

Dhala streaked past him, tagging Gyam. But he noticed Dhala's flight was not as crisp as earlier. He was tiring. He followed behind Dhala, forcing him closer to the ground. Eventually, Dhala gently alighted and turned with a scream to Gyam who was still several spans above him.

Gyam settled onto the soft ground in time for Dhala to change back to his two-legged form. His completely naked, hard-muscled, slender body. Gyam knew what he wanted. What he was hungry for, he couldn't take with talon and beak. He changed, and grinning wildly, he turned toward Dhala, equally as naked, his desire obvious. Dhala ran his finger down Gyam's spine, sending chills and causing his member to stiffen even further. Soon they were writhing on the ground, desire driving all rational thought from his mind.

Gyam drifted back to full awareness to discover the sun had slipped low against the western rim of the basin. More delightful to Gyam was Dhala's warm body in his arms. He pulled them together and gave Dhala a soft kiss. The heat where their lips touched was exciting him again. But reality overrode his bodily desires.

"Dhala, it's turning dark. We need to return to the aerie while we still are able."

Dhala twisted in his arms until they faced each other. Without another word, he ran his hands over Gyam. Dhala pressed their bodies together, the intimate embrace awakening Gyam's desire once again for the man beside him.

Dhala kissed him hard and pushed him on his back. Their eyes met, and Gyam saw the face of the fiercely loyal man he had known since birth. Then the world around them became awash in brilliant shades of green. He forced his attention to what was happening and realized somehow Dhala was shifting only his wings, encasing them in a cocoon of green.

"Still worried about being trapped in the darkness?" Dhala asked.

Gyam moaned softly as Dhala's warmth and devotion filled him. The shimmering green of a healing Chinjoka of the Athru caste filled him, and he knew of nothing else until they slept in each other's arms, protected by Dhala's wings.

Glossary

Akia Mountains — Mountains forming the northern border for the Chinjoka Basin. They are also the source of the Father River.

Anpar — Shredded vegetables stored in special jars and allowed to ferment. It is a favorite food of the Chinjoka during the winter season.

Athru — One of the castes of the Chinjoka people, and the least numerous. The members of this caste can shift completely to an avian form. They are fierce warriors and serve as the aerial reconnaissance against an attack from the Misiq.

Chinjoka — A people who make their homes in the high cliffs of the Chinjoka region nestled between two low mountain ranges that join at their northernmost apex. They live in an extensive tunnel and cave system built into the cliffs. They are divided into three castes based on their ability to shift into an avian form: Athru, Onija, and Saat. They lost two-thirds of their population due to a plague that they haven't been able to cure. Some of the Saat and Athru also have healing magic, but their skills have not helped.

Cutleaf — A large tree with deeply lobed leaves. The canopies are thick enough to make growth beneath them sparse.

Cycle — The time to visit all the seasons with no repeat.

Father of the Gods — The chief god among the Chinjoka. They believe the Father of the Gods created their world and now rules in the sky realm. The twins are his children, but some of the Chinjoka believe they are the children of his mating with the Dark God who carried and gave birth to them. Most believe the Mother carried them and they are the Mother and Father's children.

Father River — The water of the Father River gathers from numerous snowmelt streams to form a large river that flows to the edge of the granite cliffs forming the Mother Falls. The falls divide the river into the Twin Rivers. As the two smaller rivers leave the basin, they rejoin into the Father River.

First Blooding — The first game taken by a young Chinjoka is referred to as their first blooding. It is a rite of passage recognized by the tribe and the family celebrates the youth's accomplishment. It is also custom that the honoree invites guests who are important to him.

God of Darkness/Dark God — This god is recognized by both the Chinjoka and the Misiq. He rules over the Afterworld. Chinjoka see him as the god of death while the Misiq consider him the sovereign of warriors and shifting. He is also the sometimes lover of the Father of the Gods.

Great Ones — The pantheon of gods worshipped by the Misiq.

Hata — Large grazing animals that migrate through the Chinjoka territory in the spring and the fall. The herds are large enough that you cannot see the edges. They are such enormous animals that only the Chinjoka and packs of sikari can hunt them.

Long Flight — The journey the soul of a deceased person undergoes to reach the afterlife.

Misiq — A separate people who live to the north and west of the Chinjoka. They have the ability to change into a large catlike form, similar to a jaguar. They worship the God of Darkness and believe anyone who is ill or injured has to be sacrificed to the Dark God. Fortunately, their shifting ability also helps them heal faster. They were once allies with the Chinjoka, but believe the plague that has decimated both peoples is the fault of the Chinjoka. Their elders have decreed the Chinjoka must all be killed.

Mkali — Highly aggressive animals roughly the size of an adult fist. They live in large colonies in rockslides. When they are attacked, they swarm the attacker. They are the only animals the sikari avoid.

Mother of the Gods — Mate of the Father God and mother to the twins. She rules over the surface of the earth. She is also associated as a protector of the Saat caste.

Mother Falls — A waterfall marking the change of the Father River into the Twin Rivers. It is a 3,000-foot drop, and at the bottom, the river divides into its two parts. The branch that flows to the east is the Brother Twin and the river to the west is the Sister Twin. Once they pass the far southern tip of the Chinjoka Basin, they rejoin and are once again the Father River.

Nyoka — Legless amphibians that can reach lengths of an adult Chinjoka. They have the ability to constrict around their prey and crush them.

Onija — A member of the Onija caste has the ability to perform the first level of shifting, but cannot reach the avian form. It leaves them with a covering of large bony scales which provide armor for the Onija. These scales are almost as dense as iron and can deflect almost any blow. Due to this ability, they account for most of the Chinjoka warriors. When working with the Athru, they form a deadly defense, which has kept the Misiq away from Chinjoka lands.

Osa — A small grazing animal that populates the Chinjoka Basin and the lower altitude of the Akia Mountains. They move in small family groups with one stag and four or five females.

Pilea - Goddess of fire and warriors and the Sister Twin. Most often worshipped by the Athru. Also the more likely of the Twins to disobey their father.

Pilea River — The small stream formed from Father River by the falls. It flows along the White Cliffs.

Piwa - Mammal living in the numerous streams and lakes found in the upper valley of the Chinjoka. They live in shelters they dig in the banks. They have long tails that aid in their swimming ability and live on the vegetation growing along the stream bank.

Redtail — A large fish found in the streams of the lower reaches of the Chinjoka territory. Typically, the back one-third—including the tail—is a deep scarlet. The remainder is rich silver. The meat has a high fat content and is highly valued in its preserved form for winter meals.

Saat — One of the three Chinjoka castes. The Saat have no ability to change shape or form scales. They are the most numerous caste of the three, and their duties include much of the construction and maintenance of the cliff dwellings. Some family lines also have the ability to heal, both with herbs and a type of magic, but are not as potent as the Athru healers.

Sikari — Predator with dense fur and short tails, who are as tall as an adult Chinjoka when standing on their hind legs. Their jaws are strong enough to crush the thighbones of the large grazing animals. They are found in the grasslands and lower altitude of the mountains.

Skyfire - Chinjoka term for lightning.

Sky Portal — This is the opening in the sheer cliffs that allows the Athru to launch from their aeries high enough to soar directly into the thermals rising from the basin.

Soul Flight — A bonding between the souls of two people who are destined to share their lives with each other. If one soul flight dies, the other seldom lives long.

Soul Rider — Many of the Chinjoka have a spiritual guardian and advisor that comes to them in the form of one of the native animals. For those who are healers, the soul riders also have the ability to aid in their healing magic. The Chinjoka seeking guides travel to a remote area of the basin and forgo food and drink until their guardian has made themselves known.

Sun Cycle - One period of time from sunrise to sunrise.

The Twins — Offspring of the Father and Mother of the Gods. Voda is male and rules over the water and crops. Pilea is the protector of warriors, and both the Athru and Onija castes make offerings to her. All three castes make offerings to the twins. The twins will also appear to tribal members from time to time. There are situations when the twins deliberately disobey their father—to mixed results.

Voda - God of water and crops. Twin to Pilea. Guardian of the Saat caste and their primary god.

Voda River — One of the rivers formed when Father River divides into two branches when it goes over the Mother Falls. It flows along the base of the Chinjoka Cliffs.

About the Author

Jon Keys' earliest memories revolve around books; with the first ones he can recall reading himself being "The Warlord of Mars" and anything with Tarzan. (The local library wasn't particularly up to date.) But as puberty set in, he started sneaking his mother's romance magazines and added the world of romance and erotica to his mix of science fiction, fantasy, Native American, westerns and comic books.

A voracious reader for almost half a century, Jon has only recently begun creating his own flights of fiction for the entertainment of others. Born in the Southwest and now living in the Midwest, Jon has worked as a ranch hand, teacher, computer tech, roughneck, designer, retail clerk, welder, artist, and, yes, pool boy; with interests ranging from kayaking and hunting to painting and cooking, he draws from a wide range of life experiences to create written works that draw the reader in and wrap them in a good story.

Website: www.jonkeys.com

Facebook: www.facebook.com/jon.keys.773

Twitter: www.twitter.com/Jon4Keys